DEADLY BURDEN

DEADLY BURDEN
A Green Dory Inn Mystery: Book 4

JANET SKETCHLEY
janetsketchley.ca

Deadly Burden, A Green Dory Inn Mystery, Book 4

© 2023 by Janet Sketchley

978-1-989581-12-4 (epub)

978-1-989581-11-7 (print)

Permissions requests may be directed to the author via her website: janetsketchley.ca/contact or via email at info@janetsketchley.ca.

The characters and situations in this book are works of fiction and are not intended to represent any individuals, living or dead. The Green Dory Inn is purely fictional and in no way intended to represent a real location. Where real locations are mentioned, they are used fictitiously for the purposes of the story.

<u>Quotations and Scripture References</u>:

Chapter 7: "In wrath, remember mercy." Habakkuk 3:2, NIV
Chapter 8: "Marley was dead, to begin with." From *A Christmas Carol*, by Charles Dickens. Public domain.

Scripture marked NIV is taken from THE HOLY BIBLE, NEW INTERNATIONAL VERSION®, NIV® Copyright © 1973, 1978, 1984, 2011 by Biblica, Inc.® Used by permission. All rights reserved worldwide.

Edited by Brilliant Cut Editing.

Cover by E.A.H. Creative.

Interior dory image: iStock.com/Gunay Aliyeva.

Author photo by Amanda Walker Photography.

FICTION/CHRISTIAN/SUSPENSE

Published in Canada by Janet Sketchley.

A GREEN DORY INN MYSTERY
·BOOK 4·

DEADLY BURDEN

JANET SKETCHLEY
janetsketchley.ca

BOOKS BY JANET SKETCHLEY

The Redemption's Edge Series:

Heaven's Prey
Secrets and Lies
Without Proof

The Green Dory Inn Mysteries:

Unknown Enemy
Hidden Secrets
Bitter Truth
Deadly Burden

Daily Devotions:

A Year of Tenacity: 365 Daily Devotions

Tenacity at Christmas: 31 Daily Devotions for December

Readers' Journals:

Reads to Remember:
A book-lover's journal to track your next 100 reads
(Available in two cover options, print only)

NOTE TO READERS

Lunenburg, Nova Scotia, is a real town—a UNESCO World Heritage site. The Green Dory Inn and most other places mentioned in this novel are products of my imagination and in no way intended to represent real locations.

I have also taken creative licence with the inn's geography by elevating that part of the coastline to allow for the sea tunnel beneath it. One of the perks of writing fiction is being able to adjust the facts as needed to accommodate the story.

Non-Canadian readers, please note I'm using Canadian spellings in this book. You'll see words like colour, neighbour, licence, and travelling, and they're not typos. You'll also see some hyphenated words like mid-fifties and mid-size.

DEDICATION

This one's for Dad.

The character of Roy is entirely fictional—but the two of you would have had a blast sharing tales of past shenanigans.

I am beyond grateful for your love and I can't wait to hug you again in Heaven.

MEET THE KEY CHARACTERS

Anna Young: owner of the Green Dory Inn

Bobby Hawke: Landon's friend and neighbour

Ciara Williams: Landon's friend

Dee Elliston: local physiotherapist

Dylan Tremblay: Landon's friend, local police officer

Elva Knapp: woman who lives near the inn

Freesia Bachman: dog-loving woman

Gwen Smith: Landon's mother

Hope Bellgrove: Elva's visitor

Kenzie Garner: trouble maker from out of town

Landon Smith: our story's heroine, Anna's friend

Phil Kirkwood: snow globe recipient, Ciara's stepfather

Roy Hawke: Bobby's grandfather, Anna's neighbour

Starr Elliston: child who wants to help solve the mystery

Whitney Kirkwood: Ciara's mother

Vi Foley: Nigel's mother

Chapter 1

Saturday

THIS ELF COSTUME itched. Tugging at her too-short skirt, Landon Smith reached her free hand under the community centre's Christmas tree for the final present—a mug-sized box wrapped with holly-red paper and a silver bow and marked "open last." She crossed the stage to where Santa waited, white-gloved fingers spread on his knees, his red velour coat straining over a plump pillow.

A snowy beard covered his extra-wide jaw, but his smile twinkled in his sea-blue eyes. One lid dropped in a wink. "You're a natural."

It had been more fun than she'd expected. Bending nearer, she passed him the gift. "What I am, Roy, is a soft touch who can't say no to my favourite neighbour."

"Favourite, am I? Don't let my grandson hear that."

Santa Roy peered at the printed tag, then leaned toward the microphone. "Phil Kirkwood. Didn't I see you already with the other board members? You must have been an extra-good boy this year."

Around the tables, a few people paused their conversations. Heads turned to track the blond man who stood and made his way to the stage. He took the stairs at an easy jog.

The light caught a piece of glitter on his suit jacket sleeve and flared it like a sequin. Landon repressed a grin. Not even Phil's designer elegance could escape the hazards of the season.

Roy held out the box in one hand. "Tag says to open it on stage. I won't make you sit on my lap."

Phil eyed the spindly white chair. "Good call." He glanced at the gift tag. "What's this about?"

"One way to find out." Roy covered the mic. "Open up so we can be done. I'm melting in this getup."

With a smile for the crowd, Phil pulled the ribbon free and let it fall. "Thank you to someone." The red paper ripped and dropped. Then he removed the box lid and passed it to Landon.

Sparkly tissue paper rustled—more glitter for his suit—and he drew out a small jar. "A Christmas treat."

He focused on a printed label on the lid. "Christmas twenty years ago." The words came out low and hoarse. His throat convulsed.

He flipped the jar upside-down. Not cranberry sauce or pepper jelly after all—clear, sparkly liquid. A homemade snow globe.

All colour vanished from his face. His whispered curse came out like a sob. Blindly, he thrust the jar into the tissue paper and pushed the box toward Roy.

Landon raced after him to the stairs. "Phil, slow down. Let me help."

He brushed off her grasp, then clutched the railing, and descended at a cautious pace. His weaving steps carried him to his table where his wife stood to meet him, hands outstretched.

"Phil, dear, what is it?"

Even visibly pregnant, Whitney Kirkwood reminded Landon of a china doll. Petite, with long blond curls, peaches-

2

and-cream skin, round blue eyes, and now, pink lips forming a perfect *O*.

Phil's brief touch to her fingertips cut short. He sank into his chair at the wide round table. "Get your coat, darling. We're leaving."

She studied him, teeth worrying her bottom lip. Then she whirled and dashed toward the coat check.

Landon perched on the edge of Whitney's seat. "Let someone drive you home. Get your car tomorrow."

"I'll be fine."

The conversation level rose around them, people at the other tables dismissing Phil's reaction or speculating about the cause. Around the circle of his table, faces turned to him in concern and open curiosity.

Into the pause, a brown-clad arm shot between Landon and Phil and plucked his half-empty water glass from the table. "Drink."

Landon slid her chair sideways to make space for a wiry little woman with sharp brown eyes like a robin's.

The woman kept her focus on Phil until he obeyed.

Sputtering, half-choking, he drained the glass and set it on the white linen with a shaky hand.

On stage, Roy hefted his gift sack. "Ho! Ho! Ho! Santa says, have a merry Christmas. And he hopes there's some turkey left for him in the kitchen."

He navigated the stairs. Without appearing to hurry, he reached the table quickly.

"Vi." He nodded a greeting to the unfamiliar woman. Then, laughing, he clapped one white-gloved hand on Phil's shoulder. His sea-blue eyes shone hard and serious as he leaned in. "Don't give them the satisfaction."

Phil tipped his head and gave a good impression of sharing a joke. Anyone at a distance might buy it, that nothing shattering had happened. Close up, his pallor and a tightness around his eyes gave him away.

Landon knew him as her friend Ciara's stepfather. Stiff

3

and purposeful. The one soft spot she'd seen came from concern for his wife, and even then, he'd maintained control.

Whatever this snow globe meant, it mined something deep. About Whitney? He'd mumbled "Twenty years ago." That would be before they'd met.

Landon gathered her hair in one hand and let the blond strands slide through her fingers. Whatever had followed Phil from his past would touch Whitney with her high-risk pregnancy in her forties. Could it affect the babies?

Beside her, the woman in brown—Vi—stepped up to Roy. "Show me."

The old man might not have the belly for a traditional Santa, but his white eyebrows and deep laugh lines fit the role perfectly. Now, those eyebrows arched into the fur trim of his Santa hat. He looked at Phil and hefted his not-quite-empty sack.

Phil glanced in the direction his wife had taken. "I have nothing to hide. But I don't want to upset Whitney."

When Roy set the box on the tablecloth, Vi plucked the jar from the tissue paper. Instead of holding it high to catch the light, she cupped it as if to shield the contents from view. Her breath hissed through her teeth.

Fingers spread wide, Phil bounced his palm on the table. He lifted his gaze to Roy. "Who gave you this?"

Landon shook her head. "It was with the others when we arrived."

Roy dug an index finger under the furry Santa hat. "Evidence for a mischief charge. Person should know better than to mess with a lawyer."

The lines around Phil's mouth dug in deeper. "I've never been able to locate her. This time, she must be here." He pushed to his feet, narrowed eyes scanning the room.

"Oh, she's here all right," muttered Vi. "But she's not who you think."

The wiry woman darted crablike between the round tables to clutch the sleeve of a tall girl in a puffy silver coat. Despite the size difference, she hauled her toward Phil like a runaway child.

Phil stood to meet them.

The girl's sullen gaze pinned him. Stormy red surged in her cheeks. Lips locked in a tight line, she let her glare say it all.

Feet anchored in place, grip firm on the girl's arm, Vi assessed her. "That was spiteful and cruel."

The girl continued her stare down with Phil. "Why accuse me?"

Vi shook her arm. "Everyone else looked shocked or concerned. You were satisfied."

Phil broke eye contact, but with no evidence of defeat. He held up the snow-globe jar for his tablemates to see. "It's a truck smashed through lake ice. To remind me of the loss of a good friend."

Landon had barely glimpsed it on the stage before he rushed away. Not round or dome-shaped like a traditional snow globe, it was a small jam jar filled with glitter water. At the base, the tail end of a brown toy pickup truck stuck out of a dark-blue opening in the white "ice" with the cab submerged.

Phil set the jar into the box and tucked the tissue paper over the top. He spun to confront the girl. "What's your connection with Pattie Garner?"

She yanked her arm free of Vi and folded both tight against her chest. "She's my mother."

He matched her posture. "I had assumed she was sending the cards. Was that you as well?"

Behind him, Roy planted hands on hips, scowling. The Jolly Old Elf's evil twin. Angry twin, at least. The image made Landon want to grin.

The girl's mouth tightened.

A deep breath strained Phil's suit jacket lapels. Gone was the shaken recipient of an unwanted gift. His impassive features, his set shoulders—arms uncrossed now and at ease—and his voice when he spoke were pure professional lawyer.

"I have to ask why this matters so much to you. The accident happened before you were born."

"Yeah, before I was born. My father died that day because of you. It should have been you."

Sweat popped on Phil's forehead. His lips pulled in like he'd had a rush of saliva. Or bile. "I gave up wishing for that a long time ago. Regret won't bring anyone back."

He paced a slow, careful circle that brought him into her space. "Your father. That would make you nineteen. Born in August."

"So you can do math."

Phil groped for the table behind him, barely missing his dessert plate. The weight of his palm hitting the surface rattled the cutlery. He kept the eye contact. "What's your name?"

Before the girl could answer, Whitney rushed past her, wrapped in a blond-tipped fur coat. "Phil, whatever it is, let's go."

When he hesitated, she plucked at his suit sleeve and pressed her other hand on her rounded stomach. "Please. Stress isn't good for the babies."

He blinked at Whitney, down at the tan leather glove splayed across her coat front, then focused on the girl. Waiting.

"Kenzie." Her chin lifted. "Remember my name. And his."

Phil winced. "There's more you need to know. Where can I find you?"

"I'm leaving in the morning. Expect a card next Christmas."

As Phil allowed Whitney to draw him away, he focused on Landon. "Is there a vacancy at the inn?"

"Yes." Bookings were scarce this close to Christmas.

"Bill me for her room. Vi, convince her to stay."

Phil settled his hand over Whitney's grip on his arm and

dipped his head to speak softly as they made for the exit.

Landon stared after them. This bitter, disruptive stranger had hurt—and shocked—Phil deeply, and the man wanted to land that kind of a guest at the Green Dory Inn? It could be a tense few days. Followed by a barbed review if anything went wrong.

So they'd serve with their customary hospitality. And Landon would keep her thoughts to herself. She stood and offered the girl a friendly smile. "So, I'm Landon, and my friend Anna Young over there runs the Green Dory Inn. We'd be happy to have you stay with us if you'd like."

Kenzie glanced at the box Phil had left on the table. "What could he have to say that's so important he'd pay to keep me here?"

"Might be worth finding out." Landon couldn't wait to see Phil's stepdaughter's reaction to this. In the past, Ciara had accused Phil of throwing money at her to leave town. Now, he funded a malicious stranger to stay.

He'd better not be setting the inn up for any more trouble.

Vi jabbed a crooked finger at the girl. "Behaviour like yours, you don't deserve to know the rest. You have to earn the right to hear it."

Kenzie's eyes slitted. "That's not what he said." She turned her back on her accuser. "Hag." The hiss slipped out so low Landon barely heard it.

From Vi's grin, she'd heard it just fine.

Landon stifled her own mirth. "I don't know Phil well, but he doesn't waste time. If he has information to share, it's important."

"Go home," Vi taunted. "And always wonder. He knew your father better than anyone. Bet he could fill in some gaps."

Kenzie zipped her coat. "Give me the details about your inn and maybe you'll see me tomorrow."

Landon wove her way among tables of chattering people until she reached her friends. Kenzie wouldn't stay. And

Phil? The gift had shaken him. Humanized him enough that she found herself praying he'd find peace.

Anna looked up at her approach, a welcoming smile curving her generous lips. A pearly enamel snowman pin shone against her fir-green sweater.

Landon took the empty seat beside her and gulped a glass of water. Elf duty was thirsty work, especially in this hot, scratchy, and short costume. "The things Roy cons people into."

Across the table, Bobby Hawke smirked. "You're one to talk. Who nearly got me arrested in September?"

Heat prickled under her collar. It hadn't been her fault... exactly. Definitely hadn't been his.

He was the self-proclaimed "getaway driver" who'd agreed to help her. A few years older than she was, maybe in his late twenties, he lived with his grandfather, Roy, next door to Anna's Green Dory Inn. With his perpetually shaggy hair and goofy tee shirts—today's was a cartoon raisin with stick arms and legs sporting a Santa hat—this geeky writer had become her best friend.

"Ho, ho, ho." Roy deposited a steaming plate of turkey dinner in front of Landon and another at his spot next to Bobby. "Those ladies in the kitchen are treasures."

He had shed his gloves, and now he swiped the plush Santa hat from his head. A quick finger-scrub left his thick white hair sticking up like frosty grass.

The other six at the table were enjoying a second cup of coffee or tea and finishing their pumpkin pie. Roy and Landon, his last-minute helper, had rushed from distributing gifts to the children and mothers at the local shelter to a repeat performance here at the community centre for the shelter volunteers and board members.

Roy split a dinner roll and slathered it with butter.

Bobby elbowed him. "Better not do that when Mom and Dad come."

Sea-blue eyes sparkling, the old man took an enormous

bite, chewed, and swallowed. "My body, my choice."

"Gramp, that's not what that means. At all."

"Still true." Roy waved the remaining morsel at Anna. "Prepare for a guest tomorrow. A girl named Kenzie. Landon'll fill you in later."

Her heaping plate wafted Christmasy goodness, but she didn't reach for her utensils yet. "You think she'll come?"

His grin stretched until he resembled a satisfied cat. "Vi played her like a master. She can't leave now."

"This is the girl you were talking to with Vi and Phil?" Anna's expression clouded. "Phil seemed upset."

"It was mean, what she did to him." Scowling, Roy described the snow globe and Kenzie's accusation about her father. "I thought Phil was going to keel over on the spot. And now he wants her to stick around and talk to him."

Landon cut a strip of turkey. "Vi seemed to have an inside track. Who is she?"

"Vi Foley. Nigel's mother." A furrow rippled Anna's broad forehead. "I'm surprised you haven't met her yet."

To the right of Roy, their neighbour Elva set her mug down with a firm rap. "Vi knows the skeletons in every closet."

Bobby drained his coffee cup. "Most people have things they want to keep quiet. Even the geezer in the red suit." He gave his grandfather another elbow dig. "Says he's waiting for the statute of limitations to run out. I think he's kidding. I hope he's kidding."

Roy held a finger to his lips. "Some things go to the grave." He winked at Landon. "Don't tell that good-looking young cop who's been hanging around."

"You're incorrigible." Not the first time Landon had told him that. She focused on Elva. "Vi was furious Kenzie breached Phil's privacy in public."

"A real Ghost of Christmas Past." Bobby gave an exaggerated shudder.

Elva's lips made a sour twist. "That girl is trouble."

The silver strands in Anna's brown bob glinted in the overhead light. The last of her smile faded. "There's hurt there, beneath the anger. Imagine never having the chance to know your father."

"Means he could never let her down." Elva's words, sharp and final, drew a swift study from the younger woman she'd brought as a guest.

The guest, Hope, would be left to wonder. Even Anna, with her heart for misfits and the wounded, hadn't been able to crack Elva's barriers.

Landon and Elva had begun a cautious friendship after events this summer, but Landon had no idea what Elva's father had done to earn her scorn.

Unlike Kenzie with Phil. If the girl did show up, could the two trust one another? Should they?

Trust. A shaky subject for Landon these days. The risk of loss cut too deep.

Chapter 2

Sunday

A T THE EDGE of the flagstone path from the inn, Landon stopped and lifted her face to the drifting snowflakes. Their frosty kisses melted on her cheekbones. White tipped the grass, but the lacy flakes were too sparse to build up on the driveway.

Inhaling the crisp air, she crossed the wet pavement to Roy's old blue pickup. Roy had added a front-mounted yellow plow blade for the winter. Behind the wheel, Bobby wore a lumpy multicoloured hat.

When she opened the passenger door and saw it clearly, she burst out laughing. "What's that supposed to be?"

He pinched the shiny yellow star at the hat's tip, and the bunched fabric inflated, stretching into a tree hung with baubles. "Don't disrespect the hat."

Climbing in, she snickered. "It's not the hat I'm worried about. What did Roy say?"

"Who do you think gave it to me?" Another squeeze of the star let the hat slump onto his head.

"I can't wait to see Ciara's reaction."

When they reached the Christmas tree u-pick, Ciara's late-model Volkswagen Bug was already parked. Their friend scooped up her tiny Chihuahua from where he'd been exploring fallen bits of greenery and hurried their way.

Her straight-cut brown wool coat, nearly as dark as her hair, didn't show the pup's paw prints. The bright-pink silk scarf tucked into her collar matched her lipstick.

Once he exited the truck, Bobby blew up his hat again and waited.

Ciara's mouth dropped open, but for once, nothing emerged but a tiny squeak. One gloved hand shifted to cover her dog's eyes.

Priceless. Landon swallowed a giggle.

Bobby swept the hat from his head with theatrical flair. "I couldn't find a matching one to fit your pooch."

Ciara retreated, smoothing the dog's snowflake-patterned jacket. "Moxie's fine the way he is, thanks." Then she pointed to the log-cabin-style building across the parking lot. "This'll be fun. I want to check out the gift shop once we have the tree."

"Trees," Landon said. "One for Anna and one for the inn's common room."

After checking in, the three friends trekked along a frost-hardened dirt road to their assigned section. Faint strains of "I'll be Home for Christmas" followed from the gift-shop speaker.

Sculpted evergreens stood plump and vibrant in a winter-browned field, spaced to allow room to grow. Here and there, a young tree, barely knee-high, splashed a lighter green. Sawdust and fresh stumps reminded Landon they'd left this a little late in the season. No wonder there were so few cars in the parking lot.

A child's laugh rang from somewhere to the left.

Bobby pointed with the yellow-handled bow saw he'd brought from the truck. "How about that way?"

In among the trees, the heady scent of balsam fir and sharp winter air flashed Landon back to childhood. To a similar lot with her parents and sisters. Before everything fell apart.

Under the guise of brushing melted snow from her cheeks, she blotted tears with the back of a red-mittened hand. "I wish Anna had come too. How am I supposed to choose for her?"

Last year, her first as a widow, Anna had flown to spend the holidays with her daughter. Determined to celebrate Christmas in her own home again, she'd felt coming here to the same tree farm without her husband would be too painful.

Ciara twirled around, one arm flung wide and the other cradling her little dog. "This is magical. We had a real tree once, but it came from a setup in town. And once Mom married Phil, it was artificial designer decor all the way."

Bobby laughed. "That's what we had at home. Practical and a lot less mess. Any year we came for Christmas, Gramp always brought me here. Dyer's Trees... that's Anna's neighbours Blaine and Tricia."

Blaine had offered to cut and deliver for Anna, but when Bobby volunteered the truck, Landon jumped at a day in the open air. University end of semester had her brain wound too tight.

She circled one tree and then the next, watching snowflakes land on the foliage and drinking in the sharp-scented air. "They're all beautiful. And I don't want to cut any of them."

"If we don't, Blaine will. Anna already paid him." Bobby pressed the curved tip of the bow saw into the ground. "Do you want to go home empty-handed?"

"This is what they're grown for. Like flowers or fruit. Or beef." A toss of Ciara's short brown hair dismissed any concern.

Bobby pointed the saw at the tree nearest Landon. "Do you like bushy or skinny? Or we can walk further."

Ciara stamped her feet. "My toes are getting cold. I didn't want to wreck my boots in the mud."

Bobby eyed her sneakers, then cocked an eyebrow at

Landon.

"Let's get one of each." She could spend all afternoon here in this peaceful place, but there were trees aplenty behind the inn. No point turning Ciara's feet into ice blocks.

She chose two good candidates and declined Bobby's offer to try the saw.

The blade rasped, biting into the tree trunk.

Ciara set Moxie on the grass, keeping him away from Bobby's activity. The little dog darted under the nearest low-hanging branches, tangling his sparkly teal leash.

"Silly boy." Ciara bent to free him. "Listen, what can you tell me about last night? About that snow globe?"

Puffing from the saw's motion, Bobby didn't look up. "Phil okay today?"

"He says he is, but Mom doesn't believe him. And this isn't just about me wanting dirt on Phil." A corner of her mouth pinched in a smirk. "Although I do. Mom called me last night—I was at my office party."

Ciara glanced over her shoulder. "This stays between us. Phil paced around the house and then took off. Said he had to walk. He was gone for hours. Mom was terrified. I had to go over and sit with her. She kept hyperventilating, and I was so worried about the babies. If he compromises her pregnancy—"

Her features tightened, accenting the sharpness of her nose. "I guess he has a super-bitter ex who blames him for someone's death. She's been sending cards every Christmas. That's how Mom found out. There has to be more, the way he reacted last night. You know Phil. Nothing rocks him. But when he came home, he was gutted. *And* furious."

Everyone at the table had heard Kenzie's accusation. Yet if Phil had been involved, he'd have been convicted. He wouldn't be a lawyer now with that background—unless he got off on a technicality.

The chill tracking Landon's spine had nothing to do with the snow. If anything illegal lay in Phil's past and it came back to bite him now, Whitney's high-risk pregnancy could be in jeopardy.

She bit her lip. "Phil made it sound like the girl who brought the gift didn't have all the facts. What she said might not even be true."

The first tree fell to the grass with a gentle whoosh. Bobby moved to the second. "And now we'll never find out. Gramp couldn't believe she didn't show up at the inn today."

"Anna too." Landon and Anna had waited around all morning, missing church. Wherever Kenzie stayed last night, check out would have been before eleven.

So much for Anna's ideas on how to get Phil and Kenzie together for a Christmas reconciliation. Landon kept her relief to herself.

Ciara's lips formed a bright-pink line. "I need to know if this could affect Mom."

Bobby kept his head down, arm moving in a regular rhythm. "You could, oh, I don't know, ask him?"

"Does Phil seem like a true-confessions sort of guy to you? Besides, he doesn't like me." She picked up Moxie and inspected his paws, rubbing them free of snow. "Come on, Bobby. You're a computer guy. Help me out and find the accident online?"

"You can use a browser too."

"I don't know how to figure out the right questions. I tried. Do you know how many fatal accidents there were twenty years ago in December? Phil comes from Saskatchewan, but that's a lot of land—and it may not have happened there."

"I'm not going to mess with an innocent man's past to satisfy your curiosity."

He'd be remembering last time. When Ciara manipulated them to break and enter to search for evidence.

Ciara cradled her dog closer. "How can I find out if you won't help me?"

Landon agreed with Bobby, but she understood Ciara's concern. "At the dinner, Vi seemed to know the secret. Nigel

Foley's mother. She might not tell you what it is, but it didn't seem to worry her."

"Nigel? Oh, that weird man with the bicycle. He creeps me out. Phil buys natural remedies from Vi. I can go see her. Pretend I need something. Since nobody here will help me."

The second tree swished downward. Bobby lowered the saw and pushed to his feet. "Shall we go?"

Landon grasped the thinner trunk and waited for him to pick up the other. It took a minute to get her bearings before starting to drag the tree toward the parking lot.

She wanted no part in Ciara's meddling. From Vi's sharp comments to Kenzie at the dinner, the woman would have a stock of choice barbs for defence.

~~~

"I wish you'd let me do that." In the inn's basement, Landon reached for the blue rubber storage bin Anna lowered from her perch on the wooden stepladder.

Anna swiped hair from her forehead. "The ornament for Piper will be in one of these. The rest can wait until we set up the trees."

Anna's daughter had called in tears tonight at the loss of a treasured keepsake. Her young son had splintered the thin wooden cutout after it slipped off their Christmas tree.

Descending the ladder, Anna sighed. "Pregnancy hormones aren't helping, but Murdoch made that decoration for her. She's lost another piece of him."

Last month marked the first anniversary of Anna's husband's death. And this Christmas, each family member carried the added grief of knowing he'd been murdered.

Anna snapped the ladder shut and propped it against the shelving. "We'll need this again soon. I hope we can get the trees done before—"

The inn's front doorbell sounded from the main level, followed by a knock.

With no guests expected and December's early nightfall,

they'd locked up at suppertime. Leaving the boxes, Landon jogged up the stairs behind Anna. When Anna flung wide the door, Kenzie stood, hunched and shivering, on the doorstep. Fat flakes of snow stuck to the girl's hair and the shoulders of her coat.

"You must be Kenzie." Anna drew her inside and shut out the winter night. "I'm Anna, and you've met Landon. Welcome. We thought you weren't coming."

Their guest slid a backpack from one shoulder. It thudded at her feet. "I couldn't decide. Is Phil seriously going to cover this?"

"He called this morning to confirm." Anna's tone gave nothing away. Not Phil's follow-up calls to see if the girl had arrived, nor his eventual request that they text him when she did—if she did.

Anna bustled down the hall to the rear of the inn, rubber-soled slippers slapping the light hardwood floor. "I'll get your key."

Landon pushed her own forebodings away and offered a smile. Phil could handle himself. She and Anna would provide hospitality. And not choose sides. "Did you have a good day in town?"

"At first." The brief animation fled Kenzie's features. "Until I heard people talking about the dinner last night. Speculating, taking Phil's side. Without the decency to ask me when I was right there."

Anna returned carrying a pewter schooner key fob. "Landon, will you show Kenzie to her room? I'll bring the boxes up from the basement."

Leading the way upstairs, Landon addressed Kenzie's complaint. "Small towns are like that. People will defend their own against an outsider but cheerfully dig up dirt themselves. They won't be so defensive of him when you're gone."

She stepped into the Schooner Room and clicked on the bedside lamp. Not as bright as the overhead fixture, but softer and more inviting.

Kenzie plopped her backpack onto the bed's sea-blue duvet. As she took in the surroundings, her posture relaxed. "Hating Phil has its upside when I can make him pay for a spot like this. I'm a student. I could never afford to stay here on my own."

Phil had authorized up to a week's stay. Better not share that tidbit. "What are you studying? I'm at the Mount for social work." Struggling at twenty-four, older than most of her classmates, and increasingly unsure this was what God wanted for her life.

"First year at Acadia, sciences." Kenzie draped her coat over the rocking chair. "Home is Saskatchewan, before you ask. I came east to get my revenge on Phil."

She looked away. "It's too late tonight to contact him. I'll get his number from you in the morning."

Landon eased out of the room. "Anna makes a killer cup of hot chocolate. This is a perfect night for it if you want to come down. She has cookies too."

And if a little friendly conversation brought information about Phil's dark secret, it might put Ciara's mind at ease. Not that Landon was investigating.

Downstairs, she found Anna in the private sitting room, kneeling between the two open totes, her lap buried in small boxes and random ornaments. On the coffee table lay a pale wooden disc, cut away in the middle to shape a kilted bagpiper. Wood-burned letters around the rim spelled "Piper's first Christmas" and the year.

Anna indicated it with her chin, her hands deftly repacking the other items. "Murdoch made this one too. She needs it more than I do now. I'll courier it out first thing tomorrow."

Footsteps sounded on the stairs, and Landon glanced toward the hallway. "I offered Kenzie a mug of your famous hot chocolate. We could all use a treat."

"And maybe some answers." Anna climbed to her feet,

brushing flecks of glitter from her fleece pants. "I hope Phil's not making a mistake. Settle her in the common room while I get it started?"

"Settle" and Kenzie didn't mix tonight, not even with the girl slouched in the leather club chair by the front window, scattered snowflakes drifting outside. Her feet shuffled in their chunky knit socks. Her elbows moved on the armrests.

She sat up straight, staring at Landon. "Why should I trust you?"

"Um, I'm not sure. Do you want to?"

"I need answers, and I don't want to talk to Phil." Kenzie pinched a lock of brown hair, squinting at the ends as if she didn't like what she saw. "I even crawled to that Vi woman today, but she wouldn't help. Self-righteous secret keeper. Thinks she's better because she knows things about other people. One of these days, it'll blow up in her face."

"Lunenburg's like any other town, with more secrets than we know." Some worse than others. What Landon and her friends had uncovered this summer still sickened her. Vi and her son, Nigel, bore that shadow, as did the neighbouring Elva. And who knew how many others?

Kenzie flicked the strands of hair behind her shoulder. "So I have to see Phil after all. How do I even know he'll tell me the truth?"

"His stepdaughter thinks he will. And she's not his biggest fan."

Her eyes slitted. "You've been talking about me too. You all have."

"My friend is worried about her mother's high-risk pregnancy." Landon spread her palms. "It's not malice or gossip. At least not with Anna and me. We're trying to understand. You must have expected people to talk, though. Wasn't that the point of a public gift?"

"Of course. I just didn't plan to be around to hear it. And I didn't know his wife was pregnant—and fragile."

"Does it make a difference?"

"Maybe? That gift really shook him. I thought it would satisfy me." Kenzie scuffed her fingertips against her jeans.

Landon released a soft breath. "But it didn't?"

"It's his fault my father died. Time for a little payback."

Porcelain clinked in the hallway. Anna entered, her tray balancing three assorted Christmas mugs and a plate mounded with shortbread cookies and gingerbread cutouts. Once Kenzie and Landon each took a steaming mug and a cookie, Anna set the tray on the puzzle table.

She dropped into the wooden chair beside the puzzle, drink in hand. "We need to finish this to make room for the Christmas tree. Sorry it's not already up to welcome you. I should have picked an easier design. Too much white."

A slender white lighthouse rose from snow-brushed grey rocks, stormy waves behind and fat flakes blotting a heavy grey sky. On its narrow door, an evergreen wreath sported a Christmas-red bow.

"If I can't sleep tonight, I'll know what to do." Kenzie sipped her hot chocolate. "This is so good."

Anna beamed. "Whisk the powder into hot milk—or cream. And add a truffle."

Kenzie drank again, then licked brown foam from her upper lip. "Mom would love this place. Except she couldn't stand to be near Phil."

Anna selected a gingerbread cookie. "Does she know you're here?"

"Of course not." The words exploded like a sneeze. Or a plea. "Finding the right kind of truck, making the snow globe, imagining his reaction—it was therapeutic. For me, anyway."

Anna's eyes closed in what might have been a brief prayer. Then she exhaled. "Phil asks if you'll phone him by ten tomorrow morning. I'll give you the number at breakfast."

"I don't know why I'm doing this to myself. There's nothing he can say even if he apologizes." Both hands clutched her mug. "He'll try to blame my father. Some twisted form of revenge."

Said the girl whose whole reason for being here was revenge. Landon flattened a palm against her jeans. "Last night, Phil was reacting. He didn't have time to plot anything even if he wanted to."

"He's a lawyer. They think on their feet."

Phil had barely *kept* his feet. No, he'd seemed desperate— hungry—to connect with his self-proclaimed enemy. Like he truly did have details she needed to hear.

Kenzie's gaze dipped, then tracked between Landon and Anna. "You two don't seem close to him. So this place is neutral ground. Could he come here? I thought maybe a coffee shop, but this whole nosy town recognizes me now. With points and stares."

What could shake Phil so badly? And why would he risk sharing it with this stranger bent on causing harm?

Chapter 3

Monday

"WHAT HAPPENS IF he can't get here that soon?" Landon reached over the white pass-through doors from the kitchen to take the phone from Kenzie.

The girl stood in the breakfast room. She'd come downstairs shortly before ten, asking to use the inn landline so Phil wouldn't learn her cell number. And after waiting until the last minute to call, she'd given him a bare thirty minutes to get there.

Anna smoothed her holly-print apron. "You don't have to rush check out. He asked for an open-ended stay." She chopped the last word short, then added, "Unless he tells me otherwise."

"Thank you." Kenzie hiked a stiff shoulder at Landon. "If he's late, I may have trouble starting my car. Or misplace my keys. Or maybe I'll go. This is crazy."

Anna's slow exhale carried force. "Warm chocolate chip cookies should break the ice. Did you want to meet in the breakfast room? I can put on coffee or tea so you don't have to serve yourselves. We'll get out of the way."

"Can we use the room with the puzzle? A lawyer would feel safest behind a table or desk. Plus, if I score the comfy chair first, I'll seem relaxed. And coffee, please."

"Common room it is." Anna clattered her baking utensils with uncharacteristic vigour. Trying to keep from saying more?

Exactly half an hour later, a glossy black sedan cruised up the long driveway from the road.

With Anna wrangling cookie sheets in the kitchen and Kenzie planted in the common room club chair, Landon let Phil in.

He stowed his gloves and surrendered his wool coat, revealing a charcoal-grey suit. A peach tie softened the effect. At least he hadn't gone for full-on intimidating black.

Landon swallowed her nerves. If he'd come from the office, a suit could be his daily uniform. And from what she'd seen, even his casual look would be elegant. Stepping back, she gestured toward the door beside the stairs. "Kenzie's in there. You can shut yourselves in and have all the privacy you'd like."

The scent of baking wafted from the rear of the inn. "If you wait a couple of minutes, Anna's plating cookies fresh from the oven."

A smile ghosted across his lips. "Most kind of her." Serious again, he lowered his voice and gestured toward the open doorway. "May I request the courtesy of your presence? Or Anna's? I prefer not to be alone with a young woman who considers my reputation a commodity to be tarnished."

Surely, Kenzie couldn't be that malicious. Or could she? Jaw set, Landon nodded.

Phil paused inside the doorway. "Thank you for agreeing to talk. May I call you Kenzie?"

"It's my name." She stood to shake his hand before folding into her seat like she belonged there.

"A difficult name for me to speak, even after twenty years." Phil took one of the upholstered chairs, gripping the curved oak armrests to reposition it squarely in her line of sight. "I've asked Landon to join us—for both our protection."

"I heard."

Trying to hide her discomfort, Landon crossed to the wooden chair by the puzzle table.

Phil withdrew a small manila envelope from his suit coat pocket and tapped the edge on one knee. He extended it to Kenzie. "I thought you might like these pictures of him."

The girl's features froze. One hand reached. Retracted. "They'll be compromising. Or demeaning. No thank you."

So smoothly it could have been his original intention, Phil offered the envelope to Landon. "If you'd be so kind?"

Anna's arrival with a tray of coffee and cookies made a brief reprieve. Landon declined her offer of a mug for herself. She shouldn't be here. Yet underneath her shaky nerves, she understood.

Once the door closed behind Anna, Landon took a breath and untucked the envelope flap. Five pictures slid onto her lap. Kenzie's father was in his early twenties, smiling in each shot. The final image showed him with a second young man, their arms around one another's shoulders, standing in front of a weathered cabin.

She looked at Phil, down to the photo, to Phil again.

His lips firmed. "I considered omitting that one. But these were all I had."

Landon put the prints in the envelope and passed it to Kenzie. "He's enjoying life. I'm sorry for your loss. Both of your losses."

At the edge of her vision, Phil nodded.

Kenzie clutched the envelope. "I'll look at these alone. Later. Thank you."

Blinking rapidly, she walked to the table and one-handedly stirred cream and sugar into her coffee. By the time she took her seat, her lashes no longer fought tears. "My father is still dead because of you."

Phil cleared his throat. "What brought you to the dinner?"

"Sending cards wasn't enough. For the twentieth anniversary, I wanted to go big. Do something public. See if

24

it hurt you."

"Mission accomplished." His dry tone didn't waver. "How did you find me?"

"There is a—vacancy—in my heart where I should have a father. Mom made sure I knew from the beginning whose fault it was. I've been following you online. When I saw you'd be at that dinner as a board member, I had to come."

"How far?"

"The Valley. I chose my university location to put you in range."

"Your mother doesn't know you're here."

"No."

Phil made eye contact with Landon. "My stepdaughter would crow over any sordid tidbits from my past. Likely in a way that would upset her mother."

"Whitney doesn't know?"

"She knew about the accident but not the cause. I confessed the details yesterday." He leaned against the mint upholstery. "I rely on your discretion. As Ciara did this fall."

At the mention of sordid tidbits, Kenzie had leaned forward in her chair, elbows on her knees, coffee mug held between her palms, envelope of photos in her lap.

"Mom's never forgiven you."

"I've never forgiven her either."

The coffee mug jerked in her grip. "What for?"

"Your mother and I were a couple. Before you were born."

Kenzie snorted. "Obviously."

One finger tapped his pant leg, then stilled. "Whitney begged me to hold off on this until the babies are born." His lips tightened. "I'm handing you a grenade. If you pull the pin, I'll survive. But please consider my wife's challenging pregnancy. At least wait for the birth. Don't lay any more deaths at my door."

"I'll think about it."

He rose. Hands clasped behind him, he paced a cramped oval among the chairs. "Your mother and I were young and stupid. She got pregnant. I—handled it very poorly. I regret that even more than my friend Kenzie's death."

"I'm an only child." She'd straightened, arms now clamped across her ribs.

Facing her, Phil planted his feet and stood, arms loose at his sides. "I ran out on her. When I found the guts to come back—support the baby—marry her if she'd have me—"

An ugly shade darkened his skin. His throat pulsed so wildly Landon feared he was choking.

Gaze locked on Kenzie, he pushed the words out. "She said she aborted the baby. Threw that news in my face and left town."

Kenzie sneered up at him. "Mom hates abortions. You're lying."

Phil walked a slow half-circle to his seat, then dropped as if his legs had given out. "Ask her. And tell her this came from me."

She drew her knees to her chest, arms locked around them. Feet on the seat cushion. "Maybe I will."

Standing, he inclined his head toward Landon in a faint bow. "Thank you. This has been uncomfortable for us all."

He glanced at Kenzie, braced in the club chair. The rigid lines of his features softened. "Study the pictures, think about what I've said, and call me in a couple of days. One key detail about your father's been kept from you."

Swift strides carried him out the door.

~~~

Of all the nights for an invitation to share a meal at Roy's place. Landon swallowed her last bite of blueberry-sauced pork tenderloin and willed herself to relax. The delicious food and flickering ivory candles reflecting in the dark oak tabletop set a peaceful tone. Yet, hours after the meeting at the inn, Phil's agony frayed the edges of Landon's composure. And tonight, instead of casual fare and banter with her friends, the room held a dinner-party vibe. With

Bobby's parents.

"I know the perfect dishes for the lovely dessert you brought, Anna. Landon, would you help me get them down from the cupboard? They're up high."

Landon sat taller, not fooled by the seemingly innocent request. She studied Bobby's mother, Alexis, diagonally down the table. As far apart as they could have been placed at a dinner for six.

"Mom..." Bobby's groan rumbled like a volcano. Colour seeped into his cheeks.

Seated at Landon's end of the table, he pressed a foot onto her toes. "You stay. Let the hosts work."

At the opposite end, Roy's fork clanked against his plate. "Here's the chance to order your boy around, Lexie. He lives here. Heaven knows, he needs the exercise."

The woman's nostrils pinched. "A–lex–*iss*." Her eyes glittered at Roy. "You men cooked the meal, and Anna prepared a decadent trifle. You can let us contribute too."

Bobby braced his palms on the table edge, pushing back his chair.

Landon stood first, spine straight. Hoping he'd read her eyes and not escalate. She'd heard enough stories about his mother to be prepared. And ready to stand her ground.

She joined Alexis on the short walk to the kitchen. "What do you say we rearrange the shelves? Roy hates that."

"I hear you," he hollered from the dining room. "Put on the coffee while you're out there."

Alexis strode across the kitchen and tugged a folded stepstool from its niche. "I'll pass them down. You can set them on the counter."

Instead of climbing, she angled toward Landon, one hand holding the stepstool. "Robert has too much potential to be allowed to stagnate here much longer."

"Mrs. Hawke—"

"Thorne-Hawke, dear. And it's doctor. But call me Alexis."

The clipped tone stung. Landon held eye contact. "Perhaps

he prefers to work here because we recognize that and respect him as he is."

"Do you have feelings for him?"

"Of course I do. He's a great guy and my best friend."

The woman's elegant brows slid together. Her nostrils pinched. "Romantic feelings."

Landon was a committed single. Bobby knew that. Tonight, she found herself in no hurry to enlighten his mother. She crossed to the sink. "I'll start the coffee."

"I'll thank you to answer my question."

Filling the coffee maker's water reservoir allowed time for deliberate breaths and a silent prayer. *Lord, You love this woman...*

Alexis stood a mere pace away, twin spots of colour high in her cheeks. "My son has a successful future and will need a partner who can support him."

A partner who was not Landon. Message received. Landon's eyes rolled before she could stop them.

The other woman's lips flattened into a red line.

No question, Bobby deserved better. A partner without a traumatic past or any of her other limitations—some of which she'd successfully kept from him. Yet he'd said he loved her.

He'd also promised not to mention it again. They'd gone on to forge a stronger friendship. By now, his feelings would have passed, and one day he'd find a true soulmate.

Shoulders stiff, Landon matched the woman's stare. "*Dr.* Thorne-Hawke. Alexis. I am not looking for a ticket to the ball."

Alexis's expression blanked. She gave her head a slight shake.

"To dance with the prince. Cinderella?" Bobby would have gotten it. And laughed.

His mother whirled to the cupboard and clanged the stepstool into position. "Help me get these dishes down."

The pale green glass, translucent and paper-thin, must be

ancient. Beautiful but irreplaceable. Landon held her breath as she transferred them to the counter.

Bobby, his father, and Roy trooped into the kitchen carrying stacks of dirty plates. Would Roy object to his daughter-in-law's use of the heirloom bowls?

His sea-blue eyes lit. "My mother's dishes. Good choice, girl."

As they finished setting up for dessert, Landon's phone buzzed in her pocket. The third time it started, she excused herself to the bathroom and checked the display.

Three calls from Dylan. At least one voice mail. Her stomach clenched, but everyone she might worry about was here with her. Still, her finger trembled as she hit the call icon.

He answered on the second ring. "Are you home?"

Crisp, concise. Full cop mode. As she'd feared, not a social call. "Sorry, no. We're at Roy's."

"Has Kenzie Garner checked out?"

"No, why?"

"I need you and Anna to meet me at the inn. Forty minutes. Don't say anything to Ms. Garner." He clicked off.

Landon grinned at the whimsical top-hatted snowman perched on the toilet tank. "Easy to say nothing when you know nothing."

Now, to extricate Anna in a way that didn't imply Alexis was scaring Landon away.

~~~

Light glowed through the forest from the inn. Warm yellow from the windows, twinkling colours from the Christmas bulbs outlining the house and outbuildings.

Landon and Anna needed a flashlight to navigate the path home from Roy's, but the walk between houses took no longer than by car. Cold car. Walking warmed their bodies and let the crisp air clean their lungs and chill their noses. Each exhale made a cloud. Smoke from a nearby wood stove threaded among the scents of evergreen and salt, tickling Landon's nose but evoking a sense of peace and cozy belonging.

The frozen ground was mostly bare, studded with stones and the occasional stick. Arms cradling the trifle bowl, Anna stumbled.

Landon steadied her. "Careful with that. Roy may be planning to sneak over for more fat and calories. Alexis is right, but she'll never change him."

"Not if we keep enabling him." Anna glanced sideways. "She means well, even if she goes about it wrong. I assume she staged an impromptu meeting in the kitchen. You okay?"

"I'm angry. It's like she has this agenda for her son and can't see the man he really is. So she has to control his relationships and snipe at him to get with the pattern. She's half of what made Jessie such a bad fit for him."

"Mmm. What about you?" The question floated on the night air.

Landon falling for the boy next door and settling down locally? Anna's dream, no question. Not happening. "She warned me off, but it was a waste of breath."

Her spirit warmed. Bobby's love, freely offered but not received, had affirmed her value in a way even faith hadn't done—and faith had done a lot. By definition, a God of love had to love her. But a self-described "card-carrying decent guy" feeling that way said something else entirely.

"So..."

The eagerness in Anna's drawn-out word cut through Landon's introspection. Oops.

"It's not what you think. It was a waste because I'm single and not looking. If God has romance for me, He's going to have to hit me over the head with it."

She'd said that to Bobby in September. When he'd chosen friendship over trying to win an unwilling heart. She hadn't seen him with anyone else, but he never pined or moped or hinted for more. He was just Bobby. Unlikely hero and her best friend.

Her steps slowed. "I rushed us out the door because Dylan's coming. He phoned me right after Alexis's 'talk.' It's police business to do with Kenzie. We're not to warn her."

"Whatever Phil told her this morning—I hope she didn't decide to blab it all over town." Anna's grim undertone suggested tomorrow's breakfast might get singed.

Landon didn't blame her. "There's something about her father she doesn't know. Phil's desperate to make her hear him."

As they neared the inn, Landon scanned the yard. Anna's cat, Timkin, had stayed inside, but their misfit, Mister, could be out here on the prowl. No sign of the marmalade cat, but Kenzie's car in the lot meant Dylan would find her here.

Inside, the main floor was quiet. Kenzie must be in her room.

Anna's first act was to brew a pot of herbal Christmas-themed tea, which they carried into the guests' common room. As she kept saying, "That lighthouse puzzle isn't going to do itself."

Landon set her mug on a ceramic coaster painted with a lush poinsettia. "Why not move it onto one of the breakfast tables? We're not going to have a full house here over the holidays."

"We might want to have people in for a potluck. Worst case, I'll lay it in the box in sections and take it out in the new year. Even if that does feel like admitting defeat."

Landon's vision was blurring the white snow, waves, and clouds by the time Dylan arrived. At his knock, she hurried to the door.

He stepped inside with a swirl of cold air. "Brr. Wind's picking up."

As he unzipped his parka, she studied his face for a hint of his purpose here. Mouth serious, lean cheeks drawn, eyes seemingly darker than ever. Whatever Kenzie had done had hit hard.

Harder than malice alone. Landon's heart jumped. Phil. The girl hadn't killed him?

Dylan caught her watching and cracked a quick grin. "Whatever you're thinking, you're wrong." He sucked in a breath as if strapping on body armour. "Where's Anna?"

"Follow me."

Inside the common room, he shut the door. After a brief greeting for Anna, he cut his gaze toward the ceiling. "She's up there?"

"Her car's outside. It wasn't when we left at five." Anna eased toward the front of the straight-backed wooden chair she'd been using at the puzzle table, planting her feet solidly on the hardwood floor.

Dylan seated himself on the other wooden chair. "I've been all over a crime scene. The uniform may not be too clean."

Landon sat near Anna. Waiting.

He let out a slow exhale. "I do need to talk to Kenzie Garner. Information only. I'm accelerating because we don't know how long she'll stay and we at least need contact information."

Some of the stiffness seeped from Landon's spine. The girl couldn't have done anything too extreme.

Dylan leaned forward, hands spread on his knees, fingertips whitening against the dark fabric. "Wanting to speak with your guest gives me an excuse to tell you this." His jaw set. "Vi Foley died this afternoon. It's being treated as a homicide. Nigel found her. Anna, you know his peculiarities. Can you reach out to him?"

"If I can find him." Anna spoke like a marionette with no one working the strings. "He'll have taken off."

A slow smile somehow accented Dylan's sombre mood. "On the contrary, he's retrieving valuable information from his bunker—location classified unless we produce a warrant. And he'll arrange a signal system in case we need to speak with him. After that, yes, he's going to ground. If these past

32

months have taught me anything, he'll be patrolling to be sure Elva's safe, and he may stop in here for tea. If you could keep an eye out, I'd be grateful."

He settled a little easier in his chair. "And keep it quiet until the news breaks."

Pale and stiff, Anna pushed out a ragged breath. "I'd like to tell Elva."

"That was my previous stop. But Nigel is the protector in that dynamic. I doubt he'd be open to any support she could give." He grimaced. "I can't figure out the relationship there. Not that it's any of my business, except that these nuances can help me understand the wider picture."

Anna's slippers shuffled against the floorboards. "Maybe he feels he has to make up for what his father did."

Of course. Landon had thought it was a one-sided love, but that didn't match Nigel's air of responsibility. She pressed her nails into the upholstery of her seat. "It wasn't his fault."

"Fill me in, please?" Dylan glanced between them, brown eyes intent. "Remember, I'm a come-from-away."

Anna picked up a stray puzzle piece and tapped the edge against the table. "Elva and his mother had the same abuser, a generation apart. You know Nigel's a complicated man. I was a grade behind, but I remember him having a serious crush on Elva in high school. To his mind, the captain's actions must have made it inappropriate for Nigel to pursue her. So he channelled his feelings into what we see today."

Dylan's jaw clenched. Like he wanted to spit. Or swear. "Old man Hiltz was a piece of work. Yet nobody reported him. Or delivered their own brand of justice." His gaze flicked to Landon. "Sorry to bring that up."

Her grief over a friend-turned-vigilante still lingered, but she shrugged. "Captain Hiltz victimized Vi in her teens, and now more violence takes her life. Find her killer so we can see proper justice done."

"Yes, ma'am." He stood. "And you, my friend, are not

going to make my personal or professional life any harder by conducting unauthorized investigations. Right?"

"Right." How did he and his team do this day after day, case after case?

Anna frowned. "You wanted to see Kenzie. Under my roof, she's my responsibility. She's also a stranger here. What connection could she have with Vi?"

"Vi left a letter with Nigel, naming a primary suspect should anything happen to her. While we investigate that, we also need to follow up on other threads. Like anyone who's been in conflict with the victim."

"Wait, you know who did it?" Landon shot to her feet, barely stopping the next question. He couldn't reveal a name during an active investigation. She wouldn't make things awkward by asking.

A flicker of his eyebrow acknowledged the temptation. He opened the door and ushered them both into the hallway. "Would one of you ask Kenzie to come down, please? Say it's about the incident at the dinner and leave it at that. And I'd prefer to see her alone."

When Anna went upstairs, Landon asked him, "What does this do to your plans to fly home?"

"Dad will understand if I have to cancel, but there's been a reticence when we talk. I want to see what's going on." He tapped the strand of lights Anna had twined around the stair railing. "And I want this wrapped up before Christmas. For Nigel's sake and for my team. Let them have time to celebrate with their families."

"So you do need our help."

"Landon—"

She grinned. "You do the legwork. Let Anna and me pray for you."

His eyes narrowed. "Can't hurt."

Kenzie reached the base of the stairs, Anna behind her. Eyes watchful, mouth tight, she waited for Dylan to speak.

"Constable Dylan Tremblay, Ms. Garner. I have a few

questions, and your hostess has kindly offered a private space to chat."

Her lips pressed tighter as if she bit the insides. "Phil called you. The snake. I'll spread his story everywhere—"

"You misunderstand, ma'am. If you could follow me, please? This way."

His outstretched hand didn't touch her, but the power of his presence steered her to obey. Again, he shut the door.

Anna led the way to her private sitting room. "We'll hear them when they come out." She sank onto the couch. "Poor Nigel. I can't believe Vi's gone. Not like that."

Slow tears rolled down her cheeks.

Landon sat beside her. "Will he be okay?"

Shoulders shaking, Anna completely broke down.

All Landon could do was press tissues into her hand and hold her, rocking and murmuring prayers drowned out by Anna's sobs.

Nigel was pushing sixty and had lived with his mother all his life. For all his odd mannerisms, he held down a job and had the independence to build and maintain a survival bunker. In case the aliens came, but the reasoning didn't change his ability.

This level of grief went beyond losing one friend and concern for another. Tears burned Landon's eyes. She held Anna tighter. "This is about more than Nigel, isn't it?"

"It's—Murdoch—all over—again." Anna was keening now, a lost, low wail.

Barely into her second year of widowhood, reeling from the recent discovery that her husband's death had been murder, now processing another killing close to home...

Landon sprinted to shut the sitting room door. Locked it. Innkeeper duties would wait. And Dylan could let himself out.

She snagged a soft throw off the nearer recliner and draped the ivory plush across Anna's shoulders, then slid an arm around her waist and held tight. Together, they'd ride the current of grief.

Her own losses tugged at her, but this was Anna's hurt. She tucked her feet up on the upholstery and leaned her head into Anna's neck, praying when words came. Singing a simple praise song after that. Reminding Anna she wasn't alone.

This woman. Twice her age, more than a mentor, more than a friend. Anna had become her mother figure these past few years.

Since Landon had come to the inn, how many meltdowns had Anna held her through? To give back felt good. *God, be her comfort.*

Slowly, Anna calmed. The tears stopped. She wiped her eyes and gave her nose a good blow. "Thank you for staying with me." She rose and shuffled toward her bedroom. "I'm done. Will you lock up?"

"Want me to sleep on the couch tonight?" Landon had done it in June when there'd been a prowler lurking.

Anna sent a wavery smile over her shoulder. "I'll be fine. God and I have some talking to do. If I need you, I'll text."

"Okay."

Dylan had long gone, and there was no sign of Kenzie. Landon locked the front door deadbolt and stood staring through the glass into the night.

He'd visited because of their guest. Telling Landon and Anna about Vi was an extra he'd slid in on the side. With no way for them to reach Nigel tonight, hearing the news in the morning would have been soon enough.

So why had he gone to Elva's? They couldn't suspect her. Was she also at risk?

Chapter 4

Tuesday

STREAMERS OF MIST drifted past the inn's kitchen window, grey like small wraiths of cloud. Or the cobwebs people strung for Halloween. Landon turned away, haunted by thoughts of Vi dead and Nigel grieving alone.

The dismal day wouldn't keep him from roaming the woods—patrolling against what, she didn't know. His expert woodcraft meant they'd never see him if he didn't present himself, yet Landon and Anna had decided to keep a close watch. He'd appreciate a warm drink if the dampness held.

In the kitchen's warmth and cheerful lighting, she accepted a plate from Anna. She carried Kenzie's waffles and bacon through the pass-through doors to the breakfast room.

The girl set down her phone and inhaled with a smile. "This is so much better than dorm food. You have no idea."

Anna's cooking was worth the commute to the city for Landon's part-time classes. Not that she wanted the drama of a residence full of under-twenties anyway. And renting off-campus brought other issues.

Kenzie drizzled maple syrup over the blueberry-topped waffles. "Cop said I could leave town. First, I have to decide if I want the rest of Phil's story."

"It's not that far a drive from the Valley if you wanted to come back."

"If I'm going to do this, it has to be before I see Mom. I fly out next week. That's not a lot of time." She looked up, suddenly young and vulnerable. "You're sure he's telling the truth?"

Landon rested her hands on the chairback across from Kenzie. "What does your heart tell you?"

The girl's shoulders slumped. "It's probably true. And since Mom didn't tell me, it's something bad." She scowled at her waffles. "I can't go home not knowing."

Landon topped up Kenzie's water glass. "Today's probably not a good day for me to sit in on your meeting. Anna's getting a care package together for Vi's son, and I'm supposed to deliver it. She wants to stay here in case he comes around."

"Text him."

Landon shook her head. "No phone. Nigel's a bit eccentric."

"You don't think he killed her? Like that guy in the news last month who shot his parents at the dinner table."

"No." If he could have, Nigel would have exacted his own justice for Elva's attack this summer—but he'd have presented himself to the police afterward. "He's complicated, but no."

Kenzie sniffed. "Well, I'm sorry for him and all, but clearly someone got fed up with her secret keeping. Knowledge is power—either she wouldn't share or she threatened to."

Wouldn't share? That opened a different angle of suspects. Including the sulky girl spearing a fat blueberry with her fork.

The news report this morning hadn't revealed the cause of death. Deliberate murder needed a specific type of killer, but accidents happened when passions flared. Kenzie had visited Vi on Sunday before coming to the inn. Had she returned yesterday afternoon?

~~~

Nigel hadn't appeared by the time Landon went outside after lunch. The skies had cleared, but the watery sunlight made the air seem colder.

She hopped into the old blue pickup and shut the door. The sturdy cardboard box of food fit on the bench seat between her and Bobby, and she stowed the smaller bag on the floor at her feet. "Thanks for driving me. And thank Roy for loaning his truck."

"Yeah, I'd hoped Mom and Dad would drive my clunker down and fly home, but Mom said no. I'll find another way."

Bobby's main ride, a low-slung white Corvette, sat snug and dry in a heated garage in town until spring.

"You call it a clunker and expect your mother to ride in it? Would it even survive the trip?"

He reversed the truck in a tight turn and headed down the driveway. "Was she that rough on you last night?"

"What? No, I didn't mean she'd kill it. It sounds half-dead already. She's—"

"Gotcha." He snickered. "Seriously, I'm sorry about last night. I must have tried too hard to convince her we're only friends. Although she'll lean on my friends too if she gets the chance. I hope she didn't embarrass you."

"Bobby, I embarrassed myself. Why didn't you tell me she's a doctor?"

"How did that come up?"

"I called her Mrs. Hawke." The patronizing rebuke burned again. "I'm used to people thinking I'm a dumb blonde, but that doesn't mean I like it."

"You actually get that?"

"Not like I used to." It came with the learning disability. The one he didn't know about.

"Wow." The truck slowed for a sharp curve, elevated plow blade rattling. "Why didn't you use her first name like anyone else?"

"She was coming on strong, and I wanted some distance. Instead, I made it worse."

The two-lane road traced the coastline, the water outside Landon's window sullen today despite the pale sunlight.

At the edge of town, Bobby signalled and steered the truck into a convenience store lot.

A slight figure peeled away from the corner of the building and pushed a battered mountain bike toward them.

Landon collected Anna's care packages and slid from the truck as Bobby jumped out the other side. She approached the boy. "Hey, Corey. Thanks for doing this. Have you spoken to Nigel?"

Corey's knit cap slanted his blond bangs across his eyes. He peered at her through the gaps. "Not yet. He's private."

He shrugged out of his backpack, his thin brown jacket exposing bony wrists. "Gotta repack the food so I can carry it."

Landon held the cardboard box as he deftly filled his pack. Last came the bag. "This is for you and your dad. Christmas cookies from Anna."

His head came up. "Tell her thanks." He hoisted the backpack and threw a leg over the crossbar of his bike, then drilled Landon with a stare. "Miz Foley was a good person. Are you gonna find her killer?"

Landon blinked. She'd solved the last murder by accident—and had nearly become the next victim. "Nigel wouldn't want us putting ourselves in danger. Me or you."

"Whatever." Corey pushed off on his bike, pedalling hard.

She caught Bobby's sympathetic grimace and shrugged. "I can't win with him."

"Why meet him here?"

"He knows how to find Nigel's bunker. That's like a sacred trust, and he won't lead us anywhere near it. I don't think he wants us around his house either, although Anna's been there."

Inside the truck again, Landon fastened her seat belt and

snugged it in across her puffy coat. Out of the wind, she could unzip partway. "Anna texted Corey this morning and had to break the news. He hadn't heard. Dylan came last night but asked us to wait for the official statement. He also told Elva."

"Elva makes sense. And we know why he told you."

Heat prickled where her scarf lay against her neck. Anna's wishful matchmaking and the grilling from Alexis had her overreacting. Bobby knew better than to imagine a relationship. Landon stared out the windshield and tried to keep from sounding defensive. "He wanted Anna to look out for Nigel. He's just a friend."

"Actually, I thought he'd want to warn you off investigating."

Oops. "He did that too."

"So next stop, scene of the crime?"

"Now, who's the bad influence?" She studied him, the joke becoming serious. "Should Dylan have been talking to you?"

"Dunno. Nigel shouldn't stand alone." He scuffed his fingers through his hair, leaving a rumpled thatch. "I get leaving it to the professionals, but there's this drive to help."

"I think they'd consider staying out of the way a helpful activity."

"Spoken like a person who's trying to stay on Santa's nice list." Bobby snickered. "You've met the old guy. What would he say about this?"

Sparkling blue eyes snapped in her imagination, along with Roy's wide jaw in a grim set. "Don't get yourself killed, girl." She shifted sideways in the seat and tipped her index finger at Bobby. "And keep that grandson of mine in line."

Bobby's hands rose in surrender. "You nailed the intonation."

"It's exactly what he'd say. And he's right. But Nigel might even be at the house if they've released it. It's our best chance to see him, and it would let us pay our respects to Vi. With a murder investigation, who knows when they'll release her body for a funeral? Let's go."

"As you wish." He started the engine and put the truck in gear.

She poked him in the arm. "I'm not a princess."

"Oh?" The truck stopped, barely out of the parking space. Bobby let out a slow breath. "Do you want to unpack that for me?"

"'As you wish... Your Majesty.' You didn't have to say it for me to hear it." She arched an eyebrow.

"As long as that's all you heard, we're good." He eased his foot off the brake, rolling the truck forward.

Was that a challenge? "I may have heard 'Miss Princess Bossy Pants' too. Hey, it's your grandfather telling me to keep you in line. Not my idea."

Bobby snorted, shaking his head so fast his hair flew. "He's rubbing off on you."

The truck rattled its way onto the street.

"Do you know where Nigel lives?" Landon hadn't thought to ask Anna.

"Across from Gramp's physio clinic. I took *his* royal highness there a lot this summer."

Roy's broken leg was what brought Bobby to Lunenburg before Landon arrived in June. While she'd been all about returning to Ontario as fast as she could, Bobby's fond memories of summers here made the transition easy for him. Landon had stayed to switch schools and dodge a toxic professor. Meeting Bobby's mother confirmed her suspicions that part of his reason to stay in Nova Scotia was to create boundaries.

Instead of continuing toward the inn, Bobby cut left onto a narrow strip of pavement that swept along the coast. The way veered inland for a while, through evergreens and scattered bungalows. Before long, a gravel road to the left led them into more trees and newer-looking single-level homes and split-entries. The truck bounced through a pothole, and Bobby grunted. "Sorry. At least we don't raise a dust cloud when the ground's frozen."

Soon he slowed and pointed to the grey Haven Physiotherapy sign to the left. "That's Gramp's spot, and he said Vi's is the next driveway on the right."

Where the Haven Physio property stretched open and inviting, landscaped with a small parking lot, the Foley home lay fenced by bare-limbed trees and scattered evergreens. Bobby kept the truck to a crawl to navigate the rocky driveway. Atop a slight incline, he steered into a spot under an ancient pine. "No sign of Nigel, but we can get out and walk around."

The small building resembled a summer cottage more than a year-round home. Weathered boards suggested age, and moss grew on a corner of the roof overhung by a stately maple—if Landon could be sure of the tree type without its signature leaves. Crime-scene tape barred the steps to an enclosed porch. A plain spruce wreath with a bright-red bow clung to the wooden door.

They followed a path around the structure to a rust-spotted sedan parked before a building barely large enough to be called a garage. Another strip of vibrant yellow tape cautioned that the outbuilding was also off-limits. They circled the home, the frozen grass bumpy underfoot. Deep in the forest behind them, a lone jay screeched.

The day might be mild for mid-December, but the damp chilled Landon's bones. She stuffed her hands into her pockets. "Nigel can't be inside. If he's nearby, he doesn't want to talk."

"Yeah." Bobby scuffed his boot against a fallen branch. A twig snapped off, but the branch held tight to the ground.

As they were leaving, a woman strode up the driveway. Bobby stopped, lowering his window, and waited for her.

She peered in at them. "I thought Roy might be with you. Starr recognized the truck."

"Gramp says she doesn't miss much. Dee, this is my friend Landon. We're looking for Nigel."

Somewhere around thirty, the petite woman radiated

fresh-air-fuelled energy. Her cheeks still bore an outdoor summer tan. Light-brown hair swung loose at her shoulders, half hiding the shearling collar of her bulky denim jacket.

She smiled at Landon. "I'm Roy's physiotherapist from across the road. And my daughter, Starr, is our local traffic reporter."

Then she sobered. "You must have heard about Vi. Isn't it horrible? Nigel's taken off, but why don't you come over? I have a big gap between clients today, and Starr would love to hear how her 'favourite old person' is doing. She got such a kick out of him dressing up as Santa at the dinner." She focused on Landon. "I recognize you now. You were his elf. We sat at the table next to the drama. Can you believe that girl? Do come if you have time. Be warned, Starr will talk your ear off."

They waited until Dee reached the road before coasting along behind her.

As Bobby parked in the physio lot, Landon admired the house. "This place is amazing. Business must be good."

Sided in a seafoam green with white trim, the building's single storey near the road stretched to a second level under a grey slanted roof that evoked the slope of a wave. White shutters framed the upper windows. The land extended to the ocean. At the far end of the parking lot, an old-style well made of beach stones had been converted to a flower garden. It would be charming in the summer. Now, browned stalks shivered in the breeze.

Bobby stepped from the truck. "I think they lived here before Dee set up a home clinic. Gramp occasionally mutters unkind sentiments about her ex."

He spread his arms wide as if to embrace the sun piercing the clouds. His jacket fell open, revealing a surfing Santa on his shirt. "Gotta take these moments when we get them. There's more snow on the way."

The small amount that fell on Sunday had already melted. Landon inhaled deeply, filling her lungs with salt-sea air.

"Better snow than rain."

"Says the one who won't be clearing driveways."

"Don't worry. I'll be shovelling the inn's steps and walkways where Roy's big blade can't go. But it's Christmas. Snow is always welcome."

"Famous last words." He gestured to the main door, which swung inward to reveal a black-haired child. "Gramp uses the clinic entrance, and I usually sit in the truck to work. I wonder what the rest of the place looks like."

The child, Starr, was older than Landon had guessed at Saturday's dinner. Maybe ten, eleven? Forearms supported by grey cuffs, her hands gripped the posts of matching silver crutches. The way her body curved forward as she leaned into them made her seem smaller. Heavy, loose curls accented her delicate features.

"Mom had a phone call. Come and talk to me."

When Bobby started introductions, Starr's eyes sparkled. "You were the lady elf. Tell Santa Roy he needs to work on his laugh. There's videos online."

They looped their coats over pegs by the door and parked their boots on the rubber tray underneath.

Starr led them into a spacious room where a bushy Christmas tree stood crowned with a black top hat. Hundreds of tiny white lights illuminated branches bearing round white ornaments. For garlands...

Landon stepped closer. Not ribbons at all. Everyday winter scarves. "What a fun idea."

"It's a snowman tree. We got it on the weekend. Before..." Her pointed chin quivered. "You know about Miz Vi, right? I saw Roy's truck go up. He always brings me candy."

Bobby showed empty palms. "Is that like a toll we're supposed to pay? To pass the guardian?"

"Why am I not surprised to find you in here?" Dee crossed the room, the soft soles of her shoes rasping a firm rhythm on the grey laminate floor. She flopped into a charcoal leather recliner and curled up in its oversized depths.

Starr climbed in beside her and nestled in front of her bent legs. "This is our snuggle chair."

Bobby had walked to the picture window overlooking the bay. Skirting the tree, he cast an appreciative nod toward the chair before taking a corner of the couch. "Gorgeous view. I could never get any work done in here."

"He writes books." Starr's brown eyes widened as she shared this information with Landon. "About heroes and spaceships. When Roy needs a drive, he parks so he can't see the water."

Apart from the Christmas tree, Dee had decorated the space in colours reflecting the sea, sky, and rocky coast. One wall held a long rectangular print of seabirds in flight. Landon could almost hear their cries.

Dee stirred. "I should have offered you drinks before dropping anchor."

"I'm good, thanks." Landon glanced at Bobby on the other end of the couch.

He shook his head. "We came to see the tree."

"And me!"

Landon smiled. "And you. It's good to meet you, Starr. I like your name. It sparkles."

"I'm not sparkling now. Not with Miz Vi being attacked and Nigel so sad. Mom is scared."

Dee smoothed her daughter's hair. "We don't have to be scared. Whoever did this won't come back. Vi named her enemy." She looked over at Landon and Bobby. "When he found her, Nigel came and asked us to call 9-1-1. Did you know he won't use a phone?"

Landon nodded. He'd explained it was to prevent aliens recording his voice. Apparently, he thought it was too late for the rest of them. The one time she knew he'd broken that rule was when Elva could have died. Finding his mother dead... He must have reasoned a quick jog across the road wouldn't compromise the emergency response time.

"She'd given him a sealed envelope to pass on to the

police." Dee continued stroking her daughter's hair in a gentle rhythm. "Vi knew a lot of secrets she never told. She only considered one person to be a threat worth recording evidence. She forbade Nigel to read it so he wouldn't be a target too."

For all his eccentricities, the man was a stickler for protocol.

Landon shivered. "I hope the—" She'd almost said *killer*. Did Starr know Vi was dead, not hurt? "The person knows that."

"Maybe he's gone to his bunker for safety," mused Bobby. "I assumed he needed space to process it all."

In his grief, was Nigel also in danger?

Chapter 5

IS NIGEL IN danger? Landon fired off the text to Dylan before they left Dee's street.

Despite Bobby's low speed on this rough road, the rattling truck body transmitted vibrations from the tires straight to her spine. She shifted on the bench seat. "If Vi was half as suspicious as Nigel, it makes sense she'd leave information about anyone she feared. In case the worst happened."

"It's like she did the investigators' work for them, if they can find the person. And if that's who did it."

Landon glanced at him. "Come on. How many enemies can one harmless old woman have?"

"How many secrets could she learn?" The speculative drawl meant his writer's brain had kicked in. One hand left the steering wheel to pinch his chin between thumb and forefinger.

"Don't put this in a book. Even in space. A real woman died and her son is hurting."

The truck jostled onto the paved road, and Landon's bones wilted into the suddenly stable seat.

Bobby sped up. "I didn't mean to sound callous. It's a basic scenario—the more people with motive, the more complicated the plot. Except it's usually the person everybody hates. Or they're stinking rich. Vi was neither.

Although Gramp says there's resentment—and fear—about the extent of her knowledge."

"Well, I hope it's straightforward. We won't have to help solve this. We can concentrate on supporting Nigel."

How would an atypical person like Nigel process grieving? What would be healthy for him? What should they watch for as bad signs? She sighed. Assuming he showed up where they could find him.

Her phone buzzed in her grip, making her twitch.

Bobby snickered. "Phone's for you."

Ignoring him, she answered the call.

Dylan skipped the greeting. "Who have you been talking to? And what did I say about not investigating?"

A delivery truck rumbled past in the opposite direction, raising salt spray from the pavement.

"I gather you're still on the road. With your co-sleuth or did you rope Anna into this one? Put me on speaker."

Bobby toggled the windshield washer. "Guilty as charged. I heard you. But we weren't investigating."

Dylan's exhale grated from the phone. "If anything happens to her, you and I will talk."

"Honestly, we weren't investigating." Landon fumbled through the basics of the trip. "Dee invited us in to meet her daughter, and she told us about the letter Vi left for Nigel. So I'm concerned the killer might try for him next."

"Remember curiosity killed the cat."

"Not every cat. One look at Mister and you know who won."

"Last cat standing." Bobby's murmur didn't reach the phone.

Or Dylan chose not to respond. Instead, he exhaled a grumbling sound. "Listen, there's one thing you can do to help that'll keep you out of trouble."

"Really?" Landon glanced sideways at Bobby.

"There's a Hope Bellgrove staying with Elva. Have you met?"

"We shared a table at the dinner on Saturday. Why?"

"Keep this to yourselves. Her business card was found on the scene, and her story doesn't sit right with me."

That must be why he'd stopped at Elva's after Vi's body was found. Landon frowned at her phone. "You have Vi's letter. Doesn't that name your suspect? Plus, Hope only arrived on the weekend."

Bobby tapped a short beat on the steering wheel. "Loose ends."

"Got it in one. Until we have sufficient evidence for an arrest, every angle needs a follow-up. Hope Bellgrove is not considered a suspect, for reasons I won't share at this point. But she's lying about something, and I want to know why."

As Landon stowed her phone in her coat pocket, Bobby said, "Thanks for not throwing me to the wolf."

Not *wolves*. Singular. One wolf. Dylan. "What?"

"I wanted to go to Nigel's. He blamed you."

"We both wanted to." She shot him a sideways grin. "Should I set him straight?"

"Did you notice he didn't say if Nigel's in danger or not?"

"I wonder if that was deliberate." She resisted the urge to call him back. He had work to do. She'd text when he was off duty.

They'd almost reached the inn. She zipped her coat. "What if we stopped at Elva's to ask if Nigel's been around?"

"You'd do better on your own later. If we arrive together, she'll think we were sent."

They passed Elva's house, then the neighbouring one, then cruised up the driveway to the inn. A wooden nativity scene, each plywood figure cut and painted by Anna's husband, stood halfway up the front lawn. The inn's signature green dory, draped in burlap, held the manger.

From the wind's raw bite when Landon left the truck, more precipitation was coming. Rain or snow, they'd have to wait and see. This close to the coast, low-temperature rain felt colder than snow.

With the barest glance at the second car in the lot beside Anna's, Landon tucked her chin into her collar and hustled along the slate path to the rear of the inn. The front entrance welcomed visitors. This door led to home.

The two Christmas trees stood propped against the deck rails, bare of the snow that had barred them from the inn on Sunday. Trimming them was supposed to be yesterday's project. Between the news of Vi's death and the Kenzie-Phil drama, plans had changed.

Timkin, the black and white inn cat, uncurled from beneath the shorter tree and streaked between Landon's feet for the door. There was no sign of Mister, the orange stray who'd allowed them to house him for the winter.

The moment she crossed the threshold, warm cinnamon and vanilla filled Landon's senses. She shed her coat and boots and followed her nose to the kitchen. Were those snickerdoodle cookies Anna was lifting onto the cooling racks?

Landon checked the window toward the driveway, but of course Bobby had already gone. She wouldn't dare tell him what he'd missed. This close to the baking, she reached for a sample by instinct. It warmed her fingertips. The first bite practically melted in her mouth.

"Mmm. Amazing." She finished it off before asking, "Has Nigel been around?"

"Not yet."

To distract herself from craving more, she caught Anna up on seeing Corey and the side trip to the crime scene. And the visit with Dee and Starr.

Anna listened, eyes dancing with a smile too great for her lips to hold, head bobbing as if they had to get this out of the way before the good stuff.

Grinning, Landon leaned a hand on her hip and studied her friend. "Okay, what's the big news?"

A deep breath lifted Anna's chest, making the printed reindeer on her apron bib appear to leap into flight. "I didn't want to tell you in case it didn't work out. She's here."

Who would Anna be this delighted to see? Whose presence could push murder to the background even temporarily? Even if Anna were celebrity conscious, nobody famous would be touring around Lunenburg in a well-worn car like the one outside.

Landon crossed the kitchen and leaned a hip against the sturdy farmhouse table, her open palm flat on the smooth pine surface. The promise of a nice surprise washed over the day's tension. "I need a hint."

"Your mom. Gwen. She can only stay till the weekend, but she came." Anna clapped like a child. "Merry Christmas!"

Time stopped. Landon would remember this moment forever. The swishing whisper of the dishwasher. The sweet scent of baking in air suddenly too thick to breathe. The stark solidity in her chest. The glow in Anna's eyes sharpening in concern the longer the moment stretched.

Flailing blind, Landon caught the nearest chairback and clenched, the curved wood hard against her skin. Anchoring. Supporting knees that wanted to give way. She couldn't sit for this. Had to meet it standing upright.

A trickle of air reached her lungs, all they could hold without expanding. Her frozen ribs wouldn't budge.

Apart from Anna's kindness, she had no claim on the inn's safety. Her few duties didn't earn her room and board. Anna could invite anyone she chose. But— "How could you throw this at me with no warning?"

Her constricted vocal cords changed the accusation to a hiss.

Anna's clasped hands flattened against her apron front. The last light of happiness fled her face, leaving it the colour of dough.

Landon tried to clear her throat, to free her voice. "I'm sorry. I—this hurts—that you didn't talk to me. Prepare me. Give me a choice." The words clawed out in a painful whisper.

"I thought you'd be happy. Last time you mentioned Gwen, you spoke like you wanted to reunite."

Tears stung her eyelids. "I've wanted that since the beginning. I needed her, and she wouldn't even speak to me."

"She couldn't. Landon, try—"

Landon rubbed her throat muscles as if she could knead away the ache. "I understand now, as best I can. It's not about forgiveness. It's about vulnerability."

"It was hard for her to come. She cancelled twice."

"What about me?"

"You endured hell on earth. With God, you came out stronger. Your mother, not so much. This is a big step for her to be here, to see the child she loved who was taken." Anna's chin trembled. "Don't reject her. A mother's heart can only break so many times."

"I don't want to reject her. But the walls are there. They can't just vanish because I want them to. I need time."

"It's three now. You have until five thirty. Although I don't know when Kenzie will get in." Palm outstretched, Anna took a hesitant step forward. "I'm sorry. I love you like my own, and I honestly believed I was helping. Now that she's here, we need to move forward. I'll be praying. You can do this."

Get on board with the program. But Anna was right. What else was there? Move out until Mom left? A petty action that would make their eventual reunion more difficult. And, oh, her heart needed her mother and sisters.

Standing tall, she met Anna's gaze but made no move to close the gap. "I'll be here for supper."

Late December's short days would have her home before then, especially if the cloud cover held. She stuffed her feet into her boots, tugged a cherry-red tuque over her hair, and left, zipping her coat on the way down the stairs from the deck.

No sign of the marmalade cat. Hands deep in her pockets, she strode into the woods behind the inn.

These properties extended deep and wide. Many residents kept the mixed forest thinned to allow the light in and grow stronger trees. Not all had paths between neighbours like Anna and Roy, but a person could travel a fair distance behind the homes.

Once tall grey trunks surrounded her, she stopped. Stared up along the length of majestic pines arrowing toward a mottled sky.

Anna's helping had crossed way too far into interference this time.

"God, help me let go of the anger so You can prepare me to meet Mom. Thank You for bringing us together even though I don't like the way it's happening."

Pine needles rustled overhead. Sweet forest scents breathed peace into her lungs. The cold crept through her boot soles to touch her toes. Stomping her feet, she roamed among the trees, trying to absorb the stillness.

Maybe she'd meet Nigel. He often prowled through here with his metal detector, searching for evidence of aliens. And watching over Elva.

In another man, that could give off a stalker vibe. Nigel was protective. Landon could picture him as a knight of old. His armour would be dinged and scuffed, but his service would be faithful and secure.

Thoughts of Nigel and Elva must have led her feet in that direction. Elva's two-storey home appeared through the trees. A plain white-sided colonial, it jutted abruptly from the lawn. This time of year, mounds of bare earth gave a stark reminder of Elva's carefully nurtured flower gardens.

Landon picked her way through the growth between Elva's place and the nearer neighbour's. Once past the cars in the driveway, she circled around to Elva's front door.

Hope Bellgrove answered her knock. "Elva will be a minute."

The fortyish woman was about Landon's height. Her hair fell in long layers that curved in around her cheeks to minimize a very round face.

"Would you tell her it's Landon? I'm from the inn down the road. You and I met at the dinner on Saturday."

Recognition lit Hope's brown eyes.

Out of sight behind her, Elva called, "She can come in."

Landon smiled. That in itself was a complete reversal from their first encounter. Elva wouldn't call her a friend yet—Did the caustic woman allow any friends? Yet despite the almost thirty-five years between their ages, they'd become allies, bonded over similar traumas.

Inside, Landon left her outerwear and followed Hope into the living room.

Elva lay stomach-down on the floor, head and one arm extended under a paisley brocade couch that was once the height of fashion. The one her mother had kept under plastic and forbidden her to sit on as a child. Fat round wooden feet raised it barely high enough for Elva's reach.

Landon squirmed with second-hand claustrophobia. "Elva, let's move it out from the window. Wouldn't that be easier?"

Elva braced against the hardwood floor and propelled herself out into the light. She squinted at the long-handled barbecue tongs she held. "Useless things."

Climbing from her knees to her feet, she brushed nonexistent dust from her close-cropped chestnut hair. "If you're willing, I'd appreciate the help. Hope is under doctor's orders to avoid strenuous activity." She retrieved her glasses from the coffee table and fixed Landon with a narrow-eyed stare. "What brings you around today?"

"My feet."

Hope muffled a snicker, but Elva's eyes glittered in warning.

"Sorry. I hoped I'd cross paths with Nigel in the woods. Has he been around?"

Elva gave a rapid headshake. "No sign of him. Although you could have walked right past him if he didn't want to be

55

seen."

"Do you think he's in danger?"

Elva's pencil-thin eyebrows arched. "Nigel?"

"He gave the police a letter from Vi about a suspect. What if that person thinks he knows what she wrote?" Landon glanced at Hope. "Vi is the woman who was killed on the weekend. Nigel's her adult son. Have you met him?"

"Briefly. I saw Vi at that dinner. It's a shame, and at Christmas too."

"Nigel can take care of himself." Elva's lips flattened. "Now what's the real trouble?"

"Isn't that enough?"

"It's a flimsy excuse to show up at my door and make cracks about your feet bringing you."

Landon stared at a shiny red ball on the Christmas tree. "Anna hit me with something unexpected, and I took off."

"What's she done now?"

Landon opened her mouth, then gulped a breath. It felt wrong to unload her personal struggle in front of a stranger, yet Dylan wanted her to connect with Hope.

She fisted one hand and cupped the other over it, pressing in on her jutting knuckles. Facing Hope, she began. "I was human trafficked as a teen. Elva already knows. Long story, but my mother couldn't accept me back into the family."

With a shallow breath, she pushed on. "Anna and Mom were friends, and she stepped in where Mom couldn't. Anna is a natural nurturer—sometimes too much—and she's a strong woman of faith. I needed all the prayer I could get even when I didn't know it."

Elva sniffed. "Natural nurturer or meddler? But her heart's in the right place."

"Now, I find out Mom's here at the inn—Anna's idea—and I have two hours to get my head in gear to meet her in person. After nine years."

Elva moved to stand at one end of the couch, fingers like talons against the upholstery. "This could get ugly."

"Mom must be open to it, or she wouldn't have driven all the way from Cape Breton." Landon loosened her fist and laced her fingers together. "I don't do well with surprises."

"You and me both, sister." Elva's retort came out rapier sharp.

Hope's peach-glossed lips had parted. "That's awful. The trafficking. And then your mom rejecting you." Her eyes shimmered with tears. "I'm adopted. My family is amazing, but I have this... hollow space. My birth mother gave me up. I've been searching for years to find out why."

"Haven't they opened the adoption records?"

"Yes, but birth parents can veto contact. I get it, but it hits like a smack in the heart. She doesn't want me."

Landon remembered the numbness. The sense that an impact had stopped her heart and left it with a faltering rhythm. She pressed her palm into the middle of her chest. "That's what it was like for me. I want to be close again, but I don't think we ever will."

Hope fingered the simple gold necklace at her throat. "I'm not asking for close. Just to be acknowledged. And for any medical history I might need for myself and my kids."

"Is that why you came? Do you think she's living in Lunenburg?"

"I—things are tense at home, and I had to get out of the city for a while. Elva and I met this summer, and she knew my birth mother." She ducked her head and peeked at Elva, standing poker-straight beside the couch. "I hoped if she got to know me better she'd trust me with a name."

Elva's eyes glittered. "Your birth mother was a fool, and she paid the price. She gave you up so you could have a future unmarred by her mistake. That's all you need to know."

There'd been a guest at the inn this summer bent on stirring up family secrets. Thinking his pain entitled him to lay bare decades-old shame. Landon made eye contact with Hope, willing the hurting woman to hear. "If the circumstances were traumatic, what if she hasn't healed? Forcing a meeting could hurt you both."

She took position at the opposite end of the couch. "Let's get this moved."

Elva gave a curt nod.

The heavy piece of furniture squeaked across the polished hardwood. Elva squeezed through the narrow space. After a moment on her knees, she stood, one hand in a fist. Once they'd shoved the couch into position in front of the picture window, she showed Landon three tiny gold screws. "Thank you. These are too small to flush out with anything I tried."

A side table next to the couch's matching chair held an oval mahogany base, tipped on its side, attached to porcelain figures in bright clothing. Elva fitted the thin bottom plate and screwed it into place. Upright, the wood became a platform for a winter skating scene. She twisted the winding key, and the skaters moved in time to tinkly music.

Landon and Hope crowded nearer.

Elva tucked the small screwdriver into her cardigan pocket. "This was my mother's. It hasn't played in years. Hope helped me clean the mechanism. Thank you."

Hope smiled. "It's lovely. I'm glad it works again. I'm sorry I dropped the screws."

"No harm done. Murphy's Law, they had to find the least accessible place."

The fading daylight through the window sheers meant Landon needed to leave. She took a last look at the cheerful scene. "Let us know if you see Nigel? Or send him over?"

"I'll do that. He'll need support, and he may not realize it."

As Landon donned her coat, the sense of bracing herself had nothing to do with the temperature outside.

If only her relationship with her mother could be mended as easily as Elva's music box.

Chapter 6

L ANDON HEADED HOME through the trees, watching for Nigel. She'd never hear him, and Elva was right—if he didn't want to be noticed, she'd never see him.

How was he feeling? Not just losing his mother naturally but to murder?

She slipped the coat collar tighter around her neck. What would he do now? Heaviness lodged in her chest. Vi had been a single teen when he was born. It seemed like all they had was one another.

He'd probably give anything to have her back.

Then there was Hope, so desperate to find her birth mother. That information wouldn't help Dylan, but at least Landon had broken the ice.

The remaining ice to break sealed her heart against her mother.

Gwen. They'd texted, spoken on the phone, dancing around the possibility of reconnecting. Both wanting it, both afraid. Until now, the fear had won.

Sunlight pierced the clouds, tracing impossibly long shadows where it filtered among the branches. Landon forced her steps homeward. The cold air bit deep in her lungs.

"God, help me not ruin this."

She was puffing when she reached the inn, heat prickling her spine and under her arms. It made a good excuse to pause on the deck and collect herself.

A low yowl greeted her, and the battle-scarred marmalade cat emerged from behind the Christmas trees propped against the deck rail.

She crouched and held out her mittened hand. "Hey, Mister. You haven't seen Nigel, have you?"

The cat sidestepped her reach and placed a paw on the knee of her jeans. His head tipped up, eyes intent.

She didn't dare move. With this one, any contact was rare and always initiated on his end.

He blinked. Stretched to place his other forepaw on her leg.

"You want me to pick you up. Seriously." Holding eye contact—and holding her breath—she brought both palms to his sides. When he allowed her touch, she picked him up and cradled him loosely.

"We're going inside now, okay?"

His left ear, the nicked one with the permanent bend, twitched. He lay in her arms, watchful, as she stepped inside. Then he twisted and leaped to the floor. Without a backward glance, he took the hallway in a slow swagger, his kinked tail held high as if to say, "This never happened." Seconds later, he ducked through the cat flap in the basement door.

The residual peace of the contact remained as she left her coat and boots and went in search of Anna. And Gwen.

She found them in the guests' common room, working on the lighthouse puzzle. Both women stood. Anna retreated toward the bookcase, leaving clear air between mother and daughter.

A sob caught in Landon's throat. She hadn't known how to prepare for this. Or what she'd feel.

One look undid all her barriers.

Her mother's features hadn't changed. Yet they looked drawn and weathered as if she'd lived multiple lifetimes. Her mouth, stripped of its infectious smile, drew a tight line holding infinite pain.

Landon's soul ached. She held out her hands and stepped forward. "Aw, Mom."

Tears clogged her throat. This woman had endured so much, and without faith to strengthen and comfort her. This would have been Landon too, if she hadn't found God's tender care. Shattered. Barren. A husk of life.

She found herself holding her mother with the same tentative hope she'd felt with the cat. Barely touching, afraid to shatter the moment. Then one, both of them, clutching together as if they might be torn apart. Sobbing. Maybe laughing. She couldn't tell.

As they quieted, chests heaving for breath, she realized Anna had left the room.

Keeping the tight hold, Gwen whispered, "Surprise."

Landon eased backward, creating space to study her mom's tear-swollen face. "Why didn't you text?"

"I was afraid you'd run. Or I would."

With an aching slowness, Gwen reached out and smoothed Landon's hair. A featherlight touch, repetitive and soothing. A solid link to childhood security.

"My baby. What they did to you—" Gwen's mouth crumpled. She sniffed, her lips pressing tight but still trembling. Another sniff. She stood taller.

Her hands found Landon's shoulders. Her brave, bright-eyed smile broke Landon's heart.

"Look at you now. All grown up, and... whole. Are you?"

Landon let a slow breath expand her ribs. Then another. Felt the narrow floorboards against the soles of her feet, anchoring her securely in this place and time.

They'd exchanged frequent messages the past months. Her mother knew how she was progressing. Reading a digital communication, even hearing a voice on the phone, was one thing. Seeing in person, touching, was another.

She held the eye contact, feeling another tear slide down her cheek. "I've been healed, I'm being healed, and I will be healed." Those three short phrases captured her understanding of the process. "Jesus has me, and He'll get me through. Most days, yes, I'm whole."

"No thanks to me."

"Mom, don't. God knew what you couldn't do, so He gave me Anna. And—another person of faith who helped me for a while."

Yeah, thinking of Zander right now was not a good plan. She shook away the memory. "I know you're not sure about God, and that's between you and Him to work out. My counsellors could only do so much. Without Him, I don't want to think where I'd be."

The front entrance chimes startled them both. They jumped in tandem, sending each other into watery giggles.

Landon angled away from the glass-paned privacy door Anna had closed for them. Kenzie must have had an early supper to arrive so soon. She'd see the room was occupied and bypass it.

The latch snicked.

Landon stiffened, jamming her brain into hospitality mode. She ripped a tissue from the box on the puzzle table and dried her eyes.

Gwen stepped to the window, her breath fogging the darkened glass.

"Oh." In the doorway, Kenzie stood holding a small pizza box. Her curious smile shrank and vanished. "I didn't mean to intrude. It sounded fun. Plus, I have news."

Landon's eyes must be a puffy disaster. No innkeeper smile was going to hide that. She steered the girl into the hallway and left her mother to compose herself. "Sorry that was awkward for you, Kenzie. I haven't seen my mom in years, and reunions can get messy. We both jumped like spastic chickens when the door chime sounded, and you heard what happened next."

The scent of pizza made her mouth water. Pepperoni? She pointed at the box. "You can eat in your room if you prefer, but it's okay to use the tables down here. Give me two minutes, and I'll set you up a place and bring a glass of water."

"Thank you." Instead of crossing the hall to choose a table, Kenzie stayed put. "My news."

"You met with Phil again and learned the rest of his story?" Landon had no business knowing any of the exchange, but since they'd dragged her into the first part, she'd hoped to hear it all. Especially if it impacted Ciara.

The girl's eyebrows drew into a vee. "No. He's been stalling since the murder. But I heard something. Remember, I'm nobody around here, except if someone recognizes me as the troublemaker from that ghastly dinner."

Ghastly? It'd been fun until the Vengeance Queen dropped her snow-globe bomb. Landon set her teeth to keep the words in.

Kenzie didn't seem to notice. "So I'm in the pizza place, and these three teens come in. I'm bored, so I'm watching them and listening to their conversation. They're gossiping about the crime."

"Go on."

"This woman comes in, picks up her order, and leaves. Then a snarky-sounding boy stage-whispers she's his pick for the killer."

Landon's senses sharpened. "Did he say why? Or give a name?"

"Something about the dead woman reporting her, and animal control seizing a houseful of starving dogs. The police would be able to follow that, right? No name. I think he called her 'Freak Show,' sneering-like. Kids have no respect."

And Kenzie did? Fumbling her tissue to her face, Landon faked a sneeze. "Sorry."

"So can you tell your cop friend? If it's true, the lady has motive."

~~~

Landon's concern about awkward silences—or stilted

conversation—disappeared once she, her mother, and Anna settled around the square pine table in the kitchen.

When Anna blessed the food, this room, the heart of the inn, enfolded the three women into its warmth and security. The overhead light warmed the pale pink walls and reflected like a mini sun in the table's glossy finish. Anna's chicken pot pie set a comforting note that didn't lend itself to heavy subjects.

Anna had already caught Gwen up on the murder and their mysterious young guest. Landon longed to hear about her sisters, but the troubled hints she'd gleaned from Anna in the past—and her mom's avoidance of mentioning them so far—shelved that news for later.

For now, her heart craved the gentle intimacy that unfolded while they ate and chatted about the safe, mundane parts of their lives. As they lingered over cookies and tea, she noticed the time. Seven already, and she still had to contact Dylan with Kenzie's clue.

Kenzie had retreated upstairs before they started eating. Had the flow of their conversation accented her solitude?

"Maybe we should invite Kenzie to join us later." Leaning on her elbow, Landon studied her mother. "I don't want to cut in on our visit, but she seems lost. Waiting for Phil to make time to give her information she's not sure she wants to hear has to be tough."

The care lines around Gwen's mouth deepened. "It's been a long trip and an emotional day. The tub in my room sounds awfully good. We have tomorrow."

She'd be staying until the weekend. If they could get past the difficult subjects tomorrow, that should leave time to start rebuilding.

Light flashed outside the kitchen window. The motion sensors had kicked in. A staccato series of double knocks rattled the back door.

"That's Nigel." Anna hurried out.

A moment later, she returned. Nigel padded into the

kitchen behind her, his knitted grey work socks silent on the flagstone-patterned vinyl floor. While Anna made straight for the sink and filled the kettle, he surveyed the room. His grey eyes sharpened as they fixed on Gwen, his bushy salt-and-pepper brows crowding together.

Landon introduced her mother.

The grey eyes blinked twice, and he nodded. "Good you could come. Be proud of your daughter. She's a strong one."

Gwen murmured her thanks.

What did she see? A tall, scruffy, sixtyish man with days-old whiskers, in black and grey camouflage coat and cap. His open coat revealed a red plaid flannel shirt. Nothing in this picture hinted at the kindness behind his mannerisms. Or his hero heart. Or, for that matter, that his praise was never lightly given.

His affirming words touched something deep in Landon, a place barren since she'd lost her father. She left the table and approached him. "Nigel, I'm so sorry for your loss. Would you accept a hug?"

Head held to one side, he blinked. He straightened, nodding once. "Thank you."

Nigel smelled of the outdoors, of cold air, woodsmoke, and exertion. And he gave a surprisingly good hug for a man who projected as stiff and socially awkward.

Anna pulled the table out from the wall to free the fourth chair. "Stay awhile, Nigel. Your tea's nearly ready."

She tugged the metal cover from an unmarked glass jar and extended it to him. His own blend of leaves, sourced and dried himself. Landon had learned about those when they first met.

He brought it to his nose and inhaled carefully before passing it to Anna. "It's good. Thank you." He slid into the open seat with his back to the wall. "Most hospitable."

Once she poured boiling water on his tea leaves and topped up the other cups, Anna settled at the table. She slid the plate of cookies toward him.

He studied them. "No home baking in the bunker. Except what you sent with the boy."

"Nigel, are you in danger?" Landon hadn't received a straight answer from Dylan. The bunker could simply be for solitude.

He blinked twice. "Mother kept her secrets to herself. The one who killed her should know."

"We heard she left a letter naming a possible culprit. Did you read it?"

"Even that one's privacy deserved protecting—unless they killed for it." He rotated his cup by quarters until it had come full circle. "The investigators will pursue."

Landon focused on his flame-scarred hands. "What will you do?"

"Wait and see." Steam still curled from his tea, but he gulped it down and stood. "Anna, thank you. Gwen, be strong. Landon, a moment?"

Landon followed him into the hallway to the rear door.

He fitted his feet into knee-high rubberized hunting boots, then peered at her from beneath those bushy eyebrows. "Elva's visitor. What do you know?"

"Not much. She's searching for her birth parents, and Elva has information she won't share."

"Watch her. Mother said."

If Vi's letter had named Hope, Dylan would never have sent Landon anywhere near her. "You're not convinced the person your mother named is guilty. But Hope just arrived. You don't think she's the killer?"

His bristly salt-and-pepper brows pulled together. "You see what I can't. Watch her."

In one swift motion, he opened the door and slipped out into the night.

~~~

Landon's phone buzzed a text alert. She left her spot at the puzzle table and dropped into the leather club chair by the bookcase.

They'd lured Kenzie downstairs, promising cookies in exchange for help with the jigsaw. Gwen lasted ten minutes before heading for her room, but Anna and Kenzie actually expected to finish it tonight.

The picture's varied hues of white couldn't hold Landon's interest. She'd been picking at the pieces but mostly tag teaming verbally with Anna's conversation to solve the puzzle of Kenzie.

Now, Dylan had responded to her message about what the girl had heard in the pizza shop. *I need a break. Beg Anna for baked goods and her biggest mug of coffee?*

Landon shot back a laugh emoji and a thumbs-up. "Anna, Dylan's on his way. You make better coffee than I do, and he sounds desperate."

Bent over the table, Kenzie straightened, a puzzle piece pinched in her grip. "I should go upstairs."

Anna touched her shoulder. "You're welcome to stay. He doesn't bite."

His second text said, *I'm coming as a friend. If Kenzie's there, play along?*

Another thumbs-up and Landon stowed her phone. "Kenzie, I told him what you overheard, but you might be able to describe the woman or the kids for him to identify. Or even tell him what time you were there."

From the lights that swept up the driveway ten minutes later, Dylan drove his Jeep and not a police cruiser. When Landon let him in, he was still in uniform and wearing a permanent squint. She took his coat, her arm sagging under the weight. "You look exhausted. Couldn't it keep until tomorrow?"

He stared past her, a slow smile warming his features. "Anna, you're a lifesaver."

Anna gave him a giant mug, then waved a plate of cookies to lead him into the common room.

He followed like a sleepwalker. To Landon, he said, "This

way I can see you for a minute or two. The coffee's to get me home."

"You know there's a twenty-four-hour café a block from the station."

"And I do my part to keep it in business. After today, I needed to see friends, not professional servers."

He greeted Kenzie and lowered himself into the club chair. Keeping the mug level, he slouched into the leather embrace until his head rested on the seat back. Long legs extended and the mug braced between his hands on his stomach, he closed his eyes.

Landon itched to grill him about Vi's letter and how soon they might know if it named the killer. His exhaustion stopped her. It'd be like barging in on her mom upstairs, luxuriating in a tub of Anna's bubble bath, to ask about her sisters' troubled lives. Cruel and intrusive.

Anna set the cookies on a side table. "Dylan, are you going to drink that coffee or snuggle it like a teddy bear?"

His snort jostled the mug, sloshing coffee to the edge. He cracked open an eye. "Nothing spilled."

He eased himself upright and took a sip. "Perfect. It needed to cool a minute. Ms. Garner, I'm off duty, but I'm always a cop. If there's anything you don't want me to hear, don't say it. I was hoping for a casual chat with all three of you, but if you'd rather, I can come back officially."

Stiff-shouldered, Kenzie turned from the puzzle table. "You can call me Kenzie. And I have nothing to hide. It's the people in this crazy town who have all the secrets."

His lean cheeks pulled in. "I trust we'll expose those belonging to a certain murderer shortly."

With Anna and Kenzie at the chairs by the puzzle, Landon had taken one of the mint-upholstered chairs. She slid her fingertips along the curved oak armrests, the grain smooth to her touch. "Nigel told us the letter's under investigation."

He took another long drink from his mug. "Based on Vi's written testimony, we'll be having an interesting conversation with this person even if they weren't involved in her death."

"Poor Nigel." Anna pressed her palms into her knees. "Vi was a selfless, caring member of the community."

"That depends on who you talk to." Kenzie left the puzzle, fully engaging in the conversation. "I overheard gripes about her influencing others to get the outcomes she wanted. She could have been a blackmailer. Or even a witch. Maybe some do-gooder church person decided to get rid of her."

Anna's generous mouth pinched tight. "I'd question that definition of doing good."

Kenzie shrugged. "All it takes is one."

"Vi was a Bible-believing Christian. Not a witch. An observant, intuitive woman with a heart for justice." Anna's chest rose in a slow breath as if she measured her words. "She focused more on law than grace, which at times may have led her to pressure people she thought ought to pay for what they'd done."

As opposed to Landon's former mentor who'd exacted his own justice to enforce payment. Mental illness, trauma, or warped theology could twist anyone. She hadn't seen Zander since discovering his dark side. Sooner or later, they'd meet in court.

"What do you mean by grace?" Kenzie swooped her fingertips in a gliding curve. "You're not talking about dance moves."

Anna smiled. "Sorry. It's forgiving instead of judging, because of God's love."

Kenzie's eyes glittered, and her mouth hardened. She'd be thinking of her grudge against Phil.

Landon spoke before the girl could vent. "Back to blackmail. If you'd seen Vi's house, you'd know there wasn't extra money floating around." Landon and Bobby hadn't been inside, but the exterior gave a clear picture. Unless the dead woman had been a secretly wealthy hoarder who kept it all in a mattress or buried in the backyard.

Dylan scooped up two golden cookies and offered the plate around. "We're aware of the divergent views on Ms. Foley. The truth is likely found in the middle. Before I go, I'd like to hear what Kenzie can describe about her mystery woman. And if Landon's made any progress with hers."

Landon ignored Anna's sudden forward posture. "Not from a first chat. I'll find a way to talk to her again."

Kenzie's description of the teens and the woman didn't suggest anyone Landon knew. At the mention of the seized dogs, Dylan made a small nod.

Anna clasped her hands to her mouth. "That sounds like Freesia. 'Freak Show,' indeed. Those kids have no idea. Dylan, you'll have her background on file from that investigation. She's had her struggles with mental illness. She needs to be protected, not mocked and slandered."

Kenzie scowled. "The kids were mean. But it's only slander if it's not true."

Anna's lips pinched. "The poor girl had a breakdown when animal control seized those dogs. It had to be done, but all Freesia could say was they'd taken her babies. A nurturer can't kill."

One of Dylan's eyebrows gave a microscopic twitch. "That's not always so. But in this case, I hope it's true."

He levered himself from the chair and collected his empty mug. "Ladies, I'd better say good night." He extended an upturned palm to Landon. "Walk me to the door?"

Landon rose before her brain caught up. The gesture, the intimate tone, when he knew her too well to make an overt romantic move. His earlier text message had asked her to play along. She looked up into those dark eyes, and he winked.

Anna's stare burned her spine as she followed him into the hallway.

When he ducked into the kitchen, Landon couldn't resist. "Don't leave that mug in the sink, dear." She opened the dishwasher and slid out the top rack.

"Thanks for following my cue. Kenzie's still on my watch list. If you and I seem to have a deeper friendship, it allows me to drop in more often."

Arms folded, Landon leaned against the counter. "Exactly how deep is this friendship? Are we dating? I'm not going to kiss you good night."

His eyebrow twitched again. "How about I express an interest, which you may or may not reciprocate? You can keep hanging out with your getaway driver. And let me down easy when our killer is apprehended."

She fixed him with a level stare. "My mom's here. And if I don't tell Anna, she'll have the full wedding dinner planned before midnight."

Dylan laughed. "She's had that set since June. I never dared ask if she's Team Dylan or Team Bobby."

"You're not serious."

"Ask her."

It took effort to unclench her jaw to speak. "I'll tell her. This is not a game. Honestly, I love Anna like a mother, but she's pushing too hard." She bit off the budding rant. Too many times, Dylan or Bobby—or Anna—had borne the fallout.

Dylan spread his feet and rocked back on his heels. "I did want a private chat before leaving. A serious one. You've spoken with Hope Bellgrove."

"Elva knows Hope's birth mother but won't identify her. Hope wants to find the truth. I can use that connection because I've just reunited with my mom. Long story."

A tired smile flickered. "As a friend, I'd like to hear that story when we have time to do it justice. Tonight, I wanted to encourage you to keep working on Hope. Even if our initial suspect checks out, I want to know why she's lying. But you're safe to engage."

"How can you be sure?"

Dylan poked his head into the hallway. "All clear." Nevertheless, he joined her at the counter and pitched his voice low. "I told you her business card was found at the scene."

"Mm-hmm."

"This stays between us. We think the card was intended to deflect from the killer. The body was positioned on the floor in the typical casket pose." He crossed his hands over his chest. "Holding Hope's card."

"Why?"

"It's possible the peaceful positioning was a form of apology. The back of Vi's head indicates she was struck from behind. Or pushed and fell, striking an object the killer removed from the scene."

"So you're looking for a strong person. Or an angry person. But why Hope's card? She's a stranger."

"That's where the lie comes in. She says she doesn't know. She's a real estate agent in Halifax. Someone at the dinner asked for a couple of cards for a friend who wanted to move into the city. She didn't get a name."

"Vi made herself pretty visible that night. Hope would remember if it was the same person. Anyway, can you see Vi wanting to move to the city?"

"From what's emerging about her personality, no." He yawned. "Enough sweet talk. I've got to go."

As he zipped his heavy coat, he beckoned her nearer. "The thing to consider is this—Who did Hope give that card to? See if you can get the truth. If it wasn't Vi, it may have been the killer."

Chapter 7

Wednesday

L ANDON SNUGGED HER scarf closer around her neck and hunched her shoulders against the wind. The choppy waves on the bay across from her emphasized the chill.

She paced back and forth at the end of the inn's driveway.

Finally, a dark-clad figure approached, head forward and arms pumping.

Elva.

The woman barely slowed when she reached Landon. "Trouble getting away." With a quick shoulder-check, she angled across the two-lane pavement to the water side to meet any oncoming traffic.

Landon jogged to catch up, then matched her pace along the frozen gravel at the road's shoulder. "What's the matter?"

Elva's text at breakfast had asked to meet. Neither home would do. They had to walk.

Her avoidance of the inn property was rooted in long-ago trauma. Excluding her own home meant talking where Hope couldn't hear.

"Find Vi's killer. For Nigel." The force of her speech matched her sharp movements.

"Wait, what? Elva, slow down." Landon clutched at Elva's

coat sleeve and missed. Her lungs burned with each gasping breath. How could a woman over twice her age have the endurance of a track star?

Landon glanced up at Roy's grey-green ranch-style bungalow as they passed. No one in sight, but he could be watching through the window. Leave it to Roy to be on the lookout and torment her about her stamina later.

Elva waited, her face pinched with more than the cold. "He won't ask. So I will." She set off at a slower pace. "Please."

"The police have Vi's letter—"

"It won't be that easy. You mark my words. That letter was leverage, nothing else. To keep a threat in line. Vi was always one step ahead, but this killer managed to catch her off guard."

A car came around the corner toward them, and Landon ducked in behind Elva. Walking single file between the guardrail and the pavement gave her time to think.

Elva didn't trust easily. She never admitted a need for help. This was as big a leap as Mister inviting Landon to pick him up. How could she say no?

How could she say yes?

Fear made her movements jerky. She never wanted to face down a killer again. Dylan had already warned her off. Yes, he'd allowed one safe channel. Yes, he was a friend. But he was a cop first. She couldn't defy his order.

Worse than Dylan's wrath, her mother would be terrified. Gwen carried so much agony over Landon's past and over her sisters' present struggles. How dare Landon risk adding more pain?

An icy breeze slid inside her scarf, chilling her neck. Most of all, what did God want her to do? She kept forgetting to start with that.

The approaching vehicle whipped past, raising road-salt dust to her lips. She stepped up beside Elva with no immediate sense of response to her prayer. "What can I do that the police can't?"

Elva sniffed. "I don't know, but you've done it before. This time, it's for Nigel. We owe him."

Their boots crunched on the gravel shoulder. At the top of a steep rise, Landon gasped for air. "Why did we have to do a speedwalking trial to have this conversation?"

"Hope's card was found on Vi's body. She claims not to know why. But she'd been sniffing around to find her birth parents. She'd gone out that afternoon. Who better to ask than the town secret keeper?"

"Because you won't tell her? I'm not judging—privacy's important."

Landon's sight roamed over the waves below, grey today like winter slush. God gave wisdom when His children asked. That was a promise. So far, she had no idea what to do with Elva's request. Common sense would say no like she'd done with Corey. Even if it meant breaking Elva's fragile trust.

This was the farthest she'd walked in this direction. She didn't dare check the time, but she wanted to ask her mother about her sisters. *God, we're a fractured family, and we need to be whole.*

Elva held her silence. Waiting for an answer?

Landon pulled her hat tighter over her ears. "Hope said you met this summer. How?"

"I was in the city for a procedure. We met in the hospital."

"You volunteered the information that you knew her birth mother?"

The woman's sideways glance could have cut steel. "Not by choice. She needed a kidney. I was a match. Close enough to reveal a blood-relative connection."

"You gave a stranger one of your kidneys." And outpaced Landon on this hike. "Elva, wow. Live donors have so much better success rates."

The details clicked together. "You're related to one of her biological parents. You also knew Hope's adoptive family, or you wouldn't have been aware of her health problems."

Another point connected. "That's why she's here, to find

out about your relatives."

"Her adoptive mother—her real mother in all but genetics—doesn't want her to find out. Not so soon after the surgery. I have to honour that request. Hope is emotionally volatile and physically vulnerable even though the transplant was a success. The antirejection drugs come with side effects."

"So if she did go to Vi for information and was rejected, is she capable of killing in anger?" Dylan had said the death could have come from a shove.

"I don't know." Elva glared straight ahead, jaw locked. "If I brought her here and she did this—"

"It wouldn't be your fault. For what it's worth, Dylan doesn't think she did it. I'm trusting you with that secret."

"Why did he tell you?"

"He knows she lied about the card. Or if she didn't and gave it to someone else, that person may have left it at the scene."

"To implicate her."

"Maybe, but how would they know she'd have a reason to contact Vi?"

That raised another question. "Say Hope did go to Vi. Asked her question and left her alive. Would Vi have known the answer?"

Elva snorted. "She'd never tell."

Hope wouldn't be so on edge if she'd learned what she wanted.

Elva planted her boots on the frozen gravel roadside and drilled Landon with a stare. "Will you help Nigel? Help me?"

This ask came at a price. Landon could no more refuse than she could have kept from scooping Mister into her arms. "I'll do whatever I can."

"Thank you. I'm glad you came back to Lunenburg, Landon Smith." Elva crossed the pavement and set out toward home, her strides ferocious.

Lungs straining, Landon walked alongside. Had she made

the right choice? What could she even do? Follow Dylan's assignment with Hope, but then what?

"There was a child." Elva's features had gone rigid. Her words shot like a poison dart.

Landon blinked and stumbled on the gravel. She threw out a hand for balance, wobbling but avoiding the ditch. She'd been so deep in trying to think up ways to investigate that what she'd heard made no sense.

Elva marched on, eyes straight ahead.

A child? Not related to Vi. To Hope?

Realization hit like a physical blow to Landon's stomach. She held her mitts to the spot and swallowed bile. Looked over at the choppy water and wrenched her gaze away fast.

The cold air was nothing to the ice inside her skin. "Elva—"

"You heard me. Don't tell her."

"From David?" *Please, from David, no matter how badly he betrayed you.*

"No."

Landon couldn't stop the tears. Fifteen-year-old Elva raped in the inn's barn by the previous owner, her boyfriend David's eighty-year-old grandfather. Pregnant from the attack and sent away by her mother until the old man died.

"My mother would have shamed that child every day of her life. For something that was neither of our faults. I made sure she went to a good home where she'd be loved. The kidney was a risk, but I had to do it."

Frozen tears clung to Landon's lashes. "I won't say a word." To anyone but God.

"I know. Now, find out if the monster begat a murderer."

~~~

Winter's grey weighted everything on this dull day. Low, swollen clouds hid the sun. Frost-coated grass lacked the light to sparkle. Salt stains streaked the driveway. The bright-painted nativity scene on the lawn and the inn's sunshine-yellow door popped in stark contrast.

At least Anna hadn't lit the decorations. Any other time, vibrant colours drew Landon. Energized her. Not when sorrow dragged her steps and questions swarmed her thoughts. She'd process Elva's revelation later. For now, the tears lurked close behind her eyes, and her throat pained.

To have endured a trauma-forced pregnancy, rejected at home, bearing a child she couldn't keep... and then to be unable to speak when reunion was literally in arm's length. Maybe Elva didn't want to reveal her identity. Maybe her protective shell wouldn't allow it despite Hope's obvious pleas. Or did her arms ache to embrace the one she'd given up?

Landon forced her feet to keep moving. Up the gentle slope to the inn.

For all the horror she'd endured from human trafficking, she'd been spared having a child ripped from her arms—or from her body. They'd never have allowed her to carry a baby to term. She lifted her gaze to the thick grey clouds, refocusing on the God whose rescue gave her hope. Whose light gave her life. Who was making her new.

The past, hers and Elva's, was real. But they didn't have to live there.

The future lay ahead.

In the present, Landon had committed to help solve a murder. While rebuilding a relationship with her mother. And finishing a final paper worth half of her course mark.

Dylan would be steamed.

She couldn't even start with another visit to Hope. If the woman guessed she'd been walking with Elva, she'd be too on guard. With any luck, the police would make an arrest from Vi's letter before Landon figured out what to do next.

Inside the inn, she met Kenzie in the main floor hallway.

The girl towed a carry-on bag, its wheels clicking against the narrow floorboards.

"Hey, are you checking out?" Phil hadn't returned. Had

she given up?

As if she'd heard the thought, Kenzie scowled. "Phil's not coming until tomorrow. Anna said I could do laundry."

"Did she warn you one of the cats might be down there? He's been a stray, and he's not ready to interact much with us. His name's Mister."

"I've only seen the black and white one."

"Timkin. He thinks he owns the place. If you find him in your room, shoo him out. He's not supposed to be upstairs."

Kenzie rocked the handle of her luggage, dancing the case on its wheels. "Since your boyfriend's a cop..."

"Dylan's not my boyfriend." Landon put on an impish grin. "It looks like he'd like to be." There. No outright lie and no cramping of her style once she convinced Bobby to help investigate.

"Well, do you have an inside track with him? Can he find out if what Phil tells me is true? Is Phil a suspect in the murder?"

"Why would Phil be a suspect? Vi defended him at the dinner."

Kenzie's mouth twisted. "What kind of hold did he have on her so she'd support him after what he did to my father?"

From what Phil said on Monday, he trusted Vi. He hadn't sounded threatened or resentful. But if he wanted to ensure Kenzie only heard his version of the story—if that differed from Vi's—could he have eliminated that risk?

Landon squeezed her eyes shut in a long blink. Crazy speculation was no way to find the truth. First, Vi had already refused to tell Kenzie about Phil. Second, his behaviour toward Kenzie proved he had the self-control not to strike out in sudden rage.

She leaned an elbow against the wall. "If you want, I can join you again tomorrow when Phil comes. I don't know if Dylan could run a fact check on it in the middle of a murder investigation, but he might think it'd be worth confirming Phil's truthfulness."

"Thank you." Kenzie stepped toward the basement door.

Landon followed. "Could you tell me what you know about the accident? So I can compare with what he'll say? We can talk while you start the washer."

Halfway down the stairs, Landon realized she should have warned the girl about the retro-vibe basement decor. Anna and Murdoch hadn't updated the space beyond adding shelves and setting up his workbench.

Sixties-style dark wood panelling. Orange curtains in a thick textured fabric Landon had never seen anywhere else. This wasn't meant for outsiders to see. Kenzie kept her reactions minimal, but a muffled snort escaped.

Landon laughed. "At least it's not contagious." She perched on the lower steps, angled away from the washing machine so the girl could unload her suitcase in privacy. A quick survey showed no sign of Mister.

The detergent cup rattled into the machine, and the case's zipper rasped with the force of Kenzie's motion. "Phil was my father's best friend. Before Christmas, he was at this old hunting cabin, wasn't answering his phone, and my dad was afraid he was in trouble. The sole access to the cabin was across a lake. The locals drove on it once it froze. But a stretch of warm days had weakened the ice. Dad wasn't from around there, and he didn't know where the current flowed to avoid it. His truck broke through the ice, and he drowned. Alone. Because Phil is a rat."

The washer lid slammed. "I searched for him online maybe five years ago. How can he be respected and successful when my father died because of him? So I started sending him an anonymous Christmas card each year to remind him of what he'd caused. This year, the twentieth anniversary, I wanted to do more. To see if he even cared."

Her laugh rang harsh. More of a bark. "He cared, all right."

Landon stared at the mottled concrete floor. "Kenzie, the snow globe rocked him, but meeting you shattered him. I thought he was going to collapse."

"He came face to face with the cost of what he did. Want to know what they found when they reached his bolt-hole? He was passed out drunk in a mess of vomit. He could have frozen to death or died of alcohol poisoning. How's that for Mr. Upstanding Fancy Lawyer?"

"It's not pretty." Landon shifted her seat on the wooden stair to make eye contact. "A person can change a lot in twenty years, though. We all have things from the past we wouldn't want broadcast now."

What was the Bible verse about "in wrath, remember mercy"? How could she drop a seed of that into this hurting girl's heart? She rested her hands on her knees, palms up. "Your father's death was a terrible tragedy. I've had trauma too, and I'm learning that anger is a cage and forgiveness sets me free."

"He doesn't deserve forgiveness."

"You don't deserve to be trapped at the point of your loss. Bitterness hurts us more than the ones who wronged us."

Kenzie tapped a polished nail against her chest. "I hurt him with every card I send. And now with the very public snow globe. He wants to talk to me? Bribe me with stories about my dad? I should leave him hanging."

She brushed past Landon and stalked up the stairs. "I want to ruin his life like he ruined mine."

Releasing a slow breath, Landon stood to follow. "Making him bare his soul to you seems like it's twisting the knife nicely. Well played."

Kenzie stiffened in the doorway. "There's that. And you hearing it means he'll know at least one other person in the community is aware of his sordid past. I could tell his stepdaughter before I go. Maybe other people too."

~~~

Pulse skipping in her throat, Landon tapped on the Lighthouse Room door.

When her mother opened up, they stared at one another.

81

Gwen's guarded smile mirrored Landon's feelings so perfectly, she couldn't stop a giggle.

Gwen joined in.

The pressure eased around Landon's lungs. For all the distance and all the tears, the mother-daughter bond remained. They could figure out how to do this as adults.

Landon cut her gaze toward Kenzie's room beyond the cozy conversation nook overlooking the bay. "Is now okay to talk? It's more private downstairs."

After shutting the common room door, she settled in the mint-upholstered wingback chair across from her mother.

The past nine years had carved deep lines in Gwen's face. Her skin itself looked tired, like she'd been deprived of sunlight and clean air. Her hair, worn long and straight like Landon's, had aged to a darker blond and lost its sheen.

She watched Landon with a hunger. Her fingers twisted in her lap, knuckles straining. "How do we get past this? It's too late for 'I'm sorry.' But I am." Her lips pinched together as if saying more would unleash a torrent.

"Mom, it's okay." They'd talked about this in emails, carefully, slowly, piecing together a safety net for the day they'd meet in person.

Landon pulled her hair into a one-handed ponytail and let it fall. "You were right that I'd have more mental health options in Toronto. They helped me imagine what you were going through. It didn't stop with my life. This shattered our whole family."

A wan smile lifted Gwen's pale lips. "I fought to protect the two children I had left. It didn't work out so well."

Lacey and Leyna. Twenty-two and nineteen now. Landon had respected her mother's request not to contact them. She leaned forward, elbows on the oak armrests. "I've had help. Have they?"

"Not enough. I know you asked me to give them your number, but I was afraid to make things worse. Now, Lacey won't leave the house for fear of what might happen, and

Leyna took off for the city last month with some guy she met in a bar."

Gwen pressed a fist against her mouth, her shoulders curving forward. "I've been in no shape to help them. Maybe you could. They both know you're here. If Leyna shows up, you won't recognize her. Do what you can? And I'll see if Lacey will call."

How much pain could a mother carry? Without the Lord's presence to cling to? Landon left her chair and knelt at her mother's side. Taking the tight-clenched fists, she clasped them gently. A cradling contact, nothing binding.

She looked up into Gwen's pain-clouded eyes. "We can strengthen one another and be here when they reach out."

And Landon and her believing friends would pray. She was walking evidence that prayer worked.

Gwen's slow smile wavered, tightening at the edges as if she battled to keep it in place. "That's all we can do." She rotated her hands in Landon's to squeeze back. "Now, tell me. Anna says Dylan's been coming around a lot even before this act to keep him in contact with Kenzie. What about the hero next door? Bobby's the one you talk about in our chats."

"They're both very good friends." Especially Bobby after they almost died together. "Anna needs to stop match-making."

"If you have the chance to be happy, take it."

"Mom, I don't need a man to be happy."

"Of course you don't. But if love comes knocking, don't let fear chase it away."

"I'll be fine." Because love couldn't sneak past her barriers and reach the door to knock.

She freed her hands and sat back on her heels. "There's one thing we can do even in the cold. Let's check out the shops in town. I have last-minute presents to buy."

All she wanted first was ten minutes to find Dee's number and see how late the physiotherapist worked. And if Dee agreed to meet this evening after hours, to convince Bobby to join the investigation. With Nigel so hard to find, Dee and her inquisitive child might be their best starting point in the search for clues.

Chapter 8

L ANDON HOISTED HERSELF into the truck. "What's that on the back?"

"Gramp loaded up a couple of bins of sand for the driveways. Long-range forecasts claim there's a big dump of snow coming, and he wants to be prepared. Watch him when it gets closer. He relies more on his arthritis than on the meteorologists, and he says his bum leg gives him even more accuracy."

As they headed down the driveway, she peered out the windshield at the stars over the bay. "It's clear now."

"So how did Elva change your mind about investigating? What does she have that I don't?"

"A house guest she may not be able to trust." And a trauma story Landon couldn't reveal.

"Any luck with that?"

"Not so far."

With no street light outside of town, the pavement stretched in a black ribbon between the glow from the spread-out houses on their left. The water to the right caught a faint glimmer from the stars.

Ten minutes later, the truck veered from the direct route to town, and before long, they jostled onto the gravel road. The headlights transformed the hollows into pools of night.

Bobby steered around the biggest threats. "Dylan will not

be impressed. He's bound to find out."

"Speaking of Dylan." Landon angled sideways on the seat to watch his profile. "He wants to keep an eye on Kenzie, so he's acting like he's interested in me. If you hear a rumour, you'll know the truth."

Bobby gave a slow nod. "It's a good excuse."

No light shone at Nigel's. He could be at work, or maybe he was still sheltering in his bunker.

On the road's water side, multicoloured lights outlined every angle of Dee's house. More twined around the miniature evergreens framing the clinic entrance. Light-up candy canes traced the path to the main front door.

Dee opened the door before they could ring the bell. "Starr's upstairs with a book. I'd like to keep this at an adult level and not stir her imagination. Come through to the living room. What can I get you to drink?"

Landon hadn't noticed the gas fireplace before. Now, nestled in a corner of the couch with her feet tucked up beside her, she surrendered to the ambience of dancing flames and soft Christmas-tree lights. Her bones relaxed, and she let out a slow sigh. "I could live here."

Dee returned with a tray of snowman mugs and a plate rounded with cookies. "I know this isn't a social call, but Starr will be pleased if you try our treats." She set it on the middle couch seat between Landon and Bobby before carrying her own mug to the enormous charcoal recliner.

Bobby patted his stomach. "Always happy to support home baking. I even dressed the part." Today's shirt bore a plate of Christmas cookies, each missing a bite. He settled into his corner with his coffee and a pink-frosted reindeer.

Dee smiled. "I'll send a couple home to your grandfather. How's he doing?"

"I can't keep up with him, so he's back to normal."

"Starr loved seeing him play Santa. She doesn't believe the myth, but she loves to pretend."

Landon bit the ears off a green-sprinkled bunny cookie.

"Tell her these taste great."

"She's very inclusive. Tries to convince me there could have been all manner of creatures at the manger."

Resting her coffee mug on her leg, Landon focused on their hostess. "Thanks for agreeing to talk to us. We hope the police will solve this, but if we can help, we want to. For Nigel."

"It helps me too." Dee's knuckles glowed white against her mug. "I'm having a rough time with a violent crime so close to home. They say it's probably not random, but they don't know, do they? Starr is my life. I can't let anything happen to her. Or to me. We're all each other has."

Bobby unlocked his phone. "It sounds like Vi held a lot of secrets. It makes sense this would be related. Someone didn't want her knowing or was scared she'd tell. Did you notice anyone who visited lately?"

Let the writer take notes. Landon would stick with questions.

Dee leaned her head to the side, dangling her hair over her shoulder. "People drive by, but I don't recognize their vehicles. Starr saw a car leave Vi's the day of the murder. She impressed the police with her description. I don't think it helped, though."

"Did Vi ever mention anyone she was afraid of? Or angry with?" Shrinking inside, Landon pressed her arms tight to her ribs. Why had they come? The police would have asked all these questions.

"Last summer, she chased off a developer who wanted my property. The woman wouldn't accept my refusal, kept coming around trying to persuade me." She smirked. "Until I mentioned it to Vi. I don't know what she said or who to, but the developer hasn't shown her face since."

Bobby tapped the details into his phone app. "There could be any number of people she's influenced that way. Maybe we should hang out in the coffee shops and listen to the gossip."

Gossip. Unkind but potentially holding a seed of truth. Landon leaned her elbow into the armrest. "Did Vi ever mention a woman named Freesia? Anything about dogs?"

Dee's forehead cleared. "Yes. Poor thing was devastated, but those dogs—it was pitiful. A lot of them had to be put down." Her pearly nails tapped a staccato beat on her mug. "That may be the one instance when Vi took a secret to the authorities. I've heard people suggest it could happen again. Not necessarily at that level but out into the community. Maybe not even from malice. She was aging. What if she started to slip?"

Surely, most people's secrets weren't worth killing for. Landon hugged her feet in closer to her body. It only took one person to feel threatened and be willing to act.

Dee wound a lock of hair around her finger in a light-brown spiral. "I'm scared to stay here. That developer might get her wish after all, even if she's miles away. I don't want my daughter traumatized. I don't want to be waking at night to wonder who's lurking out there." She looked from Landon to Bobby. "And now I'm scared for you two. This is a bad idea, and I shouldn't have encouraged it. Go home and stay safe. Let the people with the badges and guns handle it."

Landon lowered her feet to the floor. "We'll be careful. Any leads we find will go directly to the police. Trust me, Bobby and I don't want to add to the death toll this Christmas. We won't get in the officers' way."

Beside her, Bobby took another cookie. "Nigel is our friend. He helped us with some trouble earlier this year. Now, it's our turn to help him."

"I think you should go." Dee stood, straight-backed, and walked toward the door.

Landon and Bobby followed.

As they stepped into the spacious entryway, Starr shuffled toward them in present-printed one-piece pyjamas. Concentration radiated from her determined frown and the heat in her round cheeks. She propelled herself forward on the crutches clasped to her forearms.

"You came too late. I'm supposed to be in bed."

Hands on her hips, Dee shot her a mock frown. "Yes, you are."

Bobby plucked his coat from the peg where it hung. Once he put it on, he drew a small plastic bag from one pocket. He flourished it for Starr but passed it to Dee. "Roy sent a treat in case we saw you. I'm sure your mom will keep it safe until tomorrow."

Beneath the bed-tousled mass of dark curls, her eyes lit. "I like you."

"I like you too. And you bake good cookies."

She studied his shirt through the open coat. "But you dress weird."

"Starr!"

Bobby laughed. "So they tell me."

Starr fixed Landon with a solemn stare. "Don't worry about finding the killer. I'm on the case. They can't hurt my friend and get away with it."

Behind her daughter, Dee paled. Her teeth caught her bottom lip in a locked-jaw grip.

Landon didn't need the woman's frantic headshakes to get the message. She knelt to the stooped girl's eye level. "Starr, we have to let the police do their job. If you know something, they need to hear it. Your job is to take care of your mom and let her take care of you. Keep one another safe."

As she straightened, she caught Dee's tense expression— a mix of "thank you" and "take your own advice."

Starr nodded earnestly, curls flying. "I report everything I see or remember. You don't have to worry about me. Nobody sees a kid. Especially one with a handicap."

"Well, I worry." Dee dropped to her knees to hold her daughter. "Please leave this for the professionals. We can trust them."

Leaning into the hug, Starr kept her gaze on Landon. A smile spread like honey, slow and sweet, lighting her whole countenance. "Dylan said my observational skills are impressive. Of all the officers, I like him best. He's scrumptious."

Scr— Landon covered her cough with her fist. She didn't dare look at Bobby. A preteen crush deserved respect, not laughter at swoony descriptions. "Dylan would be devastated if anything happened to you. Especially if it came from you trying to help him and his team."

He'd said the same to Landon. With brisk motions, she pulled on her coat and boots. For the child, he was right. But she and Bobby needed to honour Elva's request.

Outside, the temperature hovered not too far below freezing. Their breath puffed clouds, and the damp ocean air seeped cold through to Landon's bones. Bobby started the truck and ducked outside to scrape a light frost from the windows while she buckled in.

When he slipped behind the wheel, he stared forward. Then, lips twitching, he shifted sideways toward her. "Scrumptious? Is he really?"

Behind his glasses, his blue-grey eyes reflected a serious question. When the truck's dome light went out, he held position.

Landon shrugged. "He's not just good-looking—he's the whole package. A girl with romantic dreams wouldn't have to search any further."

"Whereas I'm likeable but I dress funny."

"Weird. She said you dress weird. Which makes people smile and is therefore funny."

He dropped the truck into gear and trundled them out onto the rough road.

Landon braced against the armrest. "Comparison kills, you know. Plus, do you want an eleven-year-old crushing on you?"

His shudder rocked the bench seat beneath them. "No thank you."

Usually his self-comparisons lined up against Travers, the

larger-than-life space hero he wrote in his novels. On one level, he must know nobody matched a fictional ideal. To start measuring against his peers...

"Bobby, are you okay?" His parents' pressure wouldn't be helping.

He swung wide to avoid a dip that spanned half the road. "Yeah, sure. Tired—I was up late to make my word count. Last night was rehearsal for the play. Are you still coming?"

"Wouldn't miss it. Although you've talked so much about the book that I already know all the best lines."

"'Marley was dead, to begin with.'" His voice had dropped into a solemn, distant tone.

He'd tried out for the narrator role, but the casting director said a guy named Bobby had to play the role of Bob Cratchit. Bobby had been antsy ever since. The behind-the-scenes story-lover didn't want to take to the main stage.

He dodged a last pothole, and they reached smooth pavement. "I'm no actor. But we're a ragged bunch, and it's all for fun. At least I'll know my lines."

The tires hummed a lulling background as Landon thought over the conversation with Dee. "If we'd asked for that developer's name, we could have researched her online. Or tried sneaking her name through the anonymous tips line so the police wouldn't know we were asking around."

"Dee cut us off too fast."

By the time they reached the inn, Landon's thoughts swirled. How would they track down Vi's killer? She had to disengage, or she'd never sleep. "Come in and say hello to Mom. She wants to meet the hero who saved me in the tunnel."

"Anna wants me to come tomorrow to set up the trees. Can we do it then? And you pointed the way out, remember?"

"Because you kept me from losing my mind when it all started."

Three grown women could handle two trees. Landon kept

the complaint to herself. Anna's matchmaking wasn't Bobby's fault.

She stepped out of the truck. "Thanks for tonight. We make a good team."

"Pray we can help and not just stir things up." He flashed a lopsided grin. "Good night."

Landon scuffed her boot heels along the slate path to the deck. Stirring things up was the only way she knew to solve a mystery. Rattle the villain and try not to get killed.

She drew her arms tight across her ribs. They'd have to be more careful this time. No more life-threatening situations. Pick up on the clues faster and deliver them straight to the authorities. Anonymously, if possible.

Inside the inn, she stopped in the kitchen and set the kettle to boil. A soothing herbal tea would help her unwind. She chose a fluted china mug, pale green with white snowflakes. Dipping the bag by its string in a slow, meditative motion, she stood staring out into the night.

"There you are." Anna's footsteps followed her voice. "How was your visit?"

"Good." Continuing to dunk the tea bag, Landon eased around to make eye contact. "Bobby said you asked him to come tomorrow to help with the trees. You and Mom and I can manage it ourselves." With a deep breath for calm, she held Anna's gaze. "I need you to stop matchmaking."

Anna retreated to the doorway. One hand went to her hip, and her eyes narrowed. "I've watched Murdoch wrangle trees into their stands. When they were too snowy on Sunday to bring them in, Bobby offered to come back and help. I accepted. Go out if you want. Or stay and enjoy the time with your friend."

Landon's molars ground together. It took a slow breath to unclench them. "I'm sorry. I just feel—pressured sometimes. Like you know what's best and I don't."

She tried to gentle her approach. "Your support means the world to me. But I need to make my own choices. I'm single.

It's okay. I don't want there to be—" What had Dylan said? "A Team Dylan. Team Bobby. Team whoever's next."

Heat bloomed on top of her foot. She glanced down at the mug in her hand. The tea bag she'd been furiously splashing. Three other fat drops of pale gold liquid dotted the floor.

She offered Anna an apologetic grin. "I don't even want to know which one you'd choose."

As she wiped the spill, she tried to settle her agitation. Waited for Anna's response. But she stowed the rag and tossed the tea bag in the compost, and Anna remained silent. Landon stood to find her mentor watching, her generous mouth curved in a faint, closed smile.

Anna's palms dangled flat against the sides of her legs. "I hear truth in what you said. I'm sorry for anywhere I've overstepped."

"Thank you. I love you."

"I love you too." Anna's eyes twinkled. "And I did pick a team. Team Landon."

She tucked her hair behind one ear. "Hope came to see you. She can't stay much longer and be back before Elva gets home."

Landon patted her pocket for her phone. "Did I miss a text? We could have been quicker."

"No, we've been chatting. She hasn't been here long."

"It's late for Elva to take off alone."

"Nigel asked her to run him into Bridgewater for a few supplies. He likes to shop near closing time. Less people."

And in the next town, he'd be less likely to meet anyone who knew him who'd want to ask how he was.

Landon carried her tea toward the doorway. "Do you know what she wants?"

"She didn't say."

In the common room, Hope looked up from her seat by the window. "Sorry to drop in unannounced. When Nigel asked Elva for a ride, I seized my chance."

Anna flicked her fingers in a shushing motion.

"Neighbours do that around here. If the timing's poor, we're honest about it and try again."

"Elva's not supposed to know you're here?" Landon settled into a chair and pressed her dry foot on top of the wet one.

"No." Hope wore a navy turtleneck, which rose now with the force of her inhale. "They say you solve mysteries. I need you to find my birth parents."

Landon's spine locked. She raised her tea for a slow sip, watching the visitor. Scrambling for words that wouldn't spark an intuitive leap from Anna. "You said Elva already has their names. You'd have a better chance of an internet search than I would."

"She won't tell me. If she finds out I've asked you, I could lose this one connection I have with my biological family."

The ancient ache in her voice, the jerk of her throat when she swallowed. A fragment of her pain transferred to Landon's chest. "Hope, Elva must know why they want to keep their secrets. What if exposure could ruin the lives they have now?"

"She said my birth father's dead. Which could mean deceased or a man she's unwilling to acknowledge. Essentially, she said my birth mother was young and stupid. Mom said she was single and afraid but sobbed when she had to give me up."

Her head tipped forward, her hair falling around her cheeks. She peered at Landon, lips taut. "It may have been a teenage fling. Or he was married. Or I could have been conceived by force. I respect my birth mother's right to silence on the details, but I need to know the genes. For myself and my children." Her mouth trembled. "I need my mother to acknowledge me."

Landon's heart tore. Hope's mother needed that too.

"Mom knew if I came I'd dig for the truth. She says I'm too fragile. I had a kidney transplant." Hope swept her long brown hair away from her cheeks. "The medication gives me this moon face, and, yeah, I'm a bit emotional. But that makes me need answers all the more."

"Can Elva find out about your family medical history?"

"I want her to trust me with the full truth."

Landon sighed, hoping her sympathy was clear in her expression. "What if she already promised not to tell?"

"That's why I'm asking for your help. Anything you can find about Elva's relatives and their relationships forty-two years ago. Small-town gossip is legendary. Somebody knows."

Anna stirred. "Vi did. She must have."

A prickle crept along Landon's spine. Hope's card. At Vi's. Yet the card's placement on the body must be a diversion. Hope wouldn't have put it there and stayed in town to be questioned. Unless she was playing a very deep game.

Sitting with them now, Hope picked at the cuff of her sleeve. "That's the woman who was killed. Nigel's mother. Would she have told him?"

Anna's lips tightened. "Nigel keeps his own counsel. If you ask him, he'll tell Elva."

"Landon could do it."

Landon seized the chance for a low-key question. "Did you get a chance to talk to Vi before she died?"

"We saw her at the dinner. I couldn't bring it up in front of Elva." Hope's fingers pleated her cuff, released it, pleated again. "I need to get back. Please find the information I need. For either parent."

Landon curved her palms around her empty mug. "I'll see what I can do."

Tears brimmed on Hope's lashes. She sprang up and reached for Landon's hands, still pressed against the mug. "Thank you. Thank you."

The moment the door clicked shut behind their visitor, Anna's hospitable smile dropped away. "I bit my tongue in there so many times trying not to interfere. Even if you could find those people's names, you wouldn't breach their secrets to her. Would you?"

"In this case, doing what I can means keeping her from asking questions. All I could think was who she'd approach next and how fast the gossip would reach Elva."

That and wondering if Hope had slipped Vi a card at the dinner to arrange a meeting. Or left one at the house in Vi's absence—or in her presence.

The pinch around Anna's mouth relaxed. "I think I'll read for a few minutes before bed. Kenzie says Phil's coming around eleven tomorrow, so I'll text Bobby we'll do the trees in the afternoon." She arched an eyebrow at Landon. "If that's okay."

Heat prickled Landon's collar. Very lightly. She'd meant what she said. "It's your inn. And he's a good *friend*. Plus, Mom's been asking about him."

"I'm glad you two are rebuilding. I'm sorry I pushed that too."

Landon drew Anna into a hug. "Thank you for bringing us together. For everything. But maybe let me have a say? And let things unfold?"

Once they said good night, Landon took the stairs at a swift jog. Light shone under the doors to her mom's and Kenzie's rooms at the front of the inn.

Kenzie and Phil. However awkward their conversation in the morning, she couldn't deny her curiosity. Ciara's straight-arrow stepfather had serious pain in his past.

Tonight, she'd text Dylan what she learned from Hope. He didn't need to know how it linked to Elva. Or that she and Bobby had begun the hunt for Vi's killer.

Chapter 9

Thursday

A BANG FROM upstairs jolted Landon upright in the guests' common room. Her lower back twinged, released from bending over the puzzle table to disassemble and collect the pieces.

Rubbing the spot, she traded glances with Anna. Before either of them could move to investigate, stomping on the stairs re-framed the bang as a slammed door.

Kenzie stalked in, her sallow cheeks flushed and her movements jerky. "The low-level, two-faced—" Her facial muscles clenched, and she let out a closed-mouth growl. The sound rose to a shrill vibrating note. In a cartoon, steam would be pouring from her ears.

Landon set aside the partly filled puzzle box. "What's wrong?"

The girl shook her fists. "He bailed on me. Like he did to my mother. Says he can't come today and to wait for the weekend. A crisis at work. He's a lying snake."

Anna took a single step toward her, palm out. "He's a partner in the firm. That gives him flexibility to meet you during the day, but it also means he has to dig in if there's trouble."

"I hate him." Kenzie flung herself into the leather club

chair. "He'll be late tonight, his wife needs him, blah-blah. And will I please meet him Saturday when he can carve out the time." Her fingers hooked jagged air quotes for the last phrase. "I'd like to carve him. Playing me like this. Why did I expect anything better?"

Anna broke off a chunk of puzzle and separated the pieces into the box, each one landing with a tiny tick. "Maybe we should give Phil the benefit of the doubt. Can you stay for the weekend? He said he'll cover your room that long."

"Oh, he'll pay all right. Pay me off—or try to. He e-transferred me eight hundred dollars, supposedly to cover my food since I came. How much does he think I eat?" Kenzie's turmoil surged like waves. "I should take the money and run."

"If he's spending this much, I wonder what could be so important for him to tell you."

Anna's calm words matched Landon's instinct. Phil might throw money like snowballs but always with a clear target.

"Yeah." The girl's pink socks shuffled on the floor, toes flicking up and down. The rest of her body held a focused stillness. Then she gripped the armrests and hauled herself up from her slouch. She stood with purpose. "Revenge shopping. I'm going to the city for the day. If he's going to pay, I'll play."

Her racing feet on the stairs left Anna shaking her head. "I hope that girl knows what she's doing."

"I'd better let Dylan know she'll be gone. She can't have been involved with Vi's death, can she? Why would she stick around for Phil? He's so desperate he'd meet her out of town."

The puckers in Anna's brow deepened. "She's impetuous, but I can't see her being this unaffected if she'd committed a murder."

"Unless she's a sociopath."

Anna's brown eyes glittered. "Thanks for that."

"I was kidding! I mean, maybe, but it's ridiculously far-fetched. We're not in a movie. She's simply a person with unresolved issues."

"I pray they'll both find a measure of peace."

"Amen." Landon stuffed down a guilty sense of disappointment that she wouldn't hear the rest of Phil's tale today. She'd dreamed some weirder solutions in the night than could be true.

Freeing up the morning left more time for her and Gwen to talk. Each conversation, each activity, flowed easier. By now, the tentative pauses and second-guessing had almost disappeared. The difficult subjects had all been broached. Her sisters' circumstances and choices lay heavy on Landon's heart, but now she knew the truth and could pray. And she could comfort her mom. The budding restoration of their relationship brought wholeness in another of the shattered areas of Landon's life.

They'd barely finished cleaning up from lunch when Bobby clomped across the deck and let himself in. "Your friendly neighbourhood lumberjack, reporting for duty. And bearing news."

"About the case?" Landon ducked around Anna and reached the hallway first. An arrest would get her out of investigating—before Dylan discovered her expanded activities. Yet Bobby hadn't sounded satisfied.

He shook his head at her unanswered question. "Vi's letter was no help. The person she named was out of the country."

She stepped further into the hall to make space for Anna and Gwen. "How did you find out?"

"It's all over town. Mom and Dad heard it yesterday in a gift shop." His lips pulled tight on one side. "They didn't think to mention it until now."

Anna asked, "Are you sure it's true?"

"Gramp phoned a buddy and got the same story."

"Yesterday." Without a peep from Dylan. "If it's out in the community, it's not confidential. I can't believe Dylan didn't text me."

Gwen cut her a sharp glance. "Please don't get involved. You shouldn't even be talking to that Hope woman, no matter how safe he thinks it is. I can't lose you again."

Landon struggled to maintain eye contact. Not looking at Bobby, her co-sleuth. Did her guilt show? Heat prickled between her shoulder blades.

Elva. She was doing this for Elva and Nigel. Sacrifices had to be made. *God, keep us out of harm's way and let the police find the killer first.*

"Maybe he was busy and assumes we'll have heard by now. Which we have." Anna pushed her hair away from her cheeks. "I don't know if Nigel ever believed it'd be that simple. I hope he can go home soon instead of staying in his bunker."

From the description Landon had heard, the bunker might be nicer than his house.

Gesturing to Gwen and Bobby, Anna made introductions.

Gwen stepped forward. She took his gloved hands and studied him in silence, tears welling.

The longer she stared, the deeper his flush. That couldn't all be from the warmth of his plaid work coat. But he didn't squirm. "It's good to meet you, Gwen. I'm glad for you and Landon."

Landon stood with them in the hallway outside the kitchen feeling the seconds stretch like a thick elastic. It wouldn't snap, but the pressure built.

A tear popped onto Gwen's cheek. "Thank you. For saving her that day. For being a good friend. It means more than you know."

"Landon's idea got us out. It took two." The colour deepened in his cheeks and spread red across the back of his neck. "I just thank God I was there to help."

Warmth surged in Landon's heart, gratitude for the love of good friends—and now again of family.

Bobby reached for the door handle. "If the tree stands are ready, bring them out to me? Less mess if I can start on the deck."

Landon bundled up to join him and held each tree steady while he cut a thin circle from the end. Fresh sawdust sweetened the air.

By the time they had both trees anchored upright in the sturdy metal stands, Gwen stepped outside in a faded blue jacket, purse strap over her shoulder. "Good luck with the trees. Sorry to skip out, but today's the only day my friend in Liverpool is free. We haven't seen each other in years."

"Enjoy." Landon waved, trying to squelch the inner voice that had been whispering since Gwen mentioned her plans this morning.

Her mother's sudden departure was innocent. Like Anna's request that Bobby help today. No matchmaking conspiracy, no hidden agendas. She snorted. If there were, it didn't matter. She needed to get her overreactions under control.

Gloved hand steadying one of the balsam firs midway up its narrow trunk, Bobby raised an eyebrow. "What's up?"

"Nothing." He'd be horrified by the idea too. "My head's playing games with me. Let's get these inside. The decorations are already in the rooms. A lot of them. You sure you're up for this?"

He gripped the tree trunk and hefted it on an angle, red metal stand pointing forward. "Get the door for me?"

In the private sitting room, open boxes brimmed with ornaments and strings of lights. A stepstool stood ready. From the wireless speaker, a smooth male voice crooned, "It's the Most Wonderful Time of the Year." Anna directed the first tree in front of the windows.

Her pale countenance and stiff-set mouth caught at Landon's heart. "Anna, you don't have to do this alone."

Bobby stooped to retrieve a broken branch tip. "Let me at least string the lights."

Anna hugged her arms across the front of her sweater. "I appreciate it, but no. This is a memory time. It's enough that you're decorating the guest tree."

Her sadness followed them into the hallway. Landon shut the door with a silent prayer.

Their tree would stand in the common room window in place of the puzzle table. The top box in the stack held green lengths of mini-lights, each wrapped around stiff cardboard and tied in place. Bobby picked up the top set. "Murdoch's work, I assume. Gramp says he took pride in what he did."

"I only knew him when I was a child. Before they moved here and before... everything." Landon unlocked her phone. "Christmas music. Any favourites you want me to stream?"

One look at the rickety folding stepstool propped against the bookcase convinced them to stretch from their tiptoes to reach the top branches. Between the upbeat tunes and sharing childhood Christmas antics, they soon had the lights strung.

"Snack time." Leaving Bobby to explore the ornament boxes, Landon headed for the kitchen for coffee and cookies. She passed Anna's door on the way. A peek through the glass showed her friend seated on the couch, an ornament cradled in her palms. A small box lay on the coffee table in front of her.

Returning with a tray of treats, she saw Anna placing the ornament on the tree. At this rate, it could take all day. But how did a person rush memories? Or grief?

"Uh—oh."

Bobby's cut-off grunt sped Landon's last few paces down the hall. She burst into the room.

He spun from the tree, one hand clutching a sparkly tree-topper star while the other supported the tree. Eyes theatrically wide, he grinned. "Nothing almost happened. The laws of physics were never tenuously against me."

Landon snorted. "You nearly made me spill our drinks. Let me set this down and help you." She placed the tray on one of the wooden chairs.

They straightened the tree and cranked the holding

screws tighter. Bobby picked up the star and grimaced at the treetop. He shook open the folded metal stool and tried to lock both steps in place. The pressure of his grip wobbled the whole thing. "The one Anna has for her tree is sturdy. Should we go borrow it?"

"I don't want to intrude. There's a ladder downstairs, but if you hold this steady, I can climb."

He knelt, knees wide for balance, and braced one hand on the top bar and one on the bottom step.

Landon set one foot in place and then the other, reaching upward. Even with Bobby anchoring, the stool swayed. She kept her movements small. "Don't let go."

"You know I won't."

She did. He'd held her steady in that pitch-black tunnel when she thought they'd die. Here and now, he anchored the stepstool.

Star in place, she retreated to the solid floor.

Bobby stood with a soft grunt. "Drinks, you say?"

He chose a candy cane cookie from the holly-print plate and carried his mug to the club chair. "So Tall, Dark, and Scrumptious didn't tell you about ruling out the prime suspect."

Landon's snort shook her arm and sloshed coffee over her fingers. She mopped the spot on the floor with her sock. "If you call him that, he'll find out we went to Dee's. Don't you dare try to pin that word on me."

She settled into the chair opposite him. "I even messaged him last night. When you dropped me off, Hope was here. She thinks her birth parents are from the area, and she wants me to find them."

"Well, it's not like you have much else to do. Like solve a murder or reconnect with your mom or nail your final paper for the semester."

"Made it under the wire. By two minutes." That close to the deadline, the stress had made it nearly impossible to decipher the submission instructions. "Elva knows the truth but won't tell her, so Hope's been asking around. Dylan agrees Hope may have been trying to get information from Vi. That could be why she lied about her card."

Bobby stretched for another cookie. "Are you going to do it? Find them?"

"There's a difference between finding and telling. Elva promised to protect the secret."

The memory of their walk—and Elva's pain—raised ghosts that crept across Landon's neck. She pressed her fingertips against the phantom chill at her hairline. Where the rough-hewn cross marked her skin. Half the length of a thumb and half as wide, on a slight angle left of her spine.

Two gulps of coffee for strength, and she jumped to her feet. "This tree isn't going to decorate itself."

Bobby stayed seated. "Why do you do that? Rub your tattoo?"

She extracted a metal hook from a half-filled glass jar and plucked a random ornament from the nearest box. Santa in a yellow slicker, in a dory. Threading its hanging loop onto the hook, she dangled it out to Bobby. "I'm surprised you don't have a shirt like this."

"Nice deflection." Through his gunmetal-framed glasses, his gaze held hers. "Sorry if I crossed a line."

She pulled more ornaments from the box. Quirky boats bearing presents, starfish, lighthouses, all nautical themes. She hung them with swift, jerky motions. Talking as if it was someone else's story.

Telling him about the terror, the excruciating pain of the trafficker's tattoo. Passing out in fear and pain to wake up branded as property. About after her rescue, the pro bono artist working with the girls to remove the ink. And her choice to let the cross cover hers instead.

Not telling him about the trusted friend who held her hand through the needle's pain while the woman worked to create art out of shame. Zander, before the gut punch revelation of his double life.

More ornaments appeared on the tree. Bobby added to her work, the two of them moving in wordless choreography to the soft Christmas tunes. "Silent Night." "Joy to the World." "O Come, All Ye Faithful." The lyrics threaded the atmosphere with a sense of peace.

The sight of snow falling outside sparked a real, if faint, sense of wonder. Landon risked a glance at Bobby. "So it's a residual ache when I remember or when I get anxious. It's also a comfort. Instead of a scar that would always remind me, the evil is covered by the cross."

She hoped he wouldn't rewind their conversation and realize she'd been talking about Elva's secret when she touched the cross. *Please, God, don't let me betray her trust.* Not that Bobby would tell.

His blue-grey eyes held warmth. A slow smile spread, and he shook his head in small, repeated movements. "You, my friend, are the bravest woman I've ever met."

When she shrugged, the side-to-side head motion intensified. "Seriously. Not hiding or denying. Going after the healing. Allowing Christ to cleanse and recreate, and slapping such a visual symbol of your rescue over the mark of bondage. People need to hear your story, and you've given them an intro to ask."

"It upset Mom. She needed to see me whole, like we could forget what happened."

Landon stepped back to assess the tree. Ornaments ringed it in a band from about waist to shoulder height. The outliers would be Bobby's attempt at balance. She sighed. "Okay, let's fix this before Anna sees it."

"Hey, it could be a new trend."

As they worked, chuckling at the more unusual coastal-themed decorations Anna had collected, Bobby occasionally paused and opened his mouth as if to speak.

After the fourth or fifth time he hesitated, slurped air, and closed again in a grimace, Landon relocated one last ornament and hooked her thumbs into the front pockets of her jeans. "If you have another question, it's okay. Go ahead and ask."

He looked away. "This is crazy."

"Welcome to my world." She leaned against the nearest chair. Waiting.

Colour crept up his neck and into his cheeks. His shoulders rose and reset. "Do you trust me?"

"Of course." The light response came easily. Even if she couldn't see how it related to whatever he'd been straining to keep inside.

"No, really. Do you trust me? As a friend."

His serious tone weighted her to the spot, pressing the soles of her feet against the narrow floorboards.

Ever since she'd arrived, he'd been there for her. Holding her together through some ugly meltdowns. Over his head with her in dangerous situations. Patiently driving, helping, doing whatever she asked of him.

Did she trust him?

Chin elevated, she matched his posture. "With my life."

The dusky rose in his complexion deepened to red. His throat worked. His gaze broke, but he re-engaged. And again.

"Your tattoo. May I touch it?"

Landon blinked at him. "What?"

"Look, I don't get visions or mystical revelations. But—" He spread a hand flat against his chest. "I have this push that says to do this. I don't know why. So will you trust me? No funny business. On my honour."

They'd passed funny a while ago. This was downright weird. If it drove Bobby this far beyond his comfort zone, she'd better pay attention.

She gave a single sharp nod, then caught her hair, and wound it into a quick rope. She dipped her head forward.

A quick footstep, and his touch connected—a pressure barely felt.

Her breath stopped.

Light as a butterfly's wing, his fingertip traced the cross.

Stopped in the centre, gentle and sure. Quieting old pain far beneath the surface and drawing light into that space.

Deep in her spirit, something broke with an almost audible crack. Her lungs unlocked, and air flowed again, sweeter than before.

Bobby's touch was the most intimate thing she'd ever experienced. Tender. Pure. A gift.

Knowledge flared a bright spark in her spirit. She loved this man with his gentle, unassuming ways. Loved his loyalty and caring heart. Had probably loved him from the moment he prayed for her underground, trapped together in the inky black.

The touch withdrew, and she stiffened, lost.

She released her hair and raised her head.

Bobby had retreated to the Christmas tree's far side. He stood watching her, arms clamped to his sides, brows drawn together. "Are you okay?"

"Yes." And no. Her core muscles shook with the effort to contain an entire sea of emotion. Curving her arms around her ribs, she squeezed. "Bobby, thank you. You've given me a—a blessing. But it woke something else, and you need to go. Now."

As he reached out, she stepped away. Sideways toward the exit.

His features fell, and his arm lowered. "I'm sorry. I should have known it was a dumb idea. Can Anna help?"

Landon dug her fingertips into her sides, speaking now through clenched teeth. "You did the right thing. It was good. You are my very good friend, and you care. So please let me work this out. Alone."

The slump of his shoulders stabbed her heart.

She whirled for the door. "I'm sorry—I need space." One hand tight over her mouth to stop the first sobs, she fled upstairs.

Locked in her room, she grabbed the butterfly throw pillow from her bed and crushed it to her chest. The ceiling slanted to a low window overlooking the forest behind the inn. She knelt there beside the rocking chair for a glimpse of Bobby when he left. If she'd be able to see him through the waves of tears.

She'd never run away from him before. Stalked off, sure, when she misunderstood a throwaway comment. Shouted at him, argued, but never fled.

He'd remained a faithful friend through it all. His comfort had held her together through more than one serious flashback. This was different. This time she'd want more. After he'd agreed to settle for friendship.

A fresh wave of sorrow rocked her body. She loved him. How could she not have seen it before—like when he still loved her?

That ship had sailed, and for the best. Single was safer. She had far too much baggage. The tears came faster. God had put her heart back together only to let it shred again when another impossible longing surfaced and sank.

Finally, Bobby's blurred figure trudged from the deck into the forest toward home. "God, help him better than You're helping me. Please. And help me stay his friend."

Seconds later, Anna knocked on her door.

Landon lurched to her feet to double-check the privacy chain in case Anna had brought the master key. She trusted the wooden door to muffle the tears in her voice. "Go finish your tree time."

"Never mind that. What's wrong?"

"This one's mine to deal with. On my own. Something triggered unexpectedly. And don't you dare talk to Mom and give her any more to worry about."

"Understood." Crisp and abrupt. "I invited Freesia in tomorrow. The woman Kenzie heard the rumour about. Are you still on the case, or should I cancel?"

"I'm on it. And thank you."

Chapter 10

THERE HAD TO be a way. Landon stalked the confines of her room, throw pillow clutched to her chest. Trying to hold her heart together.

Through the low window, the fading late-afternoon light leached colour from the vibrant butterfly prints on the wall. Their wings' black bands deepened, and the swallowtail's soft yellow slid into grey. The monarch's orange glowed defiant. Urging her to live fully, to be brave, to be the blessing she'd been formed to be.

Not to crawl back into a cocoon.

There had to be a way to ignore her feelings for Bobby and keep partnering with him to help investigate this murder. They made a great team. *Too great.* She pushed the wistful thought away.

The authorities should solve it first. Yet she and Bobby had a knack for getting into the middle of it and triggering results. Instinct shouted to avoid him until she got a handle on her heart. Logic suggested regular exposure with a non-personal focus offered a stable path.

Her questing fingers found the tattoo. A site touched with healing—she wouldn't try to fool herself it was with love. "God, in the middle of this, thank You for more healing here." Even at the cost of a new emotional cut.

A series of raps on her door spun her in a half-circle. She

rounded the end of the four-poster bed and planted her feet. "I'm not ready."

"Constable Ingerson's on the phone."

Landon flicked the wall switch for the overhead light. Blinking in the sudden change, she rattled the security chain free and opened up.

Anna's faint frown and the wariness in her posture could be hesitance at breaching Landon's boundaries. Or Ingerson had news.

"Thank you." Landon took the outstretched handset. "Do you know what this is about?"

"No, but she sounds testy." Anna headed for the stairs.

Ingerson always sounded testy. At least where Landon was concerned. Had the officer discovered Landon and Bobby were asking questions? Landon shut the door and positioned herself in front of the stretched-canvas monarch print, drawing in the bright colours like nectar.

"Hello, this is Landon."

"Are you free to join us at the Foley home? Nigel insists on your presence—now that I've gotten through to him and waited for his arrival."

Both sentences rode the heat of a breath held too long.

"I—" Not a reprimand after all. Landon's mind skidded from the directional change. She checked the time. "Of course. Why does Nigel want me?"

Another sharp exhale. "I came to take down the crime-scene tape, and it's clear through the windows that someone's searched the interior. He won't let anyone in until you get here."

No wonder the woman was annoyed. Who knew how long and complicated the signal was to reach Nigel if he was in the bunker? Now, she'd be waiting for Landon, another non-driver but without Nigel's bicycle option, to appear on the scene. "I'll see if Anna can bring me. Hold on."

Landon splashed cold water on her cheeks and frowned at her puffy-eyed reflection in the mirror. She swept up a sweater and everything else she'd need. Bobby, her natural go-to any day but today, had his play's dress rehearsal tonight. Relieved to neither see him too soon nor exclude him, she sped downstairs.

Asking a favour of Anna after telling her to butt out wasn't easy either. But mutual concern for Nigel brought a swift, if mostly silent, drive to the scene.

Anna being Anna and with suppertime approaching fast, Landon left the car with a double serving of chili to reheat in Nigel's oven. Microwaves had their own place on his no-fly list.

They both dodged around the police cruiser and crossed the uneven ground to join Ingerson and Nigel at the base of the steps to the enclosed porch.

The constable stood tall and slim, her round face tight and impatience simmering in her sharp eyes. Nigel's pose held a watchful stillness. His features under his ever-present camouflage hat revealed nothing.

Once Anna had expressed her care and driven away, Ingerson pressed a palm down on the black and yellow perimeter tape and motioned Nigel to cross.

His high-stepping motions reminded Landon of a heron. Awkward but silent.

He unlocked the door, and Ingerson followed. She'd already warned Landon to come last and touch nothing.

Their weight crossing the unheated porch set one of the wooden rocking chairs in motion. Nigel nodded at it as if his mother remained on watch.

The faded boards beneath Landon's boots gave beneath the pressure of her footfalls. No ghost here.

She glanced again at the chair, plainly constructed with straight dowels and no contours to the seat. At the worn-away paint beneath it. How many hours had Vi sat here, observing the limited activity on this dead-end road? Hearing more than her visitors meant to say? Processing what she'd learned in her cleaning jobs and overheard around town.

Shivering, Landon followed the others into the relative warmth. The house smelled damp. Already abandoned after three short days.

Nigel turned on the lights and picked his way through the chaos to a pot-bellied stove against one wall. "I'll soon have a fire going."

Ingerson put a hand to her hip. "Check inside, first. If they left anything to be burned, we do not want to assist."

"Noted." He fished a thin black flashlight from a pocket in his cargo pants and lifted the stove lid. Not content to peer in, he stirred his hand through the contents, his fingers emerging ashy grey.

"Clear." He scrutinized the top sheets of newsprint in a nearby basket before crumpling two and dropping them into the stove.

Landon stayed near the entrance, holding the meal Anna had packed. The intruder hadn't left a place to set it down.

Books and papers lay strewn across the furniture and floor. Drawers hung open, empty, from an old-fashioned desk beside the window. A large Boston fern sprawled on a braided oval mat, dirt and roots trailing from a shattered ceramic plant pot. Surprisingly, the small Christmas tree strung with popcorn and cranberries stood untouched in the corner.

"Nigel, we'll need more than you and me to clean this up."

He eased the lid onto the stove and straightened. "Your role is to see what I miss. Cleaning comes later."

"I don't even know what to look for. You're the one who'll know if anything's been taken."

His sharp grey eyes glittered at her. "If Mother hid evidence, notes... I'm blind to them. Your eyes are fresh."

"Let me finish my sweep first." Ingerson continued to prowl the room, photographing every angle.

Nigel shadowed her, muttering. Fingers twitching toward the mess and drawing back.

As the stove's warmth spread, Ingerson moved through the kitchen and started on the two bedrooms.

Landon picked her way into the kitchen, where each step crunched a mess of dried herbs and filled the air with sharp, tangy scents.

If the killer had returned for incriminating evidence, dumping the dead woman's kitchen ingredients was simple spite. Like the mess a different intruder had made in Ciara's apartment in September.

The bank of empty, neatly labelled oversized glass jars on the counter made her rethink. Hate would have smashed them. A searcher would have dumped the contents to see what might be hidden within.

She'd forgotten Vi's herbal remedies and the reputedly long list of local customers. The mash-up of scents burned her eyes. They needed to find clues, but she'd be sweeping this up the minute Ingerson gave the okay. For now, she slid the casserole dish into the ancient but spotless oven and set the temperature.

Nigel trusting her in this space meant a lot. But she had no idea where to hunt for clues Vi might have hidden—if the killer hadn't beaten them to it. A quick internet search located a list of tips.

She tucked away her phone and escaped into the living room. "Constable, what about the people who came to Vi for herbal remedies? Nigel, did she keep records? Could they point to a suspect?"

Nigel shook his head. Three quick movements. "Yes, to records when I find them. No mention from her about dissatisfied customers."

Ingerson's mouth pinched on one side, her eyes narrowing. "We won't overlook that. It fits the tossing of her supplies but not the rest of this." One hand swept the area. She focused on Nigel. "If you don't find her books, perhaps we'll have a motive for the general search. We'll need to reconstruct her list from memory—yours and other clients'."

After the officer left, Nigel produced a shovel to clear out the worst of the flour, sugar, and spices. Then he and Landon ate and set to work.

She repeated the hiding spaces she'd seen listed online. The intruder had hit each one except two, which yielded nothing to Nigel's attempts.

"Did your mother keep journals? Letters?"

"Nothing but her customer records." He described the small coil-bound notebooks she'd stored in her bedroom out of reach of prying visitors. "While I check there, see what you might observe in the living room."

Landon stopped by the pot-bellied stove, toasting her rear and the backs of her legs. Roy had claimed Vi never forgot a detail, but tracking her sales would require more than memory. She'd need records for her taxes if not for repeat business follow-up. She'd left Nigel that letter about the one person who worried her. The one the police had already cleared. Had she held other secrets that needed documenting? To reinforce the influence certain locals claimed she exerted?

Notes required a book. Pictures, documents... could be anywhere. Bobby would say notes could be anywhere too. Scribbled in the margins of a random novel. Words underlined on multiple dictionary pages like a strung-out code.

She groaned at the mental overload—and at the barrier that now lay between them. She'd get past it. She had to. Tonight, she'd text to let him know what happened while he was at rehearsal. She wouldn't let him think she was cutting him out of the mystery.

So. Books. Nigel had told Ingerson Vi never embraced computers or the internet. But if she wanted a private record for herself, she might set up an online account through the free access at the library. The police had probably checked that already, but it wouldn't hurt to bring it up.

For now, Landon would start with the papers and books

spread across the floor. One minute to replace the couch cushions and drape the multicoloured granny-square afghan over the threadbare piece of furniture. Then she scooped an armful of books and plopped onto the couch.

At least she didn't have to read it all—simply scan each printed page for any handwriting. The searcher would have already shaken them upside-down to find loose items.

When Nigel added more wood to the stove, she asked if any book titles or authors matched his mother's customers. Or anyone Vi knew, for that matter.

Matched, or could link. Bobby would be proud of her coming up with that one.

It sounded oddball, but Nigel took the question seriously and examined each cover. He set a handful aside. "Mayor's surname. Fishing boat. This one's a street in town."

"It's a long shot, but we can pass these on."

He waggled a scuffed-up paperback at her. "*Hope Restored.* Elva's guest is Hope."

Elva's guest whom Vi had rebuffed. "That's an old book. Hope didn't arrive until last weekend."

Nigel blinked rapidly, his bushy salt-and-pepper eyebrows bobbing. "She shouldn't have come. Mother said it would lead to trouble."

How had Vi known Hope's identity? "She may have seen Hope at the dinner. I didn't think they spoke, though."

His scarred hands clasped the thin book, twisting it. "She came the same day as—" His mouth snapped shut with enough force to click his teeth. He shook his frame like a dog shedding water. "Sunday. Hope visited on Sunday."

Landon laid the book she'd been skimming in her lap. "Do you know why she came?"

"Not our business. Confidentiality." He blinked sharp grey eyes at her. "Why the surprise? She left her card. The police know."

"They don't. She lied, Nigel. Said she didn't know how your mom would have her card." Landon pressed her palms against the smooth pages of the book in her lap. "Were you here? Did they argue?"

His salt-and-pepper brows crowded low. "You know why she came."

"I will respect the secret."

"Good girl. Mother would have liked you."

"I think I'd have liked her too. I'm so sorry for your loss."

Three of his signature blinks. A series of nods. "Yes. But she gains Heaven."

"And we will honour her by finding the person who did this. I'll keep going through these books. Did you find the notebooks?"

"No."

"Is anything else missing?"

"Not that I can tell. I found an unfamiliar hat. Hand-knit. Black. Hairy yarn with a thread of purple." He jutted his chin toward his mother's bedroom. "Under the foot of the bed. I left it where it lay."

"You're sure it wasn't your mom's?"

"Mother refused to wear the colour of night."

Clearly, Vi had nothing against black in general. It outlined each cheerful granny square on the couch in a stained-glass effect.

"We can show whichever officer comes this evening." Ingerson had said she'd request a patrol check-in. "And tell them Hope did visit."

Nigel's bushy eyebrows drew into a scowl. "Sunday. Mother died on Monday."

"She could have come back." If Elva's daughter was a murderer... Landon swallowed against a sudden tightness in her throat. "Dylan told me your mother appeared to have been posed holding Hope's card. That doesn't sound like a killer's confession. But whether Hope came once or twice, she was here. Maybe she saw or heard something that can help identify the real culprit."

"Perhaps. As an outsider, she might miss its significance."

Landon slogged through page after unmarked page. The books had been read, but where Vi wanted to call out the contents she'd used a torn edge of newsprint tucked between pages. Many of the scraps bore no typing at all.

By the time tires crunched outside and heavy boots hit the steps, her eyelids felt like glue, and pain pressed against her temples.

Nigel opened to the officer's knock.

Corporal Zerkowsky greeted them both, his broad frame filling the doorway.

Landon rose and stomped pins and needles from her feet. "I've been sitting too long. We thought there might be a note among the papers but not so far."

Zerkowsky's impassive nod seemed to acknowledge the worth—and probable futility—of the task. "How come I find you at every crime scene?"

"In the whole of Lunenburg County? You must have a pretty slack job."

His heavy shoulders rolled. "I wish. For the record, Ingerson said you're here at Nigel's request. I'm hoping you'll keep out of harm's way."

"The only risk here is I'll go blind from eyestrain."

"A real and present danger in this line of work. You should see the reports I have to file." He scuffed his feet on the doormat and stepped into the room, surveying the small progress they'd made in sorting through the downed items. "Anything missing?"

"Mother's notebooks. Her customer details." Nigel described them and pointed him to her bedroom for the hat.

Zerkowsky grimaced. "Were they present when we searched on Monday?"

"Yes."

"Wish we'd known about them at the time." He shook it off. "Our perp's name may or may not be recorded, but we'll want to recreate the list as best we can. Write down any you can think of, and we'll see if those folks can add more names.

Most of her customers will want to help."

He plucked the landline phone from its cradle. "May I? Nobody remembers phone numbers these days. They stick everything in their contacts."

At Nigel's assent, Zerkowsky punched buttons. "She has half of Lunenburg County in here. Nigel, neither of you have cells?"

"Correct."

"I won't leave you without a phone. We'll send a tech by tomorrow to see about migrating this list. If that's not an option, they'll have to transcribe it the old-fashioned way. Most of these people won't be customers, but it gives us a beginning."

He replaced the handset. "Anything else?"

Landon updated him about Hope's Sunday visit. "I already gave Dylan my take on why she'd want to meet Vi. She didn't get her answers because she asked me for help last night."

Mindful of Nigel's watchful stillness, she added, "I said yes to stop her digging around town and raising rumours. But I'm with Vi. It's not our story to tell."

Zerkowsky probed her with a long closed look. "She may not be an active suspect, but don't provoke her. It's supposed to be Christmas. Goodwill, not flaming drama."

He collected the hat from the bedroom. "It appears the intruder finished the task uninterrupted, so they shouldn't need to break in again. We'll drive by two or three more times overnight anyway. Nigel, are you staying in? Windchill's picking up outside."

"I will."

"Good. We can assume any light we see will be yours. Don't work all night, and let your helper go home. Fresh eyes see clearer."

Nigel's focus snapped to the pendulum clock on the bookcase. "I've kept you too long."

Nine thirty. Landon rubbed her eyes. "I can come again tomorrow. I don't want to be much later calling for a ride."

Zerkowsky stuffed the bagged hat into his parka pocket. "I can take you now if you like. Save dragging anyone else out in the cold."

"Is that okay, Nigel? I could shift the papers and sleep on the couch if you're not ready to be alone."

His bushy brows shot up. "Mother would be scandalized. Rest assured, no harm will come to me tonight."

They set a time to meet the next day. Landon collected Anna's casserole dish and bundled into her coat and boots. Leaving him by himself in the home he'd shared all his life felt callous, but she said good night and followed Zerkowsky out the door.

Light shone in the windows at the house across from Nigel's. "Dee will be glad you're doing drive-bys tonight. Constable Ingerson said she came over before Nigel arrived."

Zerkowsky rumbled a note of agreement. "She hadn't seen any cars today before Ingerson's, and I think that has her scared the killer could be sneaking around more often than we know. It's her and the little girl alone. No wonder she's spooked."

"Is that why you asked Nigel to stay inside tonight?"

"In part. He may be able to take care of himself, but I don't want to come chasing out here on a call to find he's frightened the neighbours."

The police cruiser's suspension didn't handle the rough road much better than Roy's truck. Those few minutes of jostling, on top of tight back muscles from sitting too still too long, left Landon craving a hot soak in the tub.

First, to reassure Anna that Nigel was all right. Then text Bobby. She hadn't yet read the ones he'd sent before heading out to his rehearsal. He'd better not be waiting at the inn.

She needed her game face on to meet in person—once she found one. For now, she'd keep him updated. Cutting him out of the mystery would be one more wound.

She'd already confirmed with Zerkowsky that Dylan was off duty. He could catch up on the latest events when he reported for his next shift.

The inn lot was mercifully free of Roy's truck. It wasn't likely Bobby would have driven home and decided to walk over in such a biting cold, but Landon didn't relax until she found Anna and Gwen alone in the private sitting room.

Feet up in the matching recliners, they'd been watching a Christmas show. Anna hit pause. "How's Nigel?"

"He doesn't reveal much, but I think he'll be okay."

Landon perched on the edge of the couch to tell them about the search for clues. If she settled into the upholstery, she'd never reach her bath. After a bare-bones update, she headed for the stairs. Anna might not be happy, but she hadn't mentioned Bobby at all. Not even when Gwen repeated how glad she'd been to meet him.

Locked in her room, Landon ran the bathwater and opened Bobby's texts. She could do this. Loving him didn't mean she had to turn mushy at his every word. Guilt at leaving him hanging didn't mean she had to beat herself up either. Even though she should have responded this afternoon.

He'd be beating *himself* up despite what she'd said about the touch being a gift.

A deeper healing lingered, tangible to her spirit.

His messages apologized, over and over. Pleaded for a response. *Anna says you've shut her out too. It's killing me that I've hurt you. Scream at me, throw something, anything. But let me know how you are.*

Her sight misted. He'd seen her in a triggered meltdown before. Knew how bad it could get. That's what he'd be picturing.

How to convince him this was different? *Bobby, you didn't hurt me. You healed. Thank you. I need space cuz it opened another issue. Not your fault. Good friend.*

Before she finished pecking out a note about Nigel, the phone buzzed in her hand. *May I phone? Need to hear you're really okay.*

She replied with a thumbs-up and shut off the tap, then dumped lavender-scented Epsom salts into the steaming water. Her ringtone sounded before she finished.

"Hey." She squeezed the word past the lump in her throat. "Sorry I bolted. Then Nigel needed help. I've been home maybe ten minutes."

Nigel wasn't just a diversion. This was Bobby's investigation too. Reporting on the break-in helped calm her voice to convince him she wasn't a hot mess.

She stirred the bath salts to dissolve before settling into the rocker by her window.

He seemed to accept she hadn't included him because she knew about the dress rehearsal. "I can't do much tomorrow either. I'm tied up all afternoon. I'll get Gramp to drive you if you're stuck."

"We have three drivers at the inn. I'll get there."

"But are we good? Our friendship? I truly felt a force bigger than me at work—and ever since, I've been kicking myself for not trying to discern what kind of force." His exhale came out like a growl. "If we had an extra body, they'd have replaced me at the rehearsal tonight."

Outside, the motion-sensor light snapped on. The lean orange cat, Mister, sauntered from the trees toward the barn. His swaying gait radiated satisfaction. Good hunting?

Landon pressed her fingertips to her tattoo, remembering Bobby's touch. "You were worried about me. I'm sorry. You can stop now, right? Wow the crowd tomorrow?"

He snorted. "It's a fundraiser. The crowd may pay us to stop."

"I'll let you know if Nigel and I find anything. Anna has another possible suspect coming in tomorrow—the woman Vi reported to animal control."

"Be careful. If you get hurt, Dylan will take it out of my hide."

Chapter 11

Friday

WITH THEIR ONLY guest a late riser, Landon appreciated the slower start to serving breakfast. It let her, Anna, and Gwen enjoy time together before Anna had to leave her coffee and don her apron.

Today, the girl's habitually sullen vibe had changed to a smug assurance.

Carafe in hand, Landon approached her table. "How was your shopping trip?"

"Satisfying. And I had cash left over to book in at that fancy spa for today. Phil's a snake and I hate him, but revenge spending is sweet."

Landon poured her coffee and took her order. "Sounds like a fun day."

"I've been eating on the cheap but now that he's paying? I'm going for one of those lobster-topped burgers for supper."

A motor hummed, and she glanced outside. "Slick Jeep."

It stopped in the nearest space, and Dylan emerged. He turned up his coat collar and strode along the path toward the deck.

"Ah, the boyfriend wannabe." Kenzie smirked. "He cleans up pretty nice. I like the way he looks at you a whole lot better than how he looks at me."

"He's on the job with you. Don't take it personally. Dylan's a great person."

If Landon had to fall in love, he'd make a near-perfect candidate. Strength, integrity, courage, a protector. He ticked every box except for faith. She'd want a spiritual unity like she'd seen in Anna and Murdoch.

Yet she fell for the goofy, kind of scruffy, booksy guy. She, the dyslexic who struggled for passing grades.

She pushed through the white swinging doors to the kitchen.

Dylan occupied the other doorway, the one leading to the hallway, his shoulder propped against the frame. "Morning, storm cloud. What's up?"

Ignoring Anna's twitching lips, Landon gave her Kenzie's breakfast order before summoning her innkeeper smile. "Hello to you too."

His dark, hip-length jacket hung open over black jeans and an ivory turtleneck. Scattered snowflakes melted, glistening, in his hair.

If Starr could see him now.

Scrumptious. Her snicker morphed into a full-on grin.

"That's better. I was beginning to think you didn't want me around."

"I was... ruminating." That was a word, right? "Recovering from yesterday."

He bounced his fingers against his pant leg. "You're worried about Nigel. It stinks, losing his mother like this. Christmas doesn't make it any easier. We'll find the killer. I promise."

"It's hard to know what's going on inside his head. Nigel's. Not the killer's."

Gwen pushed out a chair from the table. "You were at Nigel's a long time."

Taking the seat, Landon waved Dylan toward the extra.

He shook his head. "I phoned in to the station to catch up

on developments. Lucky you, being the one Nigel trusted to help him search. I'm here to drive you to work."

"On your time off?"

One hand dipped into his pocket and jingled his keys. "We'll get coffee on the way. Besides, I like to keep tabs on my favourite sleuth."

Because of Hope and Kenzie. And Nigel. He'd better not know Landon and Bobby were investigating further. "Are you calling me nosy?"

"Let's say things happen when you're around."

Landon stood to collect the food Anna plated for their guest. "Be right back."

She re-entered the kitchen to catch her mother's protest, pitched too low to be heard in the breakfast room.

"—should be keeping her safe." Gwen's chin jutted harsh in profile, her mouth and brow tight.

Dylan's gaze cut toward Landon as if warning Gwen of her presence. "Believe me, I've tried. Landon, were you this stubborn as a child?"

She edged behind the table to squeeze her mother's shoulder. "Please don't worry. Dylan won't let me do anything risky." Which meant she'd have to make sure he didn't find out.

From his snort, if they weren't with her mother he'd shoot back a zinger about not being able to stop her in the past. Here and now, he contented himself with, "If she insists on involving herself, I can at least direct her to avenues where I need background intel. She's surprisingly good at it."

"Why, thank you." She was good at it if he counted sheer dumb luck.

One more press of her mom's shoulder and Landon eased away. "I can go now if Anna's okay to handle cleanup."

Anna flapped her snowman apron in a shooing motion. "Scoot. I'll put your mother to work."

Landon collected her phone, purse, and an extra-heavy pair of socks for Nigel's. She'd kept her feet up last night, away from the cold floor, but had still needed that hot bath to melt the inner chill.

Her phone showed a text from Dee. *Can we meet? I want to help solve this. Too close to home.*

A lot of empty forest surrounded those two houses. At the end of the road like that, they didn't even gain security from regularly passing traffic. No wonder Dee was on edge.

Landon replied with her morning plans. *Nigel wants us to work alone, but I can come over if you have a gap between clients.*

They could talk more freely with Starr at school.

At the base of the stairs, she met Kenzie leaving the breakfast room. Landon stepped sideways into the hall. "Have a fantastic day at the spa."

"You enjoy your time with the not-boyfriend." The girl's brief smile faded. "You're helping that Nigel guy, but you'll be here tomorrow when Phil comes?"

"I promise. Tonight, if you feel like it, there's an amateur production of *A Christmas Carol* happening in town. Phil can buy you a ticket."

"Scrooge, himself." Kenzie scowled. "Guess I can't say that with him paying for everything. But he stole my father. There's no price high enough."

She sped up the stairs.

Landon shrugged into her heavy coat and felt in the pockets for her mittens.

Two minutes later, she and Dylan hit the road. True to his word, he drove past the side street that led to Nigel's road. "Coffee first. And conversation. What's your take on Kenzie hanging around? She could have gone back to campus and driven in tomorrow to meet Phil."

"And miss the chance to spend his money? Plus, a lot of students will have already left for Christmas break. I think she's trying to distract herself from wondering what more he'll say about her father."

"You're going to sit in?"

"That's the plan. If it could relate to the murder, I'll share. Phil seemed to trust Vi, though. Her death really rocked him."

"Speaking of Vi, Ingerson should have an interesting conversation with Hope Bellgrove this morning. You're likely right about the motive to learn about her birth parents, but I don't like her lying to us."

"She couldn't admit it in front of Elva and risk alienating her one family contact."

"I did leave a card for her to call later."

When they reached his favourite java joint, Dylan asked her to stay in the Jeep. A good five minutes passed before he reappeared with tall to-go cups in each hand, cradling a brown paper bag against his chest. He popped his door and passed in the cups, one at a time. "Out of trays."

"And it took you that long to load up?"

He climbed behind the wheel and shut the door, then held out the bag. "Took that long for these to come out of the oven."

Warmth radiated through the paper along with a mouth-watering scent. Landon opened it and peeked inside. Fat, blueberry-studded scones. She inhaled until her lungs protested the pressure. "Time well spent."

"I had them skip the glaze, or we'd be one big sticky mess. Got extras for Nigel, but we should sample first. Quality control."

Landon snickered.

"Close them up for now." He started the engine and reversed out of the lot.

They stopped at a gravelled pull-off overlooking the ocean. Wind whistled around the Jeep's corners. A picnic table perched on the bluff, but once the engine stopped, neither of them reached for a door handle.

Dylan peeled off his gloves and opened his coffee. He reclaimed the bag and set it in the console between them. "Help yourself."

The triangle-shaped treat, lightly browned, retained a pleasant heat. Landon took a bite, savouring the dense sweetness and plump berries. "This is amazing."

She looked out over the winter-grey waves before angling in her seat to study her friend. "Okay, what gives? You butter me up at home, and now you supply addictive baked goods. You want something."

A lazy smile lifted his mouth. "Maybe I'm reinforcing my role as the interested guy who wants to hang around the inn more while Kenzie's there. Do tell her about our private picnic."

His wink and the warmth in those brown eyes held amusement. Not romance.

"Oh, you can rest assured I'll tell her about these scones. Her and everyone else."

He sipped his coffee. "Phil hosts an annual Christmas party. This Saturday. He's making this one a fundraiser for Vi. Funeral expenses."

"You want me to go?"

"See, I said you were good." He raised his cup in salute. "He was going to cancel but decided it was a ready-made opportunity to observe possible suspects. Apparently, Vi held a lot more secrets than we knew. There's serious resentment in certain quarters—plus a surprising number of people who are almost too hung up on being positive. Makes you wonder what they don't want you to know she had on them."

Phil and Whitney lived in a Victorian mansion. Landon had been inside once, helping Ciara move out the last of her furniture.

"I don't own a dress fancy enough to get me in the door."

"They keep it business casual so we common folk can mingle with the upper class. I went last year. You'll love the food."

"Won't people expect to see off-duty local officers?"

"They'll talk more freely without us. We thought we'd

send the new guy for a presence and so he can meet people. If Ingerson or Zerkowsky and their spouses showed up or if I went, they'd all be on their guard."

Landon swallowed a smooth, creamy mouthful of coffee. "I suppose everyone will assume you're all busy on the case."

"As we will be. While Price won't be perceived as a threat because he doesn't know them. He can't pick it up if they slip."

"I won't know them either. I've only been here since June and most people I know are from church."

Which did not make them innocent. The twitch of Dylan's eyebrow said she knew that even better than he did.

She pushed the memory of her former mentor aside. "I meant I'll see most of them anyway on Sunday. But I'll go. I might pick up a clue."

"Thank you. I want you to take a date. Bobby."

Landon flinched. "Why?"

"In case of trouble, you need backup. Price shadowing you would ruin the effect."

"Ciara. It's her parents' party after all."

Dylan's eyebrows crept together over his coffee. "Those self-defence lessons I gave you both this fall will only go so far. Your white knight may not have the training, but Ciara's too easily distracted. He'll watch you like a hawk. Pun intended."

Bobby's last name was Hawke. Landon held the eye contact and did not laugh.

Dylan popped the last bite of his scone. "Anyone wants to hurt you—they have to go through him first."

"Dylan, I—now is not a good time."

He blew out an exasperated hiss. "You're single. I get it. Take your friend, keep your hands to yourself, and steer him away from the mistletoe."

Landon jerked around to stare out the windshield. She stuffed the rest of her scone into her mouth and chewed furiously, eyes wide to dry the sheen that blurred her sight.

The tasteless mass went down in a lump. It hurt her throat, raising fresh tears. She blinked hard.

Dylan squeezed her forearm through the heavy coat. "If he hurt you, my badge won't let me pound him. But I can deliver a conversation he will not enjoy."

"Not his fault." She dragged her other sleeve across her eyes, the rough weave scraping her skin. Stared out at the rolling waves and the white gulls dipping and soaring. "Turns out I love him."

"And?" No surprise. Waiting for the trouble part.

"We agreed to 'just friends.' He's past wanting more, but it wouldn't matter anyway. I'm dyslexic. Words are his life."

"All that proves is that your God has a sense of humour. How shallow do you think the man is?"

Dylan slid his seat back and angled sideways. Studying her, probably. She didn't look.

"Has anyone told you yet today to not self-disqualify? Never mind. Listen, my friend, this runs deeper than that first love you should have experienced in high school. Are you still seeing that counsellor?"

She nodded.

"Skip Anna, ditto your mom, and don't expect wisdom from me except to know this one's above my pay grade. Phone the office now and make an appointment before I take you to Nigel's."

When she didn't move, he repeated the instruction. "This is not optional. I care too, in a mostly brotherly way. Those traffickers messed with your psyche. You've come a long way, but there's another twist or two in the road."

I'm healed. I'm being healed. I will be healed. Eyes closed, she flopped against her headrest and drew in a deep breath sweetened by the scent of scones. A quiet prayer helped centre her tumbling thoughts.

After a moment, she looked at Dylan.

The crunch faded from his brow. "Didn't know if you were praying or if you'd gone to sleep. Or decided to tune me out.

Ready to make that call?"

"Yes, boss." She unlocked her phone and scrolled the contacts.

"Mock all you want. My job is to keep you accountable."

"Keep this between us." She cut him a narrow-eyed glare. "On pain of death."

"My priority right now is to find a murderer. Preferably before this case derails the whole detachment's Christmas plans. There's no time for telling tales or playing cupid."

When she ended the call, Dylan started the engine. "Nigel will be waiting."

Landon downed the last of her cold coffee and set the cup in the console's holder. "I don't think we'll find any clues, but we have to try. Any results on that hat?"

"Not yet." They drove in silence until the Jeep jolted past Dee's physio sign and into Nigel's driveway. "You've met Dee."

"Yes." The night he'd warned Landon and Bobby off investigating. Hopefully, he didn't know they'd visited again.

"She has an eleven-year-old daughter. Bright child, physically challenged. I'd be interested in your take on her."

Bonus. A ready-made excuse for the visit she'd already planned. Landon repressed a grin. "They said Dee was upset by the break-in. Maybe I can check in with her while I'm here."

"I know you two were there the other night."

Landon hunched her shoulders up to her ears, pulling her head down into her collar. "Elva is afraid Hope's involved. She asked me to find out what I can. Yes, I dragged Bobby into it with me." She sighed. "That was before. I can't cut him out now, but it's good he was too busy today to help. I know you said not to, but I couldn't say no to Elva. Not over this."

The Jeep stopped in front of Nigel's garage. "There's more you're not telling me."

Meeting his gaze full-on, she shook her head. "Elva's finally opening up to me. Refusing her would close that door.

If Hope was in any way connected with Vi's death, what might happen to Elva—another woman who knows her parentage?"

She unfastened her seat belt. "I know the positioning makes it unlikely, but you can understand why she's worried."

"That's not all."

"It's all I can give you. The rest isn't related to the case."

His low growl rumbled in the close quarters. "I've heard that before."

"I was right then, and I'm right now." She ran thumb and forefinger across her lips like a zipper before putting on her mittens. "If I told you, there'd be a new body—mine. And a new murderer—Elva."

Dylan rolled his eyes. "Let's go."

"Oh, and Anna invited Freesia to the inn this afternoon. The one from the gossip Kenzie heard."

"To prove her innocence, no doubt."

She opened her door and stepped onto the frozen gravel. "Did you ever meet a person Anna thought was guilty? Of anything?"

"She does lack the suitably suspicious mind to be a detective." He joined her, and they set off for the house. "We need more Annas in the world, and not just for the cooking."

"Don't I know it. Accepting the stragglers and the misfits. She was a mother to me all the years my own couldn't be." She drew pure, cold air in through her nose. "If you want a glimpse of God's love, look at Anna's heart."

Dylan gestured for her to precede him up the stairs. "Except the Big Guy supposedly has no blind spots."

And He didn't meddle. At least not the way Anna did.

Landon rapped on the screen door, then opened up, and stepped into the porch. Theology cramped her brain. She knew the Ruler of all loved and accepted her. That would have to do.

Again today, one of the rockers picked up a slow motion

when they crossed the faded boards. Definitely a natural cause.

Nigel met them in the living room, his camouflage cap in place even in the house. He'd worn it during last night's search too. Rumour claimed he lined it with foil so the aliens couldn't influence his brain. Given his refusal to use a phone in case they captured his voice, that could be true. Or he could be covering a bald spot.

His sharp grey eyes assessed them. "Any word?"

"Not yet." Dylan spoke over Landon's shoulder.

Crocheted afghans covered the couch and upholstered chair. The big fern drooped in a new pot in its stand at the window beside the desk. He must have filled the cedar chest on the other side with the hats and scarves that had been strewn over the floor. He'd rehung his mother's coat on the peg by the door.

Landon caught her lower lip between her teeth, her stomach hollow. He'd be surrounded by memories. The same as Anna, Gwen, anyone who'd lost a loved one from their own household.

Day by day, he'd make it through somehow.

While the two men talked, she took Dylan's scones and the food Anna had sent into the kitchen. Aside from the empty jars, now sparkling clean in their places on the open-fronted shelves, the space showed no sign of invasion.

She hurried back to the living room. "Nigel, did you work all night? You said you'd wait for me."

Spine erect, he nodded. "Your eyes are for clues. More likely to spot a hiding place once you see it as Mother did."

Chapter 12

L ANDON TIPPED HER face to the noonday sun and closed her eyes, smiling as the warmth bathed her skin.

Behind her, Nigel closed the door and tromped down the steps from his home. He stopped at her side. "Thank you. Thank Anna for the food."

"I wish I'd been more help."

"Not finding does not mean not helping. Reassure Dee and Starr that I'm well."

"Nigel, have you made that list the officers asked for? Another way I could help is to contact your mother's clients. One of them may know something." Or be the killer, so no private meetings.

"Mother would want to guard their privacy."

"I wouldn't ask about personal details. We need to know what they might have observed."

"My answer is no. To the investigators and to you who need to stay safe."

He strode toward the garage and rounded his mother's parked car. Soon he emerged, wheeling an ancient but spry bicycle with a plastic milk crate on the rear. A helmet topped his cap, and a reflective safety vest covered the torso of his bush jacket.

With a sharp nod, he mounted the bike and pushed off down the gravel drive.

133

Landon strolled after him, attuned to the sun and the occasional call of a chickadee in the nearby trees.

One of the little black-capped birds darted from cover and flitted ahead of her across the road. By the time she reached Dee's, the bird had tucked into the shrubbery. It chirped again as she passed.

The second car in the lot meant Dee still had a client. Landon used the clinic entrance instead of trying the residence door. She settled in a turquoise moulded chair that provided surprisingly comfortable back support. For a physio clinic, that made sense.

Closing her eyes, she let the gentle instrumental music soothe her tension. The search at Nigel's had been a long shot, one she should have suggested before the break-in. Vi's customer notebooks were gone, along with who knew what other clues.

Dee emerged from a side room. "Landon, thanks for coming. I'll be with you in a moment."

After she processed her client's payment and the man departed, Dee locked the clinic door. "Let's go enjoy the Christmas tree."

She led Landon through another door into the main part of the house, passing the entrance they'd used previously, and caught up a remote that operated the tree lights.

Waving Landon toward the couch, Dee sank into the recliner with a luxurious sigh. "I'm glad Starr's in school. She's got it into her head that she's a child sleuth, and it's scaring me." She tucked her feet up in the chair. "Dispatch asked me to tell her not to call with every idea she thinks up. She's limited to once a day now."

"Always hoping she'll reach her hero."

"That's right. She spoke about Dylan when you were here with Bobby." A frown chased across the physiotherapist's face. "Starr has no male role models in her life, not even at school. Her father walked out after a playground accident damaged her spinal cord and sentenced her to a life on

134

crutches. She didn't fit his perfect image."

She paused, her jawline firming. "Then the man I moved here to be with—if you haven't heard—cleaned out every cent we owned and disappeared. The police are still trying to track him down."

Her chest rose and fell in a deep breath. "He was so good to Starr—to both of us. Until it was too late. Starr obsesses over him. Like a fool, I tried to protect her at first, and now she doesn't believe it was all a con."

Both hands slapped the leather armrests. "I didn't ask you here to dump my sad story. We're doing fine now. And I have another client coming in half an hour. Here's the deal. I want to help solve this before Starr gets us both in danger—if it's not too late. I've been thinking. Vi must have kept notebooks or journals. She knew too many secrets to keep in her head."

Landon drew one foot up on the couch and crossed her arms around the bent knee. "It's not that Nigel didn't trust you to help him yesterday. He said because I didn't know Vi I'd see things differently. Not that it made a difference. If she kept notes, the intruder has them now. Along with her customer list."

Dee's lips firmed into a line. "I was one of her customers. I don't want the killer knowing about me. Or Starr."

"Do you think they'd read everything? Or destroy all the evidence?"

"All I know is I won't feel safe until this is settled. I've been racking my brain, and it could be anyone. She knew too much—about more than her herbal-remedy customers and the homes she cleaned. She had this uncanny sense. Any individual in town could have wanted to shut her up—or could have retaliated when she wouldn't tell what they wanted to know about someone else."

She smoothed her hair with both palms, then redid her ponytail. "Or it might not be secrets at all. A random addict passing through—Vi wouldn't turn away anyone in need. Or simple revenge, like that developer she forced to back down."

"Has she tried again?"

"Not yet. If she's guilty, she wouldn't be that brazen about it."

"You've mentioned her to the police, right?"

"First thing."

Dee had an even more personal reason to be invested in this than Landon did. With the physiotherapist as another partner-in-sleuthing, Landon could create a little distance from Bobby. Until her heart adjusted to the new normal.

Landon leaned back, eyes narrowed. "You know the police aren't happy with civilians getting in their way, right?"

"So we'll be subtle."

"Works for me." She grinned. "Are you going to the Kirkwoods' Christmas party tomorrow night? I hear a lot of potential suspects may be there. Bring Starr. The more ears, the better."

Maybe Dylan would accept Dee as a substitute for Bobby. Or Bobby could pair up with Starr and see if any of the girl's ideas opened a new direction.

Dee's breath hissed. "The whole point is to keep my daughter out of danger."

"We can't stop her from thinking about the case, though. This could be a safe way to let her feel like she's contributing. Who knows, she might be the one to overhear a clue. Nobody pays attention to children in a group of adults."

"Especially handicapped children." Dee flicked her fingers over the side of her armrest as if to dispose of the bitterness. She stood. "I'll think about it. She'd have to promise not to ask questions. A child interrogator would silence the entire crowd."

Landon rose too. Dee's next client could arrive any minute. "Those ideas she gives the police? Maybe send them my way too? I'll keep you posted on what I learn on my end."

No point mentioning Freesia until she had something to report. One thing she could share. She unlocked her phone and brought up the picture of the hat Nigel found. "Do you know who owns this? It was in Vi's bedroom yesterday. It may belong to the killer."

As Dee peered at the screen, her lips pulled into a tight line. Her nostrils pinched. "May I?" She took the phone and spread her fingers to enlarge the image.

"Nigel says it wasn't there on Monday when he did the walk-through with the police. Whoever broke in for the notebooks must have dropped it. I suppose it could be someone else with a secret, but it's probably the killer."

"Hard to say." Dee set a fast pace toward the clinic. An engine sound outside must belong to the next client.

Landon's phone buzzed, and she slowed to check the message. Anna, asking if she'd be home in time for Freesia's visit. She sent a thumbs-up and added, *Can you or Mom pick me up? Across from Nigel's at the physio place.*

Stuffing her phone into her pocket, she went to follow Dee through to the clinic where she'd deposited her coat and boots.

A black scarf hung from the pegs by the main door. Fuzzy, with a thread of metallic purple.

Dry-mouthed, Landon reached for it. Trailed the material through her fingers.

Behind her, the clinic door clicked open.

She dropped the scarf and whipped around.

Dee's gaze searched hers. "I wish you hadn't noticed that."

Landon edged toward the door. No boots, no coat— nowhere to run. With Nigel gone, no one nearby to hear her cry for help.

"Don't be ridiculous." The physiotherapist retreated toward her clinic, arms clamped across her ribs. Tension framed her mouth. "Yes, it's my hat. Starr lost it this week, and now I know where. This is taking investigating too far. She is in so much trouble when she gets home."

Landon held herself poised for flight. "Could she get from here to Vi's on her crutches?"

"You'd be surprised what my daughter can do." Dee's chin

lifted with the declaration. "She went to Vi's a lot. Loved that cantankerous old woman."

"If an officer calls the school now and asks Starr, will she admit to crossing the police tape and entering Vi's house?"

"I don't know, but she's a terrible liar. They'd learn the truth." Dee clutched the sides of her head, her fingers whitening with the pressure. "My baby could have been there when the killer broke in. If I lost her—"

The shared what-if fear for the girl eclipsed Landon's suspicion. "Thank God that didn't happen."

"She must have gone on her way home from school. The bus lets her off on the road, and she could have sneaked into Vi's before coming home. When I'm seeing clients, she lets herself in and does her own thing."

"Dee, the police have to be told. She breached a crime scene."

"I know. For now, I've kept my client waiting too long. Can you see yourself out? I'll message you when I decide about the party." She disappeared through the connecting door, her light-brown ponytail swinging.

Landon followed, bundled up again, and went outside to wait for her drive. Roaming the parking lot, she concentrated on her surroundings and waited for the adrenaline spike to fade.

One look at Dee after finding the scarf, and all Dylan's self-defence tips had vanished. If the woman had been the killer, Landon would likely be floating off the rocks behind the house. Or stuffed in a corner to be disposed of later.

A shiver swept her. That hadn't happened. Nor had Dee's daughter been harmed on the forbidden visit across the road.

Time to phone in a report about Starr and the hat. They weren't going to like this. And Ingerson was on duty today. Poor kid. Although maybe it was best she didn't have to confess to Dylan.

The well at the property's edge beckoned. Finishing her call, Landon wandered nearer. Large, rounded beach stones stood thigh-high. Instead of a cement slab cover or a picturesque bucket-and-pulley arrangement, it was filled with dirt. Dry stalks of dead plants stuck from the ground like claws.

She perched on the well's edge, watching the road and letting the sun do its work.

Anna arrived shortly after. "You can have a late lunch before Freesia comes. How's Nigel holding up?"

"I can't tell. He went back to work this afternoon."

"He needs to be active. To sit and brood now wouldn't be good for him."

Landon had never seen him sit for more than a handful of minutes. Barely long enough to swallow a hot cup of tea. In hindsight, she shouldn't have been surprised he'd put the house in order overnight.

She pressed the tips of her red fleece mittens together. "I appreciate you picking me up. And inviting Freesia in. Honestly, everything you've poured into my life. I do need more space to maybe spread my wings. I'm not ready to talk about what wrecked me yesterday, but I know you care. I've seen you working to be hands-off, and it means a lot."

"I'm trying." Anna drew a slow breath. "It's hard, realizing our desire to help might be pushing in the wrong direction. I see good things ahead, but God may see better ones or in a better timing. He won't move until we're ready."

"If He brings a new insight, that means I'm ready to deal with it?"

Anna let the question hang, the tightening of her mouth revealing her struggle to restrain unwanted words. Her gloved hands flexed on the steering wheel. "Not necessarily. It could be a step or a seed, helping you get ready for later. At least that's how He works with me."

"Thank you. I booked in to see my counsellor—Dylan pulled big-brother rank."

"Good man."

When they reached the inn, Landon scarfed the extra

sandwich remaining from lunch and chatted with Gwen. With Kenzie out, they chose the guests' common room at the front of the inn where they'd see Freesia's arrival.

Gwen straightened the paperbacks on the bookcase before taking a seat. Hands clasped on her knees, she studied Landon with a mother's searching care. "This time together has been a gift."

"For me too. I wish we had longer."

"My boss will give me another week if I take a shift Christmas morning. I was scheduled to be off this year."

Care facilities always needed workers on holidays, Christmas most of all. "You don't have to do that."

"I'd like to. Lacey says she's managing okay at home. Maybe next year you'll come to us, but it's too short notice now. Let me have a little longer with you."

Guilt stirred. "I didn't expect the mystery to eat up so much of our visit, but I couldn't say no to Nigel." Or to Elva. Even though it meant effectively saying no to Gwen—and worrying her.

Keeping an eye on Landon might be part of the reason for extending her stay.

Landon quashed a flicker of resistance. She was blessed to have Gwen and Anna in her life loving her. With love came concern. She needed to embrace it—as long as they didn't overdo their care.

A dirt-spattered sedan drove past the common room window.

Gwen rose from her seat. "I'll go upstairs. Anna says she's shy around strangers."

"But you want to see her and decide if she's a threat. It's okay to stay, Mom. Reassure yourself this is low-level investigating. We're ruling people out."

The stooped posture straightened. "You won't mind? Anna said it's for a friendly cup of tea, but I know why she made the invitation."

Meddling or helping? Landon stood too. "Let's go

welcome her instead of making her walk into a room of seated strangers."

In the entryway, Freesia handed Anna a rubberized purple raincoat with a thick plaid lining. She stepped out of knee-high black rubber boots with red soles, mates to the pairs in the inn's bad-weather-gear stash.

A saucer-sized red plastic poinsettia blossom clung to the side of her head above one ear, and her wavy brown hair hung free past her shoulders. The woman appeared to be maybe twenty-two or twenty-three. Chin dipped, she peered up at Landon and Gwen. A faint smile wobbled on her lips but didn't settle.

Anna made introductions and settled them in the common room, returning with a tray of tea and shortbread cookies.

Freesia accepted a mug of tea. "This is lovely, Anna. A black Scottie dog with a Christmas bow."

"I save that one for the animal lovers."

Landon had special ordered a sturdy mug with a Nova Scotian red squirrel for Roy from the local print shop. She'd wrapped it in a box within a box within a box and couldn't wait to watch him open it. The good-natured reminders of his squirrel-triggered fall hadn't let up, and Roy laughed the loudest.

She focused herself on the here and now, choosing a mug where Santa knelt at the manger. The fictional met the real, white-gloved hands clasped in prayer to the cloth-wrapped ultimate Gift.

Freesia sat with her feet and knees pressed together, cradling her drink in her lap.

Landon had seen her around church occasionally, always keeping to the fringes. "It's good to finally meet you. I guess we both love bright colours."

Polish-free nails plucked at Freesia's red and black plaid shirt. "They're strong. I live by myself, and I need to be brave."

Anna had said she lived in an old mobile home at the edge

of a field, far from the road. Lonely by choice?

Extending one leg, Landon pulled up the cuff of her grey sweatpants—intended for the morning cleanup—to reveal hot-pink socks. "Me too. Colour also gives me energy. I've been at the Foleys' helping Nigel. Someone broke in yesterday and left a mess."

Freesia's blue eyes rounded. "Poor Nigel. After he lost his mom too." She dropped her gaze, gripping her mug. Her chin trembled. "I didn't want him to lose her. But I didn't want her anywhere near me, not after what she did."

A prickle crept up Landon's spine to her hairline. She glanced at Gwen, then Anna. That sounded a lot like a confession.

Tight-lipped, Anna gave a tiny headshake. "Freesia, it must have been devastating to lose your dogs. Do you know Vi never talked about it in the community? Never said anything unkind about you. She spoke to animal control in private. Unless the news story lied, the dogs needed more care than one person could give."

Apparently, Freesia—like Anna—couldn't resist a stray. She'd ended up with too many dogs until she was skimping her meals to provide for them when they couldn't hunt enough rabbits and squirrels to feed themselves.

In the end, she'd stolen food from the restaurant where she worked and lost her job. Unless Anna had misread the situation, Vi's report saved the lives of not only the dogs but also Freesia herself.

It had left her barred from keeping pets and required to volunteer at the local animal shelter. Officially, the supervised service was to demonstrate her ability to care for their well-being. To Landon, it sounded like a judge's kindness to a struggling woman who loved animals.

A desperate love—for animals or people—could erupt in a violent shove like they thought killed Vi.

A shudder rocked Freesia's body and nearly dislodged the poinsettia clip from her hair. She clasped the Scottie mug with both hands. "They took every single one. Stripped me of my comfort, my reason for living."

Her rapid blinks couldn't stop the tears. "Vi knew I need a therapy dog. She wouldn't side with me to keep one. Now, she'll be judged for what she did."

Landon rested her hands on her thighs, palms up. "Freesia, did Vi keep in touch? You said you didn't want to see her. Did she respect that?"

The tear-shimmered gaze swung on her. Freesia's embrace of the dog mug switched from two hands to both arms crisscrossed. Her full lips parted. "She called sometimes. I always hung up. You think I killed her. Everyone says it but I didn't. It wouldn't bring my babies back."

She set down the mug and bolted from the room.

Landon waved the others aside and skidded into the hall. "Freesia, wait."

Instead, she raced out the door, purple coat trailing from one arm.

In her house shoes and without a coat, Landon followed her. "Hey, you can't drive like this. Give yourself a minute, please."

Freesia reached her car and yanked open the driver's door.

Landon opened the passenger side and jumped in. Her brain caught up, and she held the door wide open.

The woman glared at her, anger seeming to break the sobs. "I don't want you."

Right palm outstretched across her body toward Freesia, Landon spoke gently. "I don't think you did it. Want to know why?"

Colour fled Freesia's face until she could have been an ice sculpture. "Why?"

"Because you want your babies back more than you want revenge." *God, I'm taking a chance here.* "Am I right?"

A sudden gulp restarted the tears. "Yes." The word came out in a wail.

Landon glanced toward the inn. Anna and Gwen stood in

the breakfast room window, Anna holding up a phone. Landon waved what she hoped was an all-clear.

She dared to reach for Freesia. "Will you come again? Can we be friends?"

"Maybe. Animals are safer."

"There are people we can trust." Thoughts of Bobby brought a smile.

Landon held eye contact, trying to project acceptance and low risk. "What you did today, coming and meeting strangers, sharing some of your hurt—that's brave. You know Anna's heart. I like to hope mine's the same."

She stepped from the car and leaned in, holding the open door. "The police will find who did this. I'm doing what I can to help."

Freesia ducked her head, peering through her lashes. "You want to know who killed Vi? Follow the clue."

She shifted the car into reverse and let it roll, forcing Landon to shut the door and step away.

Landon tracked the car until it disappeared from sight. "Follow the clue." Singular.

"Freesia, what do you know?"

How can I find out without breaking your trust by reporting this?

Chapter 13

Saturday

"SHE'LL BE DOWN in a minute." Landon took Phil's coat and ushered him into the common room.

According to Kenzie, the office crisis had resolved. He wasn't working today, and he'd lost the suit and tie. Instead, a dress shirt collar crowned the softest-looking camel-hued sweater Landon had ever seen.

Facing Kenzie's brand of spite must call for every resource he could muster.

He might think it tacky, but Landon's light-up necklace of Christmas mini-bulbs provided the same effect for her. The multicoloured lights glinted in a long loop down the front of her sweater.

Instead of taking a seat, he stopped in front of the tree, studying the ornaments. Did he see whimsy and folk art or a hodgepodge mess?

Kenzie's shoes clattered on the stairs.

Shoulders set, he executed a controlled turn toward the doorway. Jerked to a stop and swore, low and vicious.

Following his gaze, Landon crinkled her brow. Kenzie's dramatic entrance included a makeover. Her long brown hair draped across one shoulder in a braid instead of flowing free. She'd added makeup and found a pair of skinny jeans and a baggy Aran knit sweater.

One hand propped on her hip, she leaned against the door frame with her chin raised and a tiny smile curving mulberry-tinted lips.

Phil spun to Landon. "I apologize. I need—Could I have a glass of ice water? Please."

"Of course."

Kenzie pattered behind her along the hall. "Don't leave me alone with him."

In the kitchen, Landon shook ice cubes into a tall, holly-printed glass and topped it up with filtered water.

When the girl gloated at breakfast about a special outfit, Landon had assumed she'd made an extravagant buy to flaunt his money. Instead, this? "What's with the getup? You nearly gave him a coronary."

The little grin morphed into a full-on smirk. "The photos he gave me. One shows Mom dressed like this." She reached under the hem of her sweater and tugged as if the waistband was too tight on her jeans. "People actually wore this stuff. I can barely bend over."

"Want a glass of water too?"

"Nowhere to put it. Oh, wait. Yes, please. Maybe he'll give me an excuse to pitch it at him."

Landon took her time pouring the second glass. "Kenzie, you're our guest, but you're also his guest. Please dial back on the hostility."

"I'm leaving today anyway. If he cuts me off, no impact."

"For your own sake, then. This is not who you are." She thrust the water glass into Kenzie's hand and walked away.

Phil sat in one of the wingback chairs, legs crossed, fingertips tapping the carved oak armrest. He accepted the glass with thanks. "Again, I apologize for the language."

Landon cut her gaze up and to the side, toward the girl following her, then nodded. She thought Kenzie would claim the comfy club chair, but the girl matched Phil in choice and in posture.

Dropping into the seat nearest the door, Landon prayed again for reconciliation. She scrubbed her palms against the heavy weave of her pant legs. Drew strength from the bright lights dangling in the bottom of her sight line. Eased into the wooden back rest and waited for the sparks to fly.

Kenzie clamped her arms across her bulky sweater and hiked a brow at Phil. "Well?"

"You don't merely look like your mother. She's shaped you to act like her too." Phil had already half-drained his glass. He took another sip. "It must have been painful growing up without your father and learning about the tragedy."

"Spare me the sympathy. I want the facts that my mother allegedly withheld." She saluted with her glass. "See, I can speak lawyer too."

Phil's mouth pinched. "Did you ask her about the abortion?"

"No."

"I thought not."

He set his glass on the floor and gripped the armrests with both hands. "As I said, when I got my head on straight and tried to make things right, she informed me I'd forfeited all rights to fatherhood. Even fatherhood in absentia. She ended an innocent baby's life—my daughter—in justifiable anger at the fool I'd been."

Kenzie started to argue, but something in his expression shut her down.

"Or so she said."

In Landon's head, an imaginary judge rapped a gavel once. With finality.

Kenzie had a half-sister, given up for adoption? Even that faint a connection would burn her.

The girl's palms pressed into her stomach. "What do you mean?"

"When she said she was pregnant, I ran to my grandfather's hunting cabin and proceeded to get blind,

147

stinking drunk. Wouldn't—couldn't—answer her phone calls, and she panicked. She called my best friend—the first Kenzie."

He pinched the bridge of his nose. "You know what happened to the truck. After they found him, they found me. I checked myself out of the hospital for his funeral, but they wouldn't let me in. The whole town knew I'd cost a good man's life, even if they didn't know why. So your mother came outside. Not to let me crawl for forgiveness. To gut me with the loss of our child. She left town directly from the church."

Shoulders bowed, Kenzie rocked forward and back in her chair, her focus never leaving his face. Her lips parted, and it took a few tries to find her voice. "That would mean—"

"You lost your father the day of the accident, but he didn't die. He just wished he did."

Phil rose and paced a tight oval in the middle of the room. Hands clasped behind him, he stopped in front of Kenzie. Feet together, spine erect. Every inch the lawyer making his case.

"Your father is alive. I understand if you want nothing to do with me except for a share of the inheritance when I die. But if you're at all willing, I would value the chance to start over... and to be part of your life."

Bright spots flared in Kenzie's cheeks. "Funny Vi died before you said any of this. She can't tell me the truth. Did you kill her too? Or did your wife? How bad was what you actually did for this to be a step up?"

"Your mother could confirm it. But she won't."

"She won't because it's not true. My father is dead, and you killed him." Kenzie shot to her feet and bolted, setting the Christmas-tree ornaments swinging. Seconds later, a door banged upstairs.

Landon watched the rowboat Santa rock slower and slower. She'd been intrigued by the secret, but she shouldn't know this. Shouldn't hold part of these people's pain. Was this how Vi had felt with all her unshareable knowledge?

Except Landon would have to dump this on Dylan. It shouldn't play into Vi's death, but Kenzie had gone to see her once. Could have made a second visit.

Eyes closed, Phil seemed to take a moment to gather himself. "When she calms down, you might perhaps point out how the pictures show her mother and the deceased Kenzie both with blue eyes while hers are brown. Like mine."

He pulled out his wallet and extracted a credit card from the supple leather. "Is her room available for another week? Bill me for her stay to date, and we'll see if she runs."

Once he'd paid and greeted Anna, Landon walked him to the front entrance to retrieve his coat.

As he slid his arms into the sleeves, he cast another upward glance toward the bedrooms. "Constable Tremblay says you'll be present this evening. I'd appreciate it if Kenzie doesn't hear about the event. She can't be allowed to intrude and upset my wife."

"How's Whitney taking the news of a stepdaughter?"

"She's... concerned. As if she and the twins won't matter as much to me. Or perhaps she thinks Kenzie will push Ciara out in the cold." He tucked a pale grey cashmere scarf around his neck. "Those two together would be a perfect storm."

After he left, Landon carried the water glasses to the kitchen and filled the kettle for the most tension-taming herbal tea in the cupboard. She phoned Dylan while waiting for the water to boil and gave him the basics of the Kenzie-Phil relationship.

"There's more to it than that, but if it's relevant to the investigation, you'll need to ask Phil. He'd appreciate this being kept quiet."

Dylan chuckled. "Soul of discretion, that's me. When my informant is willing to tell me anything."

"It's not about you—it's other people's secrets."

"You and Vi would've made a good team. Speaking of teams, have you asked Bobby about tonight?"

"I'm trying to get Dee to go. If not, I thought I'd ask Mom. Or Anna. They're protective."

A laugh rang in the background. He must be at the station or perhaps his coffee hangout.

His exhale carried through the phone. "My next call will be to your neighbour. Dee has a child to worry about, and don't you think it's asking too much of your mother to be your bodyguard? Go with them if you want. Expect to see him there too."

"Dylan—"

"I want two sets of ears at that event. You're simply being friends and doing what you do. You can do this, and it's non-negotiable."

"Or what? You'll ask Phil to blacklist me?"

"I'll tell Anna and your mother it's too dangerous for you to help. Where will that leave you with Elva?"

He was right. She could do this.

She tugged a handful of her hair. Loving Bobby was an extension of liking him. It'd be fine. If she didn't get greedy. "I'll text him when we finish."

"Thank you. Keep your ears open tonight."

~~~

Nigel had said Vi refused to wear the colour of night. To Landon, black made a perfect foil for vibrant colours like the sapphire silk blouse she'd found last year in a thrift shop.

Tonight, that left her trying to climb up into Roy's truck without dragging the hem of her skirt against the salt-stained running board. While holding the bag containing her sandals.

Bobby's gaze barely skimmed hers before veering away. "The Two Investigators ride again."

She could do this. Slip back into the friendship and banter—and ignore her heart. "Thank you for coming with me. I know it's out of your comfort zone."

"So was the play, and I survived. You didn't miss much."

"We were there. We didn't stick around after, though. It's been a long couple of days. You made a good Bob Cratchit."

"Even when I dropped the Christmas goose?"

She laughed. "So don't give up your day job. Travers needs you. Seriously, all I know of the story is what you've said. Maybe it needed more than your team could give, but people enjoyed themselves."

"Gramp said he didn't see you."

"I saw him. He and your parents sat way up front. We were late coming in and stayed at the back."

"Out of range of falling geese. Smart move."

"Hey, the one who caught it threw it back."

"Pastor Vern's son. He's a good kid." Bobby picked up a plain-wrapped package from the seat between them and offered it to her. "For you. Not a Christmas present."

"Feels like a book, but it's the wrong shape for one of yours. Can I open it?"

"That's why the dome light's on. And it's not Travers. This is a classic that stands the test of time."

If it was too old to be available in audio, she was in for a headache. Landon tucked a fingernail under the tape and pulled open the paper.

Glossy red cover, gold lettering. *A Christmas Carol* by Charles Dickens. "Because you thought I missed it?"

"To keep the spirit of Dickens from rising up like a vengeful Ghost of Christmas Literature Past. I love this story, and I want you to know it at its best. If Anna has a DVD player, I can lend you my favourite versions."

"There are enough for you to have multiple favourites?"

"Trust me." He eased the truck down the driveway. Opposite the pavement, the ocean lay like a vast black void on this overcast night.

As they drove, Landon filled him in on the search at Nigel's, her crazy fear at Dee's when she'd seen the scarf, and any of her other discoveries she felt free to share. Silence with Bobby was usually comfortable, but tonight being alone together had her emotions in flux. Besides, he needed—deserved—to be up to date.

Her phone buzzed, and she fumbled to unbutton her coat pocket before the call went to voice mail. "Hello?"

Silence on the other end. Then the faintest whisper of breath from a person who didn't want to be heard. With a hitch that conveyed nerves.

She'd had two hang-up calls on Friday from this number. Tonight, the caller hadn't bailed yet.

"Hey, I'm here. Talk to me. Do you need help?"

The connection cut. Landon exhaled a whoosh of frustration. She shoved the phone into her pocket.

"What's up?" Bobby slowed, signal light clicking.

"It's a Nova Scotia area code. They call, they hang up. This was the longest connection. Whoever it is, they sound scared."

"Or it's the killer making a statement. You need to report it."

"That would be... menacing. Intense even if the person didn't speak. This is—I don't know, tentative. Like it's risky to make contact, but they have to do it. This might be the clue we need. I'm not reporting it. The police would look up the number and scare this person silent."

"Promise me you won't meet this person alone. No matter what they say." He took one hand from the wheel to grasp her arm. "I need to hear you say it, Landon. To know you'll keep it as a promise—not like us deciding to investigate after Dylan warned us off."

She bounced her knuckles on the book in her lap. "I've almost died twice this year." Once with him. "I have no interest in going for three."

"I know you, my friend. Say the words."

"I promise I won't go anywhere alone with anyone remotely connected with this case—present company and officers of the law excluded. Satisfied?"

"It'll do."

The Kirkwoods' house resembled a winter fairy tale when they arrived. Tiny white twinkle lights outlined the two-storey Victorian's wraparound veranda, its roof, and every window. More white bulbs shimmered in matching sculpted shrubs.

The truck might have fit in the wide double drive with half a dozen other vehicles, but Bobby drove past. He U-turned to park behind the other attendees at the curb.

"Okay to walk? I don't want to box anyone in."

"Sure. It's a beautiful night."

He stopped the engine but made no move to exit. "When Dylan texted to be sure I'd come, he warned me to keep my hands to myself. Did you tell him about Thursday's disaster?"

"He gave me the same spiel. And to steer clear of the mistletoe. Trying to be funny because I didn't want to do this." Her cheeks warmed in the dark. "Thursday is just between us. You did a beautiful thing, and I feel cleansed at a whole new level. Someday, I'll tell you what else it uncovered, and we'll both have a good laugh." She hoped. Definitely not laughing now.

"You're sure that's all it is? He's not clearing the field for a more personal relationship? I need to know where I stand."

"You traded texts. We talked in person. Believe me, that was not the intent." Not with the confession she'd dumped on the poor man.

"Okay. Speaking of relationships..."

Landon's heart flipped. He couldn't still care. He wouldn't break his promised silence even if he did.

Her entire body hushed. Waiting.

"Mom and Dad may drop in tonight. I'll keep my distance from you. Work the room separately with one eye directed your way in case of trouble."

Tears pricked her eyes. Relief? Or disappointment?

"Ashamed of me?" Had she said that aloud?

"Hardly. It might keep Mom from targeting you."

"I already told your mom I'm not trying to dance with the

prince." Landon huffed. "It didn't win me any points. She didn't get the Cinderella reference."

"I'm no prince."

"She thinks you are."

"Whereas you know the truth."

"I know you're my best friend and getaway driver. And the hero God has used more than once to touch me with His love." She flicked the door lever and jumped from the truck before she embarrassed them both. One ankle wobbled on the uneven ground, and she sucked in a sharp breath.

"You okay?"

"I landed funny. That's all." She rounded the front of the truck, glad to be on flat pavement. "I hope this works."

"Me too. I'd hate to have to schmooze for nothing."

"Food. There'll be food."

He snorted. "Tiny little canapés with caviar and other stuff I hate."

"What'll you do when one of your books hits the big screen and you have to walk the red carpet and survive one of those elevated cocktail parties?"

"Eat before I go. And make you go with me because you brought it up. But it won't happen. I've kept the film rights, and Travers stays out of Hollywood."

"Why?" She'd listened to the first book in the series, and it'd make a great sci-fi action movie.

"I don't have the clout to keep them from changing my vision and making a travesty of Travers. They'd have him brawling and slashing across the galaxy and hopping into bed with anyone with the appropriate body parts—of any species."

Bobby shook his head, seemed to try to shake off his agitation. Slowed and stared up at the night sky as if looking for a star. Or a spaceship. "Not with his name attached to a story like that. Nor with mine."

"Good for you."

Landon swung the bag with her sandals between them as

they walked, then dropped behind him to thread through the vehicles parked in the drive.

When they reached the cobblestone walkway, she drew in a gasp. A series of ground-level solar lights marked the path to the front door, each casting beads of changing, multicoloured light onto the fresh dusting of snow. Delightful.

The Kirkwoods' open-air veranda, swept free of snow and with its summer furniture safely in storage, made a stark contrast to the cramped and cluttered porch attached to the Foley home. Landon's boots echoed on the wide planks as she and Bobby crossed to the front door and rang the bell.

Faint Westminster chimes sounded within. Seconds later, a young woman in caterers' basic black and white opened up and welcomed them inside. She whisked away with their coats.

Landon switched to her sandals, hissing at the cold floor-level air. She surveyed the immaculate foyer, now dominated by a statuesque evergreen draped in silver and blue.

The buzz of multiple conversations flowed from guests beyond a white-framed doorway. She caught herself reaching for Bobby's hand and pressed her palm against her skirt instead. "Someone here knows something. Let's see what we can stir up."

Chapter 14

"YOU CAN GO in. I want to look at this first." Landon crossed the foyer toward a tall square table beside the Christmas tree, her skirt swishing around her calves.

"Splitting up to hunt for clues does not mean letting you out of my sight. Don't you watch any mysteries?" Bobby matched her pace. "I didn't see my parents' rental, so we can stick together for a first pass. Plus, I told them what we were doing. Casual interaction between friends is natural."

The table, curved wooden legs under a frost-white linen cloth, held a photo of Vi with her printed obituary and a green-tinted glass vase. The vase's wrist-width neck opened to a round chamber half full of different-coloured bills and coins.

Landon dug in her purse. "I forgot to tell you they're collecting for funeral costs and charity."

She curled up a bill from her wallet and slid it to join the others.

"Hush money for the dead." The dry voice came from behind them.

A squat woman stepped into view, her sparkly red dress hugging each roll and curve. She peered over black-framed glasses as Landon's offering unfurled inside the vase. "Huh. She couldn't have had much on you."

"I'm sorry?"

The woman's laugh scraped against Landon's nerves. Her eyes sparkled almost merrily. "Note the brown bills, honey. The hundreds. This isn't about Vi's funeral. It's atonement money for secrets kept."

Her wink slid into a leer. "For the superstitious, it's a bribe to seal her lips in the afterlife." She stuck out her hand. "Valda Burke. Dropped a couple hundred in there myself to be on the safe side. We had our share of run-ins, but I respected Vi. She always shot straight from the hip."

Landon clasped her hand and introduced herself and Bobby.

The woman cut her gaze between them and laughed again. "It'd be fun to guess what she knew, but you'd be trying the same on me. I've heard about you, Landon Smith. When you go after the truth, you find it."

Bobby stepped nearer, his arm brushing Landon's. "We're friends of Nigel's. Neither of us even saw Vi until the weekend before she died."

"You think that shields you from her scrutiny? The woman was uncanny."

"She respected secrets." Chatter moved into the foyer, and Landon lowered her voice. "Speaking of which, could you assume we're here like everyone else to check out the party of the season? We won't pick up any clues if the killer's here and on guard."

Those dark eyes glittered. "Or the one who shares them might not wake up Christmas morning. Noted. You'll have to take my word it wasn't me. But it wasn't. Time tempers all fury."

Bobby's supportive touch dropped from Landon's arm as the woman moved on to a new target. She felt the loss.

Keeping close enough to be heard, he mused, "All fury? Why do I doubt that?" He dropped money into the vase. "Phil sounds like he cared a lot for Vi. Probably could have covered the expense himself. Maybe she's right, and he's twisting the guilt on someone—or someones."

"He should take his suspicions to the police and not risk Whitney."

"Says the girl who won't stop investigating. On that note, let's get to work."

They stepped through a white-framed doorway, its glass doors flung wide. Conversations washed over them in waves.

Phil detached himself from three other men and crossed to meet them, his host's smile stiff. "Did Kenzie leave?"

"No. She heard about tonight, but I don't think she'll crash your party. She wanted to. The idea of everyone watching her and gossiping seemed to shut it down."

"Thank you. I'll contact her tomorrow."

Phil nodded at Bobby. "The snow-globe girl. I'm not sure how much you know."

"Landon gave me the basics because of the Vi connection but no details."

The lines edging Phil's mouth softened. "If we reconcile, those basics will become common knowledge. My wife is aware, but we're uncertain how to proceed with Ciara."

"Ah." Bobby arched an eyebrow. "I'd get my side of the story in before she heard a more negatively-charged one. Although Ciara doesn't seem prone to believe simple truth."

Landon pressed her lips together. Ciara's long-standing prejudice against her stepfather had mellowed. Yet believing the worst of him came naturally, and Kenzie's drama-queen abilities rivalled Ciara's own.

Phil excused himself to greet other new arrivals. Smiling at strangers and greeting acquaintances, Landon and Bobby passed among clusters of guests into a second room where Landon had first met Whitney in September.

Tonight, the divan was tucked into a corner and joined by clusters of folding padded chairs that lined the walls. At the opposite end, a velvet-jacketed woman played a grand piano.

Soft jazz notes swooped and improvised around classic Christmas carols.

Bobby exhaled. "This kind of party, I could like."

Landon eyed the appetizers on a passing server's tray. "That looked tasty. Not posh."

"I'll take one for the team and let you know. For now, drinks. What would you like?"

He reappeared bearing two goblets of ice water and a satisfied smile. "Mini quiches are amazing."

"You have a crumb on your chin." Landon took her glass as he brushed away the pastry flake. He'd have shaved tonight anyway to match the brown wool blazer, pale button-down, and sensible tie, but now that she thought about it... "What happened to Mr. Only Shaves for Church?"

He rolled his eyes. "Parents. Choose your battles."

"I'm sure your mom loves your graphic tees."

"Precisely. Now's probably a good time for us to start circulating separately. Promise me you won't leave the room without me? Eye contact first and a nod for direction?"

"Watch your own back too, hey?" She hadn't felt this fear before. "We need a code word. For either of us."

Eyes slitted, he stroked his jawline like a supervillain. "Lavatory. Not something we'd accidentally say, but easy to stick in a sentence if necessary."

"What, because tiger pit's too weird?"

"You remember that?"

She remembered everything. Every joke, conversation, nuance, all sweetened now with a backward-glancing affection. She twitched her shoulders in a shrug. "You think up good lines. What can I say?"

Brows edging together, he studied her. "You're nervous about this too. We'll be okay. We make a solid team."

"Yeah." Here in this buzzing crowd with the soft music, all she wanted to do was linger close and watch the light in those warm blue-grey eyes. Instead, she snapped the connection and let her gaze roam the room.

Not recognizing anyone she knew to join a conversation, she wandered among the standing groups, glass in hand, listening. Among the expected holiday chatter, Vi's name cropped up. Once, she caught it linked with Freesia.

Another speaker tossed out a reference to a you-know-who. Landon hadn't met anyone in that group and had no excuse to insert herself into the conversation to ask for a name. She worked her way to the edge of the space, keeping Bobby in sight, then tapped a brief description of the three into her phone to share with Dylan later.

As she looked up, Bobby's parents entered. His mother spared her one calculating glance before moving toward the pianist.

Remaining on her feet so he'd be able to track her easily, Landon continued to mingle. A sampling of appetizers—and zero clues—later, she spotted him and his parents angling toward the front room. Bobby caught her eye and tipped his head.

She nodded.

As he stopped to speak to an older man, she slipped through into the other room. The music wasn't as discernible out here, but she'd hoped for another chance to admire the spun and blown glass sculptures scattered on the polished wooden shelves edging the space.

She positioned herself with a side-eye view of the connecting doorway, ears open to the flow of voices around her, and drank in the sight of delicate purple flowers woven into a gossamer tracery of clear strands.

How did the cleaning staff ever dust these?

She recognized more faces now, people she could engage with. After half an hour of casual chat, mentioning Vi wherever possible, she'd gained nothing to take away but vague hints about the killer being afraid of what Vi knew about them. One man suggested Freesia again, but his wife scoffed.

Landon's mouth was dry from talking, but if she didn't ration the water, she'd be asking Bobby for an escort to the bathroom. Her feet hurt too.

The crowd was shifting, and a solid tip could arrive any time. Leaving was not an option.

Across the room, Bobby was snacking on another tidbit. She was about to suggest they return to the room with the chairs when Dee strolled in from the foyer with Starr.

At last. The physiotherapist's text this afternoon had expressed hesitation about the event.

People parted to make space for the girl's crutches, and a soft murmur spread across the room. A sound mother and daughter both ignored.

Greetings flowed around them as Dee led Starr toward the farther room, warm tones of genuine pleasure. Dee had clearly won a place in the town's heart. From the fond glances at Starr, she may have been the catalyst.

Suddenly the girl squealed and veered toward Bobby. "Did Santa Roy send any candy?"

Bobby made a show of checking his pockets, coming up empty. "I didn't expect to see you." He stage-whispered, "Catch one of the servers with the cupcakes."

She leaned forward on the aluminum crutches. "Chocolate?"

"The best kind."

Dee beckoned Starr, and Landon navigated through the crowd to follow. Bobby joined her but veered off to where his parents stood chatting with Phil.

Their host didn't linger long in any conversation, working the knots of conversation to ensure his guests were at ease.

Whitney had floated through the rooms at intervals, smiling brightly, shielding her rounded belly with her arms if anyone stepped too near. Mostly she'd observed from the corner divan in the piano room, welcoming anyone who stopped to visit.

Her wide eyes and delicate mannerisms with the princess-style dress gave the impression of a porcelain doll or a child despite her obvious pregnancy. And despite her firstborn being over twenty.

Good genes and careful makeup could do a lot. Landon hadn't seen Ciara yet this evening, but mother and daughter could pass for sisters.

Starr limped straight for Whitney and claimed a spot at the foot of the divan. They shared quiet words. Then Starr cracked a joke that left them both laughing like kids. When Bobby approached with a cupcake, Starr's eyes lit.

Landon eased into the group and took the chair between Starr and Dee. "It looks like you two know half the people here."

"I do. From Mom's clinic and Miz Vi's." Starr's nimble fingers stripped the cupcake of its Christmas-tree paper.

"Vi used to mind her occasionally when she was little." Dee sniffed. "That may not have been the best idea."

"Miz Vi was my friend, and I miss her."

Whitney's features pinked. "She knew too much about people. Always watching. Pushing those questionable remedies." She stood carefully. "Excuse me."

So Whitney hadn't been one of Vi's clients. Landon couldn't picture her attacking the older woman anyway, even in a fit of pregnancy hormones. She'd be too concerned about protecting her babies.

"Starr, when you went to Vi's the other day…"

The girl darted a glance at her mother. "I miss her. I go there when I'm upset."

Dee's mouth pinched. "We're all upset right now, love, but it's not a safe place for you to go. What if you'd been there when the killer came back?"

Landon shivered. Thank God that hadn't happened. "Did you see her notebooks or any journals?"

"Mom said they took her notebooks." Her voice shook as if this theft was one more act of violence. "I made a list of everyone I know."

"Good for you."

Dee twisted her fingers together until the knuckles whitened. "If the culprit was one of her clients, they would have taken the books that first day."

"Not if the car I saw interrupted them." Starr licked icing from her fingertips. "It didn't have to belong to the killer. If they didn't want to be seen, even if they didn't know they'd get into a fight, they'd have come in the back way. Lots of her clients did."

Landon sat forward. "There's a back way?"

The girl wiped her fingers before reaching into her pocket and producing a folded white paper. "I drew this for the police. To go with the list." She peered hopefully past their heads. "Is Dylan coming?"

The fancy blue dress and the silver barrette shining among her glossy curls came into sharper focus.

Landon shook her head. "They're working to find who did this. And patrolling around your street. One of them can pick up your clues tomorrow."

"Can you take them? The lady cop ordered me not to interfere." Starr frowned. "I have to help. For Miz Vi and for Nigel and so Mom won't be so afraid."

"What scares me is my daughter endangering herself over matters best left to the professionals. Let me see this map."

Starr unfolded it with a snap of her wrist but seemed reluctant to let it go. She stretched it wide. "See the park behind their house where he could have left his car? There's a trail there and another one from the next street. He could have parked there too. I copied from the internet."

Dee studied it, brows tightening. "You added our house too, Starr. And the old well. That's not relevant at all."

"I like it. Miz Vi and I used to sit there. She said it was a connecting point."

"Well, it has no bearing on what happened across the road."

Starr snickered. "*Well.* It's a pun."

Groaning, Bobby stood. "Santa Roy would've appreciated that one. If you ladies will excuse me?"

"Didn't he like my joke?"

"I'm sure he did." Landon leaned nearer. "Bobby and I are supposed to be moving around listening to people, trying to find a clue."

"Stay with me a little longer? Most adults don't know what to say to a handicapped kid."

Or to kids, period. Landon settled her weight in the chair. "Of course."

Dee stirred. "While you two chat, I see people I should catch up with."

"Listen for clues, Mom."

She smoothed the girl's hair before walking away, her posture taut as wire.

Handing Landon the map and another sheet that must be Vi's client list, Starr stared after her mother. "She doesn't smile since Miz Vi died. It's like when Toby ran away."

Landon tucked the papers into her purse. "Was Toby a pet?"

"He was Mom's boyfriend. He left his dog when he left us—a beagle named Weasel. She got hit by a car. Mom found her. I never got to say goodbye to either one."

Toby must be the one who emptied their bank accounts. Landon squeezed the girl's knee. "I'm glad you and your mom have one another."

"Me too. My dad didn't want me. Mom says Toby didn't either, but he did love me, at least at first." Her mouth quivered. "I still hope he'll come home. It's like nobody will love me and stay—because of my crutches. Miz Vi said to trust a special person will come along to love me for who I am."

An ache stirred in Landon's heart. She'd felt the same about her inner crutches until Bobby came along. Her special person. What happened when you missed the chance to welcome that person's love?

She took the girl's hand. "Starr, you're funny and clever and brave. There's plenty about you for people to love."

"Dylan listens. He sees me, not the ugly old crutches."

"He's kind to me like that too. It's who he is."

Starr pushed herself up straighter on the divan. "Is he your boyfriend?"

"No—a friend, but no."

"He's adorable." Starr breathed a romantic sigh. "There's even mistletoe up there on the chandelier."

Despite Dylan's wry joke, Landon hadn't bothered to check.

Seeing it dangling there, a tiny sprig, stirred a longing to know a real, love-filled kiss. Not the horror she'd endured as a trafficking victim. Her sight followed her thoughts to Bobby, standing with a bulked-up guy whose muscles strained his sweater like a superhero's.

Bobby caught her gaze.

She snapped her attention back to Starr. "You're too young for kissing."

Fingertips pressed to her cheek, the girl smiled. "Here. I wouldn't want him to get in trouble."

"Even that, Starr. He's very careful to avoid anything inappropriate. It comes with the uniform."

Landon had observed the way he balanced friendship with his career. Times she'd been upset and he'd held back instead of offering a hug. The self-defence lessons he'd given her and Ciara this fall, explaining any necessary touch beforehand, keeping as hands-off as possible. Insisting they both be present for every session, not allowing even the impression of impropriety.

Starr's brown eyes took on a dreamy shine. "I know I'm too young, but he's single, right? He could wait for me."

A sincere heart deserved respect. And honesty. Landon studied her. "What's a good age to get married?"

"Maybe twenty?"

"Let's think. He's past thirty now. So when you're twenty, he'll be what? Over forty?"

Starr's face puckered like she'd bitten into a giant prune. "Gross."

They were giggling when Dee returned. "Okay, young one, come choose one more treat, and then it's home to bed."

As Starr moved toward the nearest tray-bearing server, Landon rose and caught Dee's sleeve. "I see what you mean. She's not stopping at all. School finished yesterday, right? What if you took her away for the holidays to break up her sleuthing? The case could be solved before you came home."

"If I have to, I will, but I don't want to cancel clients when I've already blocked off a week over Christmas. We could go to my parents. I won't let her fly unaccompanied. You may not have noticed, but Starr can have... episodes. Unreliability. Emotional instability."

Dee's eyes sparked. "And plain preteen stupidity, like crossing police tape into a forbidden house. I was going to keep her home tonight, but Constable Ingerson read her the full riot act at school yesterday. Poor kid's suffered enough. You're right—I have to channel her into safe angles. And solve this before she puts herself in danger."

Chapter 15

Sunday

DYLAN ARRIVED THE next morning, in uniform, while Landon and her mother handled kitchen cleanup. When Landon waved him to a seat at the kitchen table and poured him a tall mug of coffee, he took it with a heavy-lidded blink and a deep inhale. "You're an angel. Speaking of which, I'm sorry to interfere with your church time."

"I'm toast anyway. The party went late, and we didn't want to miss anything."

She swiped her tea towel across a coffee drip on the glossy pine tabletop. "Starr may give you more space now."

"What did you tell her?"

"I encouraged her to do the math. You're old."

"Thanks. I think. I worry about that kid. If the wrong person learns she's playing detective, her mother won't be much protection."

"Dee gives a pretty strong mama-bear vibe. I asked a couple of her clients last night if the thieving ex was abusive, and the opinion was he wouldn't have lived to leave town."

"That was before I arrived, but I guess 'furious' is putting it mildly."

Landon dried the griddle Gwen had set on the counter.

"Let me get out Starr's papers before you crash on us."

Gwen refilled her coffee. "I'll go upstairs so you two can talk freely. If Kenzie comes down, I'll let you know."

With the map spread out on the kitchen table, Landon explained Starr's idea.

He downed the last of his coffee. "We've been exploring that angle."

"Starr said a number of Vi's clients didn't want to be seen. For herbal remedies. Honestly, it's not like the woman was a drug dealer." She glanced up. "Was she?"

"Would Nigel allow that to pass?"

"No, you're right. This speculating is messing with my head." At the end of Starr's list, Landon had added the names and descriptions she and Bobby had gleaned. "Valda Burke is an interesting character."

"You can say that again. Solid alibi though."

"Dee called me this morning. Basically, she heard the same things Bobby and I did. Gossip puts Freesia top of the motive list, but people mentioned Valda Burke and others."

"Again, I'd rather Dee not be involved living unprotected and so near the scene. Our patrols can only do so much."

"She's scared but trying to be strong for Starr. I didn't realize Valda Burke was the high-pressure developer who gave her such a hard time. The one Vi influenced to back down. Dee was upset last night to learn the woman had been at the party. They barely missed one another."

While he studied the list of names, Landon topped up his coffee and plated a couple of Anna's fresh pumpkin muffins. She settled in the chair next to his.

His forefinger tapped where she'd described the people whose names she didn't know. "Wish you could've discreetly captured a photo. I'll ask Phil what he can tell me."

"Maybe Starr's list will help. It sounds like Vi knew private details about half the population of Lunenburg. Maybe beyond. The killer could be anyone."

"Which is why I want you to be careful." He stretched his

arms up, then out to the sides. "We're going around the clock, trying to wrap this up so most of the team can take holiday leave. It sounds cold, but closure is the best thing we can give Nigel. Christmas is brutal for so many people. His will never be the same."

"Will you get home to see your dad?"

"He'll understand if it's deferred." He stared into his coffee, then gave his head a brisk shake. "Ingerson got Hope to admit being at Vi's. On Sunday, which matches what Nigel said."

"Obstructing an investigation, lying to law enforcement. That can't have been a pleasant chat." Landon had been on the receiving end of Ingerson's wrath before.

"Hope tried to spin it that Vi wanted an impartial property assessment. Repeated what she'd said in the first interview, that she'd given the card to a stranger who passed it on to Vi."

"Why would she keep lying? Unless Elva was present."

"Come on, Ingerson's smarter than that."

"Then why? And why didn't Ingerson confront her about the birth-parents search?"

"We don't know that Hope asked anyone other than you and Elva. Plus, if she thinks she's safe she may slip up. Has she contacted you again?"

"No. I need to find out about health history on her biological father's side. It's all I can give her." Landon wrapped her arms around her ribs, drawing her shoulders up toward her ears, already imagining the rant she'd endure from the man's one relative who might provide it.

His intent gaze bored into hers. "Jack. And Elva. You don't have to say the words. The horror comes across loud and clear. And I can connect the same dots you did."

"You can't tell her. Dylan, she's—"

"Elva? Not on my life. Hope? Not my business, like you said. But I don't want Hope finding out you know. Tell her you're still trying."

"Why? In case she went back to Vi's and attacked her? She hasn't harmed Elva, and she knows Elva is withholding the answers."

He flattened his palms on the table. "She knows Elva's a blood relative and could even suspect the true connection. You, on the other hand, might be expendable. Like Vi."

A chill climbed Landon's spine, one vertebra at a time. Her fingertips brushed her tattoo.

The touch reminded her of Bobby's, warming and loosening her tight muscles and freeing her thoughts. "You thought the body positioning with the business card meant Hope was safe."

"Unless she's playing us."

The back door swished, and Timkin sped into the kitchen in a black and white blur. He nosed his empty food dish, then stalked to the table. He stared unblinking at Landon, the tip of his tail twitching.

Dylan snickered. "We know who the boss is around here. I can't believe he and the stray don't fight."

Landon went to retrieve the can of cat food from the fridge. She started toward the counter, peeling off the plastic lid.

The cat wrapped himself around her ankles.

She jolted forward, both hands flying. "Hey!"

Timkin bounded to safety.

"Nice footwork." Dylan's chortle filled the kitchen.

Anna joined them. "That animal is a traffic hazard. Dylan, you should ticket him."

He rose, collecting the map and list. "I'll be a witness for the prosecution at his trial."

"Anna, did you see Freesia?" Landon picked up the cat's blue dish and stepped to the counter.

"She works this afternoon, but she'll come for lunch tomorrow. I think she was pleased I asked."

"Ladies, do I have to cite you both for meddling in an active investigation?" The joking had left his voice.

Landon spun, holding the bowl. Timkin paced a narrow figure eight at her feet. "I know she's on your list. She needs a friend, and I don't believe she's guilty."

He pressed his lips together and exhaled through his nose.

Imagination supplied the words he'd barely bitten back. About the others she hadn't believed were guilty—who'd tried to kill her. About how she was turning into Anna, trusting everyone blindly. How much harder it made his investigation if he had to worry about her.

"I'm sorry." She extended a hand, and Timkin mewed. Oops. Still held the food dish.

She offered Dylan a wry smile. "You don't want this as a token of my apology. For Freesia, I'm not a trained professional, but she doesn't fit. She calls her lost dogs her babies. Anna, you heard her. Revenge won't bring them back, and she knows it."

"What if she has new dogs? Illegally? What would she do to protect them from the woman she blames for her previous loss?" Dylan's crossed-arms stance and drawn-together brows left no room for argument.

Not that she had one now.

He held eye contact until she nodded. "Thank you. I'm sure you two will be safe with her here. Try to keep the conversation light. Don't do anything foolish."

What would he say if he knew Landon had jumped into the woman's car to keep her from driving away? She eased toward the counter to serve up the prancing cat's meal. Praying Anna wouldn't enlighten Dylan and he wouldn't question her obvious guilt.

Timkin rushed the dish before it hit the floor, took one sniff, then sat, and began to wash himself.

When they stopped laughing, Landon raised a palm toward Dylan. "I promise not to go anywhere with Freesia. I feel like she knows something. And that uniforms scare her."

"They do."

"If we can encourage her to share safely, I'll report it."

"Deal. Now, if you have no more bombshells to drop, I need to get to the station."

"Not explosive but so you know. Dee said Starr wants Bobby and me to go with them on a wagon ride tonight. With other people too. Okay?"

One corner of his mouth twitched a hint of a smile. "If that's okay with you, it's okay with me. Never know what you might hear."

When the door shut behind him, Landon released a slow breath. "Thank you for not ratting me out."

"What would it do? Other than raising his blood pressure. The man needs a break." Anna's hands settled on Landon's shoulders. "He has a point, though. Be careful."

"And trust no one. It's like living in a crime drama."

~~~

At least twenty cars crowded the parking lot beside a thick-railed wooden fence. Boots had trampled the new snow into slush. In the white field beyond, a team of horses pulled a wagonload of laughing passengers.

Landon and Bobby found Starr and Dee at the fence, the girl's elbows planted on the top rail. Her crutches leaned at her side, propped against the lower rail.

"Here come the horses." Starr spoke without losing her focus.

Dee greeted them with a tight smile. "It's a perfect night."

"So clear." Landon studied the bright stars and let the cold air cleanse her lungs. "Anna and Mom came too. They stopped to talk."

Starr wore a knitted scarf looped over her dark curls and around her neck. Fuzzy black yarn, threaded with purple. The matching hat probably lay in an evidence locker at the police station. "Where's Santa Roy?"

"Are you going to call him that in January? He stayed home with my mom and dad. His leg's bothering him. But he sent candy."

A small, knit-gloved hand shot toward him, palm up. Grinning at Landon, he pressed a mini candy cane into Starr's grip.

"Thanks." She unwrapped it, plastic crinkling, and stuck the straight end in her mouth. Her focus returned to the horses rounding the field's far end.

Dee said, "I can fit Roy in this week. We'll be closed over Christmas, and I don't want him to be in pain the whole time."

"I'll tell him. Thanks. He says, if it's the storm bothering him this far ahead, we're in for a wallop."

Anna and Gwen found them, and Landon made introductions.

Two big workhorses, chestnut brown with midnight manes and tails, laboured up a slight incline, snuffing and steaming. In the wagon, children begged for more.

The driver, bundled under a heavy work coat and watch cap, slowed the ride with a "Whoa, now." He jumped to the ground and lifted the children down one by one as the teens and adults dismounted.

Starr grinned. "This will be so much fun."

Dee hugged her and passed over the crutches. "We're overdue for a treat, Starr-ling."

A spasm crossed her face, and she clutched her daughter again, hard against her chest. Head bowed over her daughter, she stood frozen until Starr wriggled free.

Starr fitted the crutches' cuffs over her coat-insulated forearms and gripped the handles, leaning forward toward the gate and the massive horses.

Landon shared a compassionate glance with Dee. "They'll find the person soon, and you'll be okay."

Dee stepped nearer. "What did Dylan say about Valda Burke? Knowing she's back in action has me afraid she'll be at my door again."

"Not her. Alibi."

Instead of reassuring the physiotherapist, Landon's

whisper brought widened eyes and pinched lips. "Who, then?"

"The whole force is working overtime, and I think they've brought in reinforcements. They'll solve this, Dee. We can keep our ears open for anything that might help."

"Vi never turned away anyone in need. Drifters, vagrants. Not so much this late in the season, but it could be someone living rough." She clutched Landon's arm. "If it was an outsider trying to rob her, they're gone, and we'll never identify them. Or they'll come back and find Nigel—and Starr and me."

The night seemed suddenly unsafe. Anyone could lurk in the trees' cloak, watching even now. A chill unconnected with the temperature formed in Landon's core.

She fought it with logic. Vi's death had been an act of emotion, not calculation. Maybe with immediate regret. The killer would be dangerous if cornered but wouldn't be randomly scouting new victims in this crowd.

Shadowing Nigel and Dee and Starr was another matter.

"I feel so alone." Dee strode ahead to catch up with Starr and shepherd her into the line.

Landon let out a puff of frosty breath. Words wouldn't help. Dee needed—they all needed—the killer to be caught. *Please, Lord.*

The driver hoisted Starr into the wagon with a laugh and steadied Dee to join her. Soon a dozen or more riders filled the benches ringing the interior. After he delivered his safety spiel, he climbed into his seat and took the reins. "I hoped to bring out the sleigh tonight, but the snow's still teasing us. Midweek, best guess. If we get half of what they're forecasting, we'll have a white Christmas for sure."

Seated beside Landon, Gwen murmured, "Let me get home first."

She'd already asked her boss for an extension and had to be at work Christmas morning. For all the dire predictions for the coming snow, she'd chosen to stay until the storm was imminent.

Kenzie had also decided to stay. Tonight she'd gone to meet Phil and Whitney and Ciara for dinner.

Bobby's parents, on the other hand, had already rebooked an early flight home to Ontario. His mother was scheduled to speak at a medical symposium and claimed it was unprofessional to risk a travel disruption.

Seriously, who scheduled an event like that between Christmas and New Year's? And how bad would the coming storm have to be to keep them from flying out on the weekend? More likely, it made a good excuse for Alexis to cut short her exposure to Roy. Their planned two-week stay sounded about ten days too long.

Opposite Landon in the jostling wagon, Bobby bent his head to Starr, listening attentively. He'd better be careful, or the girl would have a new crush. At least until she processed his age too.

Unassuming and self-deprecating, he had no idea the treasure he was. What if Landon opened up, risked asking him to remember how he'd felt three months ago?

If he couldn't, she'd give him the same gift he gave her then—friendship without strings.

If he could? This afternoon, she'd encouraged Kenzie to risk a relationship with Phil. "What if it does work out? You'll always wonder if you don't try."

Harder to do with her own heart on the line.

That heart shrank like a trembling bird, wounded and seeking cover. Better to tell herself he'd moved on than to hear the words from his lips.

He looked up and caught her staring. Smiled that offbeat, accepting, platonic smile.

What could she do but smile back before tuning into the tail end of her mother's sentence?

The wagon jolted across the field and out onto a narrow dirt lane, wending along to a small picnic park.

Starr called out, "Driver? What place is this?"

"Tan's Rest."

She crowed. "I thought so. From the map I made. This is the place behind Miz Vi's where—"

Dee shushed her.

The driver peered over his shoulder. "That it is, young miss, but you're safe with me and the boys. These horses don't take no guff from nobody."

Starr was looking everywhere at once, head swivelling like a bird's. As if she could see any clues in the dark the police had missed in daylight.

An older man near the front of the wagon chuckled. "Drawing a map for Santa, were you?"

"For the police. To help find the—"

"Starr, the families don't want to hear this. Let them enjoy the ride." Dee's gloved hand settled on her daughter's leg. She leaned closer and whispered more.

The girl's scowl faded. She studied the other riders, perhaps counting the younger children who could be scared if she continued. Six of seven smaller ones, bundled up tight, snuggled against their parents' sides.

She faced forward again. "Driver, will we see bears or anything?"

"All asleep tonight. Look up at the stars. Bet you can't count them beauties."

Landon tipped her head back. Constellations shone with bright, cold fire, jewels in a black expanse so vast she could lose herself in it. Worship rose in her spirit for the God who created such magnificence and yet who saw her in her small piece of the universe.

Across from her, Bobby's arm extended skyward, index finger pointing out the Big Dipper and other familiar names before the conversation drifted into scientific-sounding words. As if he'd felt her gaze, he paused and focused in her direction. "This kid's a pro."

"Wish you were up there?" With Travers and the rest of what he called his imaginary friends?

The grin reappeared. "Maybe."

The trail continued through a thin forest at the edge of residential lots, house lights winking through the trees. Ten minutes later, the horses emerged into the field where they'd started.

When they reached the parking lot, Anna drew Dee and Starr aside. "If you're not too cold, I brought hot chocolate."

The girl clapped her mittens together. "Please, Mom? We can watch the horses a little longer."

"I saw a man out there skulking in the trees."

"We're here together where he can't sneak up." Starr's shoulders rounded forward, hunching her parka and making her seem younger. "I saw him too. When I asked about bears. Then he vanished."

Bobby grumbled about being right beside them. "Daydreaming, and I missed it. You were wise not to spook the whole ride. It was probably Nigel patrolling."

"Nigel's working tonight. We invited him to join us." Dee tugged Starr closer. "Home, kiddo."

"We'll follow you home to be sure you get in okay." Anna made it a statement, not an offer.

"You can bring the hot chocolate and see our tree."

Dee sighed. "A certain eleven-year-old does not want to go to bed."

"Speaking of spooking the ride..." A man with a thick navy scarf joined their cluster. "You're clearly an intelligent girl. I think the best way for you to help the police is to grow up to join the force." He winked. "That might mean staying out of danger by not visibly involving yourself."

A little older than Dylan, he'd been in the wagon with them, apparently alone.

Anna introduced their group, and he touched fingertips to knitted cap in response. "Constable Matteo Price. New posting, I've been here a month. Joined the tour tonight for a different view of the terrain and to meet people."

Starr's eyes rounded. "Did they show you my map?"

"You have a good eye for detail. I like how you added the garage at the Foleys' and the well on your property. It gives perspective."

"See, Mom?" Not waiting for her mother's response, she extended a crutch and stepped nearer to Price. "If I can help now, it's good for this case. Then maybe you'll help me find a missing person."

Dee groaned. "Starr, no."

Price dropped a knee in the snow, positioning himself slightly below her eye level. "Has this already been reported?"

"It has indeed." Dee squeezed Starr's shoulders, her black gloves stark against the girl's light-blue coat. "My ex cleaned out our savings and disappeared three years ago. There's a warrant out for him."

He tilted his head to look up at Dee, then Starr. "We don't forget these things. One slip, and we'll find him. Don't worry."

"Nobody understands." The girl jerked free from her mother's grip. "Maybe he didn't love Mom anymore—or even me. He loved his dog. Why didn't he take Weasel?"

Dee reached for her again but let her hand drop. "He could have left her for you. He knew you loved her more."

"It broke her heart. That's why she kept running away, trying to find him, and coming home like she wanted us to help search." Starr gulped a sob. "Until that car hit her and she couldn't come home."

Now, she slumped into her mother's embrace.

Constable Price stood, brushing at the mud stain on his knee. "If the dog ranged free, it's possible he couldn't find her when he left."

Dee scowled. "Or whoever picked him up refused to take the animal. The theory is that he left his truck behind so we wouldn't know what vehicle to hunt for."

Starr twisted toward him. "Toby Doyle. Please. He could have been threatened by a spy ring. Maybe they made him take the money and then kidnapped him so he couldn't tell."

"I'll read the file. Now, how about I follow you home like your friends suggested? Just in case."

She sniffled. "Did you see the person too?"

"I did. We'll check for tracks in daylight."

Chapter 16

Monday

"**I**F YOU HAVE to go home before I have answers I'll message you. Or call. It's not too far to make another trip if your birth mother agrees to meet."

Phone to her ear, Landon paced the inn's upper storey, circling the entrance to the stairs. Winding among the cozy blue chairs in the conversation nook. Narrowly missing the coffee table with her shin.

A floorboard creaked behind her, and she whirled.

Kenzie closed her bedroom door and stood waiting, lips upturned in a little grin. Under her open coat, she wore the silky peach sweater she'd gloated about buying with Phil's money.

Landon had thought everyone else was downstairs. She listened to Hope's protest and again promised to do what she could. "I've been more focused on finding clues about Vi's killer."

Ending the call, she motioned Kenzie ahead of her.

"What is this, family secrets month?" At the top of the stairs, the girl trailed her fingers along the banister. "Ciara's working today, but we're meeting for lunch in Bridgewater. We agree Phil's a bore but being stepsisters could be fun."

"Now, you won't be outnumbered by the babies."

"Talk about an age gap." Kenzie fished her keys from her pocket. "See you. I think I'm eating at Phil's again tonight."

"I'm glad you have the chance to get to know him before you fly home for Christmas."

At the base of the stairs, Landon headed along the cream-walled hallway to the kitchen. She helped Gwen finish chopping vegetables for a salad while Anna pureed a butternut squash soup.

Freesia arrived late, her movements jerky and her cheeks glowing. The poinsettia clipped to her hair hung sideways. "I'm so sorry. I was at the shelter, and one of the dogs had puppies. My supervisor let me stay and help."

"We're not on a deadline, and I'm sure they appreciated the extra help." Anna took the woman's coat and pointed her to the main floor powder room to freshen up.

When Freesia reappeared, she'd fixed the flower. The light lingered in her eyes. "Five pups, three girls and two boys. I'll be allowed to have one when they're weaned. Enough time has passed, and the supervisor's going to vouch for me to my case worker."

"Fantastic!" Anna folded her into a hug, then guided her to the kitchen.

Over soup and salad and Anna's homemade biscuits, Freesia shared her plans for the puppy she'd already chosen. "They agree I'll do better with a support animal and little Fritzie loves me already."

She dipped a biscuit in her soup. "The shelter manager promised to take any strays that come to me in the wild, so I won't get overwhelmed with caring for them. It's a no-kill shelter, or I wouldn't help there."

The mention of strays reminded Landon of Starr's runaway beagle. "How far do you live from the Foleys?"

The girl's spoon clattered into her bowl, and she dabbed a napkin at the splashes on her placemat. "I don't go there."

"No, I was thinking about the Ellistons across the road from Vi. When Dee's ex took off on them, he left his dog.

They said the poor thing kept running away and coming back until she got hit by a car. I wondered, since dogs like you, if you might have helped her get home. A beagle named Weasel."

Freesia's chin firmed. "That Dee is a liar. Vi told me about the posters her little girl made, and I went looking. When I found the sweet little beagle, I called. Dee told me to tie Weasel and not let her come back. Or she'd drop her at a kill shelter."

"Starr said—" Landon tried to process it. "Dee must have told her about the accident without letting her see the body."

Gwen toyed with her water glass. "It sounds so sad. I wonder if the dog reminded her mother about her ex's betrayal. At least she didn't euthanize the poor thing."

"I was still living at home then. Clear out to Blue Rocks. The other side of Lunenburg. She'd been driving Weasel out and dropping her off. That's cruel."

Yet the animal kept finding her way home. Landon frowned. "The dog was more faithful than her master. Maybe he left her behind on purpose to mess with Dee."

Gwen sniffed. "He sounds like a real winner. Good riddance."

Except for the money.

Landon scraped up the last of her soup. "Anna, this is delicious. Freesia, you know we believe you about not harming Vi—"

"I wish everybody else did."

"When the police find the killer, people will know. On Friday, you said to follow the clue." Hands open on the table, nonthreatening, Landon offered a gentle smile. "Could you tell me about it? One clue might be all we need."

Freesia's mouth clamped shut. She clutched her empty water glass.

In the silence, Anna topped up all their water.

All Freesia did was shake her head. She flicked her gaze face to face, like a trapped animal desperate to escape.

"I'm sorry." Landon rested her hands in her lap. "I didn't mean to upset you. I thought, if we solve this, the gossips will stop blaming you for something you didn't do."

"I didn't." Her eyes narrowed to slits.

Anna reached out, but Freesia angled away.

Landon studied their guest. "Maybe the police are already following the clue. We'll leave it to them."

She cast around for a safe topic. "We went on a wagon ride last night under the stars. The horses were huge."

No mention of Dee or Starr. As they took turns telling about the experience, Freesia slipped into an easier posture.

Anna had set a plate of cookies on the table and was filling their mugs when a knock came on the front door.

Landon rose. "I'll get it."

Instead of a package on the step, she opened up to the broad frame of Constable Zerkowsky. Beyond him, a police cruiser occupied the driveway.

Lines edged his mouth, and his heavy eyebrows crept together. "I need to speak with Freesia. We thought here among friends would be better than approaching her alone at home or embarrassing her at work."

Landon tensed. "She's super skittish."

"That's why they sent me. Best with pets and timid folk, despite my size."

Short, stocky, and immovable, he looked built to stop a train—or a violent offender. Yet his kindness had touched Landon more than once.

She retreated to let him in. Freesia was so not going to like this. "Okay, how do you want to handle it? You follow me to the kitchen, or I ask her to come out?"

"I'll do it. It might embarrass her more, but there's less cause for her to blame you. If you're a friend, she'll need you later."

"You're not here to arrest her?"

"Just a talk. Simple questions."

Her footsteps echoing in her ears, Landon marched along

the hallway. Zerkowsky was right. She wasn't betraying Freesia. Even if her gut disagreed.

She entered the kitchen. "We have a visitor. Mom, Freesia, this is Corporal Zerkowsky."

Gwen supplied her name with a polite smile.

Landon registered it peripherally, focused on Freesia's widened eyes.

A swift tremor shook the poinsettia in the woman's hair. She stared at the officer as if all her fears had formed a body to loom in the doorway. Inescapable.

Zerkowsky's benign smile encompassed them all, even Landon where she'd retreated to the edge of the room. She stood, palms pressed into the counter's edge behind her.

"Ms. Bachman, I'm sorry to intrude, but I need a few minutes of your time. Anna, might there be a spot for a private conversation?"

Freesia's sudden pallor made her hair seem darker and more wild. Gaze locked on him, she slid from her seat and approached as if compelled. Then she broke free and ran. Not to the kitchen's other exit for escape.

To Landon. To clutch her forearm in a bulldog grip.

"You come too. Please." Her pale blue eyes were pools of terror. "You know I didn't do it."

"Of course I'll come. We'll use the guests' common room." Landon swallowed a groan. The interrogation room, if this kept up.

"Freesia, take your tea, dear." Anna passed her the Scottie dog mug.

Despite Freesia's frantic headshake, Landon reached for the drink. "In case you want it later."

The woman didn't release Landon's arm until Zerkowsky shut the common room door behind them. She moved to the Christmas tree, touching not the ornaments but the bristly green needles. Stroking with such a light touch the branches barely shivered.

A deep inhale lifted her shoulders, and she spun to stand

with her back to the tree, gaze once again locked on Zerkowsky.

Landon shepherded her to a seat and took the one beside her. She placed the Scottie mug on a side table in easy reach and clasped Freesia's hand.

Zerkowsky shed his jacket and settled on one of the straight-backed wooden chairs. "Ms. Bachman—Freesia, is that okay?"

She nodded.

"Freesia, when you said you didn't do it, what are you afraid I think you did?"

Colour seeped into her features. Not a lot but it erased the waxy hue. She directed her attention to the floor. "Attack Vi Foley. People say. But I didn't."

"I'm sorry you've heard unkind gossip." His fingertips whitened against his uniform trousers. "We talked before, but I need to ask you again—Did you visit the Foley home on the day of the murder?"

"I didn't. I didn't. I—" Her mouth snapped shut. Hand clenching Landon's, she stared at him. "I didn't hurt her."

"See, the thing is, we have witnesses who saw your car at or near the parking lot for the picnic spot up behind the Foley home. Around the time of the murder. It's a ten-minute walk through the woods. Faster if a person runs."

"I—" Tremors rocked her.

Landon felt the vibration through their joined grip. And the drop in Freesia's temperature. "This doesn't make sense. Hurting Vi wouldn't bring back Freesia's lost dogs. She'd lose them even longer in jail."

A keening whimper broke through Freesia's lips.

Landon scooted her chair nearer. Swapping her left hand into Freesia's, she looped her right arm over the trembling woman's shoulders and pulled her close.

Zerkowsky was not the enemy here. She met his gaze directly. "Your team know their jobs. The witnesses must be credible. They can still be wrong."

Something flashed in his dark eyes. "Freesia, I need you to breathe. Maybe take a sip of that tea before it gets cold. Your car was seen."

"Allegedly." Landon pressed the point.

"Allegedly seen." His jaw flexed. A tiny motion revealing what it would mean to cross this man. "Please hear me. It's possible someone came on the scene after Vi's death. Someone who felt unable to do their duty to report it—but who may be able to help bring the killer to justice."

Landon cleared her throat. "Someone who left a clue. Freesia, I didn't say anything."

His gaze hardened. "You knew?"

"She mentioned a clue. I don't know what it is." She sat taller, leaving her palm pressed flat between Freesia's shoulder blades until the woman's trembling slowed. "I didn't even know how she was involved. Asking over lunch created stress, so I dropped it."

He leaned back in his chair, his expression unreadable. "Landon Smith. I wish I could add your middle name in there. You, my friend, are skating very near the edge. Need another chat with Ingerson about obstructing an active investigation?"

"No." Now was not the time to argue loyalty versus justice. Even though she'd only wanted to help.

Zerkowsky's features gentled. He focused on Freesia. "I'm not saying you were or weren't present at the scene. Before, during, or after the event. If by chance you were, you might be able to help us understand certain... inconsistencies. That would free us to exclude details that don't point to the killer."

Freesia shuddered. "Everyone blames the person with mental illness."

"Do I look like everyone?" He let the question hang. "I blame the person who committed the act. Once that is proven in court. I'm trying to make this as safe for you as I can, but I need your help."

She sniffled. "I've never harmed anyone in my life. I rescue spiders—even ticks."

"Then don't be afraid to tell me." His steady tone, slow like syrup, spread through the room.

Freesia's posture relaxed, and Landon withdrew her hand as the woman's spine found the chairback.

"A stranger called me from Vi's phone. They said I wouldn't believe what they'd found and I should come fast before she got home."

"What did they find?"

"Vi keeps secrets. I didn't know if she'd been spying on me or if it was something I could use to make her leave me alone." She shivered. "I parked up behind, so she wouldn't see me if she came back too soon. When I sneaked out from the side of the garage, a woman ran from the house. She jumped in a car and raced away."

"Did you know her?"

"No. I went inside—the door was wide open—and Vi was there on the floor. She was dead and there was blood and"—Freesia drew a shaky breath and wrapped her arms around her ribs—"I couldn't help her."

"And you were afraid to call the police." Zerkowsky's soft words held no accusation.

"I did the best I could. I fixed her clothes, laid her out nice and peaceful, so it wouldn't be so awful for Nigel to find. That woman—the one who ran—her business card was there on the floor. It had her picture. So I put it on Vi's body." Her forehead creased. "Why didn't you follow the clue?"

"We can follow it clearer now, Freesia. Thank you. We know the woman visited Vi previously. A killer is unlikely to position their victim so carefully and then leave their card as a confession. So we believed her when she denied seeing Vi the day of the crime."

"So I'm not accused?"

"Nobody's accused yet, not even the woman you saw. First, we follow the evidence. You did slow us down, but no harm done."

Her shoulders wilted. "I can stop being afraid of sirens in the night." She lifted her mug from the table, sipped the tea, and grimaced. "And I won't lose my puppy when he's ready to come home."

Zerkowsky had opened a notebook and begun scribbling. Now, he set it down. "That ban is nearly done. You've picked out a new dog already?"

For the next five minutes, he listened to her raptures about Fritzie the puppy, his questions bringing more details whenever she slowed. He could have had all the time in the world. He even suggested he and his wife bring their German shepherd and meet the puppy next spring at the dog park.

With Freesia settled and content, he picked up the pad and finished his notes. Finally, he tucked away his notes and smiled at her. "Thank you for helping. I'm sure Anna will zap that tea for you or make a fresh cup."

They rose, Landon hanging back for a chance to speak. Searching for words that wouldn't be perceived as further interference.

Zerkowsky hiked a brow at her. "You go ahead, Freesia. We'll be right along."

As her footsteps receded along the hall, he studied Landon, his smile fading. "What's troubling you?"

"Am I that transparent?"

"Your mind was churning so hard I thought butter'd come out your ears."

She couldn't stop a snort of laughter. "Raised in dairy country, were you? Good one."

Palms scuffing the sides of her jeans, she struggled not to look away. "It's Hope. You know why she'd be at Vi's. That's not a conversation to have in front of Elva."

His expression set, a microscopic flattening of the mouth and slight dip of the chin. Bracing. Or warning. "You're not coming with me."

"I wasn't—"

"There's a confidential note in the file about the link

between Elva and Hope. For information only. None of us wants to see Elva hurt further. I'll ask to see Hope alone."

"Or I could invite her here. Tell her upfront you have more questions. Leave the two of you to talk in private. Please don't add to Elva's pain until you're sure."

"What if she runs?"

Landon sank into a chair, palms dropping to her knees. "I don't know. It's—Elva's already half afraid of news like this. Can we not make it worse if we don't have to?"

"There is no *we* in this decision. However, I'm not so arrogant to reject common sense—even when it comes from a meddling civilian. If Hope will come here, fine. If not, I'll go to her. She has twenty minutes." The corners of his eyes crinkled. "That'll let me move my car out of Freesia's way and hit up Anna for a coffee."

"Thank you." Landon stayed in the common room until her text brought a call from Hope.

"You have news?" The woman's question came out hushed, quick. Elva couldn't be far away.

Palm to forehead, Landon swallowed a groan. How could she have not anticipated this would be Hope's first reaction? "Not exactly. Hope, there's an officer here who's heading to see you next. If you don't want Elva to know they're asking more questions, can you come over? He says he won't wait long."

A ragged breath rattled the phone speaker. "All right. Give me ten." She clicked off.

Chapter 17

"THIS IS FOR Anna. It was all I could think of."

Landon accepted the square plastic container and stepped aside to let Hope in.

The woman's round face glowed with exertion. Her gaze darted non-stop. "Flour for baking. Elva sent me through the woods, and I was afraid I'd be too late. His car's still outside."

Freesia's had gone the minute her way was unblocked.

At a heavy tread in the hallway behind her, Landon said, "Here comes Constable Zerkowsky now. Have you met?" She motioned them into Zerkowsky's temporary office and lifted the flour container. "I'll deliver this to the kitchen."

"Will you come back?"

Hope's shaky question stopped Landon in her tracks. She pivoted to Zerkowsky.

He said, "I thought you wanted privacy."

"From Elva, yes, but I need—Should I be asking for my lawyer?"

"No, ma'am. Unless you want to come in to the station and have me book you. In which case, you'd need to give me a reason. The investigation has uncovered inconsistencies in your statement that I need to pursue."

Hope fanned her fingers in front of her face. "I don't want to be alone with you. Landon, please?"

At Zerkowsky's nod, Landon agreed. "Let me update

Anna on the remote chance Elva should call and mention baking."

As expected, Anna was less than impressed with the deceit. "What's done is done."

She sent Landon down the hall with glasses and a water pitcher. "Hope was hustling when she passed the window here. You could have told her to come to the back."

Landon had assumed she'd drive. Now, the woman waited outside the common room, insisting Landon enter first. After filling the glasses, Landon took the same seat she'd occupied before.

Hope, unlike Freesia, went for the other wooden chair. Spine erect, head high, she betrayed her nerves through her twining fingers. She held the stiff posture as Zerkowsky informed her she'd been seen leaving Vi's home after the murder.

"The witness placed your business card on the body, thinking you killed her." He stopped there, watching Hope. Waiting.

Landon held her breath. Someone killed Vi, and that person had to be found. But Hope? How badly were the woman's emotions jumbled by the transplant medications? Could she have attacked Vi?

Zerkowsky sipped his water, apparently content to let the silence stretch.

"I didn't." Hope's tongue darted across her lips. "I didn't kill her. She was already dead."

"Please describe the scene when you arrived." The notebook appeared in his hand.

"She—she was face down. Arms out a bit, like she'd tried to catch herself. The back of her head was a mess of blood." Her eyes narrowed, fixed on Zerkowsky. "That's all I saw. I ran. So how do you know your witness didn't do it? I was tricked into going."

"Did you notice anything out of place from your first visit?"

"It was my first dead body, Constable. I ran so fast I nearly fell down the stairs. If I'd broken my neck, you'd have had your murderer—but it'd be the wrong one."

"Please think back. You're safe here. Can you picture the scene? Perhaps a detail that stands out as suspicious?"

Closed eyelids trembling, Hope drew one shuddery breath. Another. Her cheeks puffed out, and she clapped a palm to her mouth. Her eyelids popped open.

She swallowed hard. "I can't go there."

"We may need to ask you to. Literally. I understand it's difficult. Did you remember anything?"

"No." Hope reached a shaky hand for her water glass. Her first sip missed, splashing a dark blotch on her baggy grey sweatshirt. She replaced the glass and gulped air instead. "So you believe I didn't kill her?"

"Taking you at your word leaves enough questions for now. You initially denied any contact at all with the victim, not admitting to the first visit until evidence confirmed it."

His gaze drifted toward the Christmas tree. "The same pattern for this second visit. You told Constable Ingerson that Vi had asked for an impartial real estate appraisal, which was not completed at that first time. This left a natural opening for you to return, and yet you said you were tricked. By whom?"

"I don't know. The murderer." She'd resumed twisting her fingers together. Releasing and twisting again. "I missed a call from Vi's phone. The message said to come back. The sound was bad. I assumed it was Vi because of the number, but it could have been anyone. Male or female."

"Or Vi herself, before the attack?"

Hope's eyes flew wide. Her jaw dropped. "If—oh no."

Zerkowsky leaned forward, then back, rocking in a stationary chair. "Now would be a good time to tell us what this is about. You went twice, tried to deny both contacts. It's not protecting a possible client's privacy."

Tears slid down her blotchy cheeks. "Maybe I did kill her."

"Ms. Bellgrove. Hope. I suspect if you did, you'd have been aware."

One hand flailed, like swatting a fly. "I mean by my questions." She reached for Landon. "Don't dig any more for me."

Landon's thoughts did a sharp skid to track this new angle. "You're afraid Vi was going to give you an answer and was stopped?"

Zerkowsky cleared his throat. "What was the subject of your research?"

"I came to find my birth parents. Elva knows but won't tell—Constable, please, she's in danger, and it's my fault."

When he didn't immediately move to call it in, she jumped to her feet. "She's alone there. Send help or let me call and warn her."

Earlier this year, Elva's attempt to breach a secret almost cost her life. Landon shivered at the memory.

Hope pounced. "See? She feels it too."

Zerkowsky traded a glance with Landon. He raised his left hand, his wedding ring catching the tree's twinkling lights. "Let's talk this through. Your purpose with Vi was to ask after your birth parents?"

"Elva's a biological relative and my link to the rest. She doesn't want me asking, and she's barely trusting me as it is. I... may have exaggerated a teeny bit about stresses at home bringing me here." Perched on the edge of her seat, she managed a drink of water. "At that dinner, when Vi lit into the girl about the snow globe? People say she knows— knew—everything. So I found her to ask."

"Did she know?"

"She refused to even hint." Hope flattened her palms against her heart. "If my biological father heard her call me— " She gasped. "Nigel. He's always hanging around Elva's property. He killed his own mother."

"Hold on—What?" Landon gaped at her. Looked to Zerkowsky to see if he'd kept up.

193

His fingers tipped in an after-you gesture. Then he grinned and stuck his pinkie in his ear.

Checking for butter. Churned.

Landon smothered a giggle. Her brain caught up. "Hope... Nigel's not your father. Elva told the truth. That man is dead."

"Can you be sure? Dead could mean really bad, stay away."

"He was that too." As too many local girls had learned. Captain Jack died long before Landon came to the inn. Before she was born. His crimes didn't affect her directly. Yet she found herself having to forgive him. Over and over again. Hoping each time would be the end of it.

"If I may..." Zerkowsky's voice dropped to a deeper rumble. "You expressed concern your biological father would kill to keep the secret. You're convinced your birth mother wouldn't? Are you already aware of her identity?"

Landon bit her tongue. How had she missed that?

Hope ducked her chin, then made quick eye contact with each of them. "It's Elva. You can't tell her I know. The blood match for my kidney transplant was too close. It had to be an immediate relative, and she has no siblings."

Tears welled again. "I need her to acknowledge me, but not if it puts her in danger. I'll leave right now."

Landon stretched out a hand. "Hope, he's dead, and there's no one left to be a threat. Vi would never have called to tell you. It had to be the killer."

Zerkowsky dipped his chin. "Which brings us to your original statement about being set up. The killer calls, you come, and we have a ready-made suspect."

"So is your witness the killer?"

"I'd rather not speculate."

Freesia had received a call too. Before or after Hope's? Plan A and plan B?

A pressure headache brewed behind Landon's eyes. All the drama snowballing. She pressed her fingertips to her temples. "Hope, how much time passed before you heard the message?"

"No more than five minutes. I saw it come in but didn't want to listen when Elva could hear."

She stared at Landon. "You know my birth father's identity. If he's dead, why won't you tell me?"

"That's Elva's decision." Landon focused on the Christmas tree. The little dories, the lighthouses. "She didn't want any of us to know, and she's still hurting."

Zerkowsky tapped his notepad on the back of his wrist. "We'll need to see the call's time stamp. And hear the message."

"I didn't save it." Hope unlocked her phone and passed it over. "You can see the time in my call history."

"With your permission, I'll screenshot this and forward it to our files."

He'd done the same with Freesia and told Landon they'd confirm with the women's phone provider.

His questions seemed endless. By the time he closed his book, Hope wilted in her chair.

"I'm free to go?"

"We may need to talk again." He stood. "Go slow with Elva. If you don't push, she'll probably come around. It'd help her too if you could connect."

Hope's countenance shuttered. "I liked to hope the pregnancy was from a teen sweethearts' fling, but I always knew the story might not be happy."

Landon took her arm. "You're here now, and the two of you are building a bridge. You can have a happy ending."

"I hope so." The woman opened the door and was gone.

Landon pitched her voice low so it wouldn't carry. "Satisfied she's not the killer?"

He scratched his head. "Crazy good liar if she is. You going to tell Elva she knows?"

"Later. She wouldn't have a chance to process it now before Hope gets back." She waited until he stowed his notebook and zipped his coat. Then she said, "Elizabeth."

He winced. "Another suspect you've dug up?"

"My middle name. For next time."

His brows came together. "There'd better not be a next time. Quit before your luck runs out."

~~~

"Uncertainty ramps up the anxiety. When you know, you can move forward."

"Maybe." Landon held eye contact with her counsellor on the video call. Cross-legged on the four-poster in her bedroom, butterfly pillow supporting the laptop, and her shoulders against the wall, she already needed the bedside lamp in the growing dusk. It'd be dark by five tonight.

A counsellor who shared her faith brought that extra level of trust. At the start of each check-in, she and Sabina prayed together before diving in.

That didn't mean she felt at ease with the way this conversation was going. "It's easier to believe he's already over me and be grateful he loved me at all."

Sabina looked into the camera, her grey eyes steady. "That love was a gift. It sounds to me like part of you wants to know if it's still available."

Landon pressed her shoulder blades against the wall. "There's too much that's not good enough about me. I'm not what he needs. Won't he realize that?" If not, his parents would point it out. Not that he'd let them influence him.

"What I'm hearing is we need to keep working on your identity as a child of the Most High God. That's where your value lies. The more you believe what He says about you, the less you'll hear those not-good-enough lies." Sabina's gaze dipped briefly. "Time's nearly up. You don't have a deadline. Think and pray and see what unfolds. We'll set another appointment to delve a little deeper."

"Thanks for fitting me in today." Landon booked a follow-up appointment and logged off the video call. Stowed the laptop and picked up her cell. Stared at it in her hand, then up at the bright-orange monarch print on the wall. Back at the phone.

Trust. She'd meant what she told Bobby about trusting him with her life. She could offer her heart too. If he didn't love her now, he'd be at least as kind as she'd been to him. More.

He valued their friendship. He'd work with her to keep it, like she'd done with him in September.

Breath held, she typed a quick text. *Free after supper? Catch up on the case?*

If she wimped out on the rest, he'd wouldn't know.

His reply landed almost immediately. *Perfect. Here or there? Mom and Dad left today, so there's no inquisition panel.*

I'll come to you. Less danger of anyone here getting ideas or seeing her fall. If her hopes didn't work out, she'd have the solitary walk home to compose herself.

Roy would be disappointed his family couldn't be together for Christmas. Even if his behaviour had deliberately pushed too many of his daughter-in-law's buttons.

At the kitchen table with Anna and Gwen, Landon picked at her meal despite the mouth-watering scent. She crumbled more cornbread into the rich, thick chili than she swallowed. "Sorry, Anna. This is amazing, but today's been a lot to process."

"It'll reheat. I didn't know inviting Freesia to lunch would deputize you to be Zerkowsky's assistant for the afternoon."

Gwen's spoon scraped the bottom of her bowl. "Let's watch a feel-good Christmas movie tonight. Eat popcorn and forget about unhappy endings for a while."

Happy endings. Landon's stomach did a slow roll. Would she have the courage to reach for one?

A small bite of cornbread stuck in her throat. It took a full glass of water to wash it down. "I told Bobby I'd go over and give him the latest. Can't keep my investigative partner out of the loop."

"Don't sound so excited about it." Anna winked.

Gwen rested a gentle touch on Landon's forearm. "You're tired. He'll understand."

A sappy movie and early bed offered the perfect escape. Except she'd be facing this same confession tomorrow.

"Tempting, but I'd better go. I won't be late."

Before she'd finished eating, a rapid knock on the back door startled them all.

Anna stepped out and returned with Bobby, ruddy-cheeked and wrapped against the cold.

Holding fogged-up glasses in one mittened hand, he grinned at Landon and her mom. "I didn't realize how cold it is. Want me to go get the truck or are you up for a walk?"

"Or take my car." Anna was stuffing a lunchbox-sized container with cherry cake.

Landon pushed away from the table and covered her bowl for the fridge. "I'll eat this later."

Bobby waved her back. "I'll wait. We didn't set a time." He removed his mitts and scooped the fur-lined hat from his head. His hair stuck out in all directions.

"I'm done. You didn't have to come get me. Flashlight on my phone, remember?"

"Bad guys in the woods. Remember?"

Gwen gasped, and Landon hurried to reassure her. "It only happened once."

"Let's not go for twice. Especially in the dark." Without his glasses, Bobby's blue-grey eyes carried intensity.

Gwen gripped the table's edge. "I don't like you involved in these mysteries."

"I think that goes for all of us." Anna handed the container to Bobby, who accepted it with a smile.

"I don't like it either. Yet they keep finding me." Landon slipped past Bobby into the hall. "Enjoy your movie."

As she burrowed into her parka, she heard Bobby ask them which movie.

Gwen said, "We haven't decided. Nothing heavy."

"Anna, do you have a DVD player? I offered Landon one

or two of my *Christmas Carols* so she could see how it's supposed to be done."

"Why, Bob Cratchit, that would be lovely. And you did a fine job."

He tugged the earflaps down on his hat and re-wound the heavy knit scarf around his neck. "Ready when you are."

Outside, Landon's first breath set her coughing. Two, three cautious inhales, and her lungs adjusted. "It's the damp that makes it so bitter."

He caught his scarf's flailing end and tucked it into his collar. "That and the windchill. North Pole, ho."

Anna's container tucked under his arm, he left the deck steps and aimed a narrow-beam flashlight toward the path to Roy's.

Head down against the wind, sticking close to Bobby's side, Landon focused on her footing. Any number of watchers could have seen them pass. Although anyone standing still for very long would have their own problems.

The warmth inside Roy's house hit her chilled cheeks like a blanket. "Whew."

Bobby's first act once he closed them in was to take off his glasses. "Contacts don't fog up, but tonight they might freeze to a person's eyeballs."

After they peeled off their outside gear, he set the cherry cake on the kitchen counter. "I feel guilty about how much Anna feeds us."

"Here's a secret. The more she gives away, the more she can bake."

"That's fair. If you get hungry, we'll share. Gramp made peanut butter balls today too. As much to annoy my parents with his dietary choices as for the taste."

"Did I hear my name taken in vain?" Roy walked in, his white thatch of hair shorter but every bit as dishevelled as his grandson's.

Bobby took one look and pawed his straw-coloured haystack into better order. He replaced his glasses. "Anna sent cherry cake, Gramp."

The old man patted his stomach, then rubbed the sleeves of his green plaid flannel shirt. He hooked a thumb in his belt loop. "Not fit for man nor beast out there. What's so important to drag you out on a night like this?"

Landon copied his arm-rubbing gesture. The house's warmth couldn't penetrate the cold in her bones. "Vi's mystery."

One white eyebrow dipped as if he'd sensed Landon's full purpose. "Too bad we don't have any gadgets that let people talk at a distance. Oh, to be young again."

She held his stare, projecting innocent curiosity. "Bobby makes better notes than I do. This way we can see them together."

"What are you going to do when he's gone?"

"Gramp."

Bobby's tone whipped her attention from his grandfather.

The rosy hue of a cold-weather face had changed to heated brick. His pulse flickered beneath his jaw. "What part of 'don't tell a soul' did you not understand?"

"I didn't think your partner in crime counted."

"She's a soul."

Landon hauled her gaze away before he could look her way to read the anguish that must paint her features in vivid strokes.

Back to Roy, his sea-blue eyes sharpening, penetrating. Knowing.

Bobby hadn't finished. "If you breathe one hint of this to Mom and Dad, I'll—I will round up a posse of squirrels and set them loose in here. Worse, I'll clear out. Immediately."

"If you don't make a move, you'll always wonder." Roy spoke to his grandson, but his focus drilled into Landon.

She was undone. Completely. This grandfather figure who'd accepted her as his own saw depths she'd barely discovered. Knew. And had just blown a secret for his flesh-and-blood grandson.

Would he expose her too? She couldn't open up to Bobby now, not if he was leaving.

She filled her lungs, tasting air flavoured with whatever they'd eaten for supper. Clicked her spine into correct posture. Blanked her expression. If being trafficked had taught her anything, it was how to suppress, conceal, deny her true feelings and reactions. Time to step back behind that mask.

The black memory drew a wince that she smoothed away in an instant. Concentrating on the solid floor supporting her sock feet, she stared at Roy. Confident and unruffled.

His mouth flattened, and he gave his head a tiny shake. The glint dimmed in his eyes. "Not the way to handle it."

Bobby grunted. "It's my decision to make. Not yours. Definitely not Mom and Dad's. If you hadn't been there when the call came, you wouldn't know."

Roy's chest caved, stooping his shoulders. Deepening creases in his face emphasized every day of his age. "Forgive me. I'm an old fool, and I've hurt you both."

"No fool like an old fool." Bobby's voice brimmed with resentment.

Roy's wide jaw pulled tight. The joints bulged, tugging down the edges of his mouth.

All Landon read in his eyes now was agony. She stepped forward for a hug. "It'll be okay."

His arms barely made contact. A light touch recognizing her fragility. The bristly head of hair tickled her temple. "Talk to him, girlie."

Behind her, Bobby huffed. "There's nothing to say."

Landon squeezed Roy's ribs with all her strength. "Not one word."

The sight of him shuffling down the hall and closing his bedroom door cut deep. This sorrow, she could allow Bobby to see. She let her gaze skid across his.

He exhaled with a sharp whistle. "I have to work it through on my own. I'll tell you when I know what I'm doing."

"Sounds like the reverse of a conversation we had the other day."

Misery brewed in his eyes. "This is not petty payback."

"I know you better than that."

"Pray for wisdom and clarity? I should've asked."

"Of course." For both of them. "Also for you and Roy to make peace. I don't think he meant to break your confidence."

"I don't know what got into him. I hope he's not starting dementia." He produced the saddest goofy grin she'd ever seen. "On that cheery note, let's get to work. He even put the fire on for us in the living room."

"You don't have a chimney."

"Come and see."

In the living room, the wall-mounted television played the fireplace channel, complete with crackling flames and instrumental Christmas tunes. Bobby swept a hand toward it. "Come and warm yourself, milady. You might have to stand pretty close."

Her laugh died in the trying. After briefly admiring the miniature Christmas village scene on the display table below the television, she plopped onto the sofa.

He settled beside her. "You pointed out I always do the notes. Your turn."

"Um." Her counsellor had advised she see how the situation unfolded. Bitter recklessness swelled.

No way would she uncover her feelings for Bobby if he was on the cusp of moving away. Loyalty might make him stay, give her a chance, and miss his own.

Which meant she had nothing to lose. "There's something you should know. It could change things."

He stilled, shifting sideways on the couch to face her. Shoulders straight, no breath moving his body. Those blue-grey eyes keen. "I'm listening."

"I have a learning disability. I'm dyslexic."

"Oh."

A subtle sag in his posture suggested his thoughts. Not that her best friend would judge her. He could be disappointed, though.

She tucked one foot under her other leg. "So you do the writing, okay? What works for me might not make much sense to you."

"I should stop giving you books. Here I thought your hesitation was you weren't interested. In Travers, I'm wounded but I understand. But *A Christmas Carol?*"

"I'm an audiobook girl. I've only listened to your first book so far, but it's fun. Travers is—I don't know—a larger-than-life you. With Scrooge, this real-life mystery hasn't let me get far."

"You take that back about Travers. Them's fightin' words." His grin slid into normal goofiness. "If the narrator's good, you'll enjoy Scrooge. It's shorter than you'd expect."

His jawline softened. "Dyslexia, huh? Must make school rough. Not that it's standing in your way."

She read acceptance in his eyes. Not pity, not withdrawal. "I have strategies now. I do read. School takes everything I have."

"Well, I'll be the official notetaker and designated driver. That should get me a pay raise." He stretched an arm and retrieved the clipboard from the coffee table.

"You can cross a couple names off your chart, but there's not a lot to write. Or there's been too much drama. I'm toast." Landon massaged her forehead. Too bad she couldn't rub out the creases the day had folded in her brain. Sagging against the couch, she picked her way through the key points of Freesia's and Hope's stories.

Bobby listened, pen scratching occasionally. He added a sympathetic sound at intervals.

The mental strain of following those conversations was nothing to the emotional wallop from Roy. She didn't go there. Instead, she finished with, "I'll phone Elva when I get home. Since Hope already knows, they can bridge that chasm."

Bobby dropped the clipboard in his lap. "Our suspect list is nonexistent. Freesia and Hope weren't strong contenders anyway, but who's left? Do you think that developer could have faked her alibi? Or the person Vi named in her letter?"

Glancing at his notes, Landon didn't bother fitting the letters into words. "It's a mess and we're lost. It could be any of her customers if they got into an argument. Or one of the people whose secrets she knew." She smothered a yawn. "Or, like Nigel and Dee have both reminded me, Vi sent nobody away. It could be a complete stranger passing through who's already moved on."

"Remember the watcher at the wagon ride. He's still around. Or she is." Bobby shoved his hands through his hair, leaving a thatched heap. "We have to do better than this for Nigel. Without interfering with the police investigation. Let's go over the customer list again. We can keep rebuilding that, look for connections."

"We should talk to Nigel again. I wish he'd tell us more. When we were searching, at least once he started to mention visitors by name and cut himself off."

"He'll be checking out his own suspicions."

"Yes. Alone." Nigel navigated the forest with more stealth than a deer. He could take care of himself.

Landon shivered. Unless he underestimated his mother's killer.

Chapter 18

Tuesday

FOOTSTEPS ON THE deck below her window woke Landon the next morning. Full daylight sneaked around the closed blinds. She hauled the duvet over her head and groaned a prayer for sleep. Or for strength to face the day.

When Bobby drove her home last night, Anna and Gwen had taken one look and sent her to bed. With orders not to get up for breakfast duty.

Her brain—her soul—ached from yesterday's drama. And from her lost hopes.

But her feet had to hit the floor if she was going with Bobby to track down Nigel.

An image passed behind her closed eyelids of a mighty flood-surge river. Old Testament priests stepping into it. The flow piling up into a wall to make a dry passage across.

They obeyed first. Then came the power.

"Okay, God." She swung her legs over the side of the bed and pressed the soles of her feet into the woven mat. Braced herself and stood.

Remembered she hadn't phoned Elva last night. Pecked out a quick text. *Hope knows. About you, not him. She told me yesterday.*

When Elva didn't reply, Landon dropped the phone on her bed.

A hot shower loosened her muscles but did nothing for her foggy brain. She'd be no help at all visiting Nigel today.

But if Bobby was leaving—and he would, she prayed he'd be wise and seize his opportunity—she didn't want to miss a single chance to be together.

Towelling her hair, she tried to laugh at herself. Twenty-four, and finally hitting the high school crush stage.

Except it wasn't funny.

She rooted through her closet for a plain forest-green sweatshirt and faded jeans. She'd dressed a little nicer for Bobby last night, and now she needed to let herself slide farther off his radar. No amount of bright colour could energize her today anyway. This one would be on whatever strength God gave and what fuel she found in caffeine.

As Landon left her bedroom, Kenzie waved from a chair in the conversation nook. "They told me not to wake you, so I waited."

Skirting the stairwell, Landon crossed to the alcove between the two front bedrooms. The three windows of the inn's extended dormer made a perfect spot to watch the bay. And to enjoy the morning sun—or today, the fat flakes of snow drifting past.

Kenzie peered up at her. "You okay?"

"Tired. Yesterday was brutal. How are you getting along with Phil?"

The girl's expression soured. "Whitney doesn't like me."

"You did upset her husband pretty badly."

"I thought he deserved it." She tugged her turtleneck collar closer to her ears. "It's like she's scared I'm the competition. Serious insecurity happening."

Whitney had always seemed fragile, and people said pregnancy hormones did weird things. Add in another murder and no wonder the woman seemed threatened.

Landon leaned on the nearest chairback, fingers kneading

the soft blue fabric. "How about Ciara? You two are surprise stepsisters."

"Our feelings about Phil unite us." Kenzie's smirk faded. "He ordered DNA test kits for me and him, but I believe him. Unless he's crazy, he wouldn't make up a story like that."

She clutched a throw pillow from the chair tight against her stomach. "I don't know whether to fly home tomorrow and blast Mom for stealing my father from me. Or stay here for Christmas and ghost her."

Yesterday, she'd driven back to campus to pack so she could leave the inn directly for the airport. Despite the hype about the winter storm advisory and true to Roy's prediction, the system had stalled in New England and wouldn't be forcing Kenzie's departure—or snowing her in.

Landon lifted a noncommittal shoulder. "They both made some bad choices, but we all do."

Kenzie snorted. "What I wanted to tell you is Whitney's furious about Phil's attachment to Vi. His fundraiser will cover the burial costs, but he's setting up a scholarship in her memory. For a student interested in herbs and natural remedies."

"That's kind of him."

"I overheard her say she'd hoped they'd be rid of Vi now but he wouldn't let go." Kenzie jabbed a finger toward Landon. "What if she killed Vi to cut Phil free?"

Landon leaned forward, palms grinding into the chairback. Phil's name was on Vi's customer list, but her defence of him at the dinner had kept Landon from considering him as a suspect.

He'd been open about this part of his past. What worse secret could Vi hold over him?

Yet Whitney, petite but able to lunge at Vi in the heat of emotion... How deeply might she resent her husband's bond with this secret keeper who knew more than his wife?

Cold prickled along Landon's spine.

Phil would have been in the office on Monday when Vi

was killed. Had Whitney gone to demand Vi share what she knew?

Kenzie stood, hugging herself. "I may not like Phil, but I don't want to see him hurt more. Or see Ciara lose her mom to jail. But it's possible, isn't it?"

Landon sucked in a breath. "I have to tell Dylan."

"He was here earlier. I saw the car when I was finishing breakfast."

"You didn't talk to him?"

Kenzie's gaze drifted toward the window. "He doesn't trust me. I hoped I was making things up, but you think it's possible too. I don't know if that makes me feel good or bad."

"Motive isn't proof. Don't mention this to Ciara? She's had enough hurt this year." Landon excused herself and jogged downstairs. Dylan might have told Anna if he'd be back.

She found her mother and Anna lingering over hot drinks in the private sitting room.

Anna set her snowman mug on the table beside her recliner and lowered the footrest. "Looks like it's a coffee morning. I'll start breakfast for you. What sounds good?"

"I can do it myself in a minute. Did I miss Dylan?" She ignored the spark in her mother's eyes and the tiny curve of a secret smile. "Kenzie brought up a possibility he needs to hear."

Gwen's exhale carried disappointment.

"He said to phone when you caught up on your beauty sleep." Anna settled into the teal recliner and reclaimed her drink. "It didn't sound urgent."

"Thanks for letting me sleep. My brain hurts from the drama overload."

Landon crossed the hall to the kitchen and filled the tallest mug she could find—a silver-trimmed Christmas-tree design—with coffee and cream. While she waited for Dylan to pick up, she plucked one of Anna's cranberry-orange muffins from the cooling rack. The sugar-strewn crown warmed her fingertips.

Dylan answered before the call went to voice mail. "You'll never make it in police work if you can't go forty-eight hours straight with no sleep."

Phone wedged between shoulder and ear, she carried her mug and plated muffin to the table and slid into one of the hoop back chairs. "Never mind the hours. It's the brain strain. Zerkowsky told you about yesterday's revelations?"

"And Anna said you spent the evening going over it all again with your co-sleuth. Are we on speaker?"

"No."

"That all you talked about, or are things good?"

Landon winced, eyes screwed shut and air hissing through her teeth. The top edge of her phone dug into her ear.

"I'm sorry." His voice deepened. "Sounds like I shouldn't have asked. I'm rooting for you, kid."

Her burning eyes held no moisture for tears. "Thanks. He's got other stuff going on right now, and the timing's wrong. Don't bring it up to him. On your honour."

"Understood. Did you figure out anything about the case you're not supposed to be working on?"

A sip of coffee eased the tightness in her throat. She inhaled deeply. "We want to find Nigel today and also see if we can add to the customer list Starr tried to reconstruct."

"The list that's here in the office. Took a picture before you brought it in, huh?"

"He knows names he's not sharing. Did you identify the woman Hope saw on her first visit? Or the guy at the wagon ride?"

"Interesting you'd mention him. Dee called today and said her ex could be back in the area. I can't see what he'd have to do with Vi, but it's one more question in the mix."

He muffled the phone for a moment as if responding to a colleague at the station, then continued. "If anyone recognizes him, he may find his welcome not so warm.

People love Dee and Starr."

"Poor Starr. She'll get her hopes up, and the truth will crush her."

"Dee asked us to keep it quiet. According to the file, she's at least the third woman he's swindled. He's slick at getting the money into offshore accounts and then turning up elsewhere with a new identity."

Landon's stomach rumbled, and she tried to satisfy it with a mouthful of coffee. The muffin in front of her tantalized. "Kenzie has an idea."

"Which she couldn't have shared with me this morning?"

Landon recounted what Kenzie had overheard. "Whitney's tiny, but she may not be as fragile as we think. She's definitely threatened. Good luck getting past Phil to talk to her."

"Zerkowsky. Maybe. If he took you along."

The thought of another emotion-heavy encounter set Landon's brain buzzing. She broke off a chunk of muffin and chewed quickly.

For Nigel, for Vi... for the truth. "What if I go by myself?"

"Would you defend yourself against a pregnant woman if she attacked you? This needs two people."

Zerkowsky's gentle manner should calm Whitney, but the uniform and marked car in her driveway might overstress her before he reached the front door.

She broke off another chunk of muffin—with a juicy red cranberry. "I could ask Phil."

"She wouldn't confess in front of her husband."

"He'd catch her in a lie faster." She popped the chunk of muffin into her mouth.

"Why am I even having this conversation with a civilian?"

"You're right. Phil will insist on being present. You don't need me, especially if the officer goes in off-duty clothes and a plain vehicle."

"It's special treatment, but her condition warrants it."

Landon drew her mug nearer, ready to gulp the cooling

coffee. "Go easy on Phil. He's been through the grinder already with Kenzie."

"You sound more like Anna every day. I mean that with all respect." Chuckling, he clicked off.

With a frown at the phone, she tucked it into her pocket and stood.

Her mother had been here a week. They'd been rebuilding the relationship, but the mystery kept pulling Landon away. Despite her anger at Anna's interference, this reunion was knitting another hole back together in her heart.

Now, Bobby would be here in an hour to go find Nigel—if they could. Landon refilled her coffee, snagged a second muffin, and went to join the others in the sitting room.

An hour would have to do.

By the time he arrived and she climbed into the truck, she had her composure nailed down tight. "Do you miss your summer ride?"

Bobby's smile flipped her heart. Not a good diversion after all.

"Compared to this beast? You know it. Especially with the plow mounted."

He slid the truck into gear, and the elevated yellow blade rattled when they started forward. "In space, this'd be a tug or an ore hauler. The muscle cars you see around town, they'd be heavy cruisers. Mine is streamlined and agile, closer to one of Travers's ranger ships."

"What about ordinary cars like Anna's?"

"In-planet commuters. They wouldn't even break out of the atmosphere." His careless delivery dismissed them.

"How much thought have you put into this?"

He laughed. "About two seconds, just now. Except for the Corvette. Hence the RANGER1 custom licence plate."

When they jostled onto Nigel's road, Landon offered, "At least this rig can tackle the worst potholes."

Bobby cut the wheels back and forth, dodging the deepest. "Each to their purpose. I hope Nigel's here."

"If not, we check his work next."

Once he rolled the truck to a stop under the ancient pine, they climbed out.

Vi's car hadn't moved from its position in front of the ramshackle garage, but that told them nothing. Nigel's bicycle was nowhere in sight.

Breathing in the soft forest scents, Landon rotated a slow circle to scan the surroundings. No sign of anyone among the trees, Nigel or a stranger. An extra car across the road at Dee's, likely a client.

She hurried to catch up to Bobby as he climbed the steps.

They opened the screen and crossed the porch to rap on Nigel's door. The sound bounced back hollow.

Bobby stuck his hands in his jacket pockets. "He could be anywhere. I wonder how the police find him when they need to."

"Leave him a note? He'll find us."

"Good idea." He unzipped to retrieve a coil-bound notebook and pen from an inside pocket, then waggled his eyebrows at Landon. "A writer is always prepared."

After leaving the message tucked under a container of Anna's oatmeal-raisin cookies, they wandered the treeline. Fewer birds sang this time of year. Even the squirrels had left off their chattering.

Landon toed a tuft of yellowed grass. "Nigel will have searched these grounds even more thoroughly than the investigating team."

Big and glossy black, a crow glided from the heights, angling downward on silent wings. It landed, hopped twice, and aimed a keen eye at them.

A thump sounded from the house. They whirled to see Nigel emerging from an attached doorway set at a flat angle from the ground.

Landon had forgotten the root cellar from their previous visit.

Nigel heaved the wooden door over the opening before he

approached. Despite its rough appearance, the hinges made no sound.

He lowered the brim of his camouflage hat although loose grey clouds hid the sun. "Developments?"

"Questions." Landon pointed toward the front door. "Anna sent cookies."

With a jerk of his head, Nigel indicated the house. He scooped up the container and the note on the way by. Inside, he hung his coat on a peg and stepped out of his heavy brown work boots. His hat remained in place.

"Tea?" Without waiting for an answer, he strode into the kitchen, soundless in thick woollen socks.

Landon found a peg for her coat, remembering the scarf at Dee's and the matching hat Starr had dropped here. Thank God the girl left before the killer arrived. No wonder her mother had been terrified.

In a building this size, Landon didn't need to raise her voice to reach the kitchen. She walked closer anyway. "Have you seen anyone prowling around? Dee's afraid it's the killer, but it could be her ex."

Nigel's gaze cut her way, then dipped to the container of tea leaves he'd been spooning into diamond-patterned cups. Vi's empty herbal-remedy jars lined the shelves opposite the stove.

"He can't return. Mother knew."

Bobby leaned against the door jamb beside Landon. "Dee made sure the police knew too. Surfacing anywhere in Canada would bring him jail time."

"Dylan said she expressed concern." Landon eased toward the living room.

Bobby caught her staring and smirked, drawing thumb and forefinger along his jawline to his chin like a movie supervillain. "Sounds like we should pay a call on the lady."

"No wonder she's scared, living there alone with a child to protect. After what he did, why would her ex come back? Unless he's the killer." She focused on Nigel. "What your mother knew—Could he have tried to, I don't know, buy her off or threaten her? And it went sour? But why now?"

His grey eyes glittered. "Impossible. This person will be a local who feared my mother. For reasons we may never know."

He gave them each a mug and carried his toward the living room. "Fearmongers suggest a transient came begging and became violent. Foolishness."

Landon took the rocking chair, leaving the afghan-draped couch for the men. "Why?"

Nigel sat almost primly, knees and ankles pressed together. He peered at her over his tea. "Why sow fear?"

"Why is the idea foolish?"

One sip and Bobby blinked hard. He lowered the mug to rest on his leg. "Because a stranger wouldn't have an isolated violent outburst and vanish with no further trouble. Nor would they lie low and come back for round two in the same place. A local might be horrified by what they'd done and feel they needed to break in for damage control."

"Precisely. Finish your tea. Strengthens the immune system and sharpens the brain cells."

Bobby hunched in his seat. "I don't—What's in it anyway?"

"Never you mind. Drink."

Landon's first mouthful brought tears to her eyes. The bitter scent filling her nostrils seemed to flow from the back of her throat. She locked gazes with Bobby. "What doesn't kill you makes you stronger."

"I was happy being weak."

Breath held, eyes closed, she chugged it. With an explosive gasp, she blinked at Nigel. "Have you given the police the name of the woman Hope saw leaving on Sunday?"

"Unfinished business, that one." His bushy salt-and-pepper brows crawled low. "She should return."

"Nigel, they need to interview every possibility. Don't you

want them to find the killer?"

His scarred hands gripped his mug. "I search alone. Among the trees. Visiting Mother's customers. I can discern guile."

Bobby winced. "I think the police prefer a more formal interview process. A paper trail, and all."

"I honour her commitment to privacy."

Landon clicked her fingernails against her empty mug. How to ask without offending him? "What if you find the person? When you went after Elva's attacker, we were afraid—"

"I will not mete out justice. Mother walked her own path and accepted the element of danger in her calling. Elva was an innocent victim."

"Your mother was an innocent victim too, and we're sorry you lost her this way. Especially at Christmas."

Bobby choked down the last of his tea. "Will you help us rebuild her client list for the investigative team? Exclude your mystery visitor, but let us have the rest. What if a customer picked up a remedy and saw the killer arrive?"

"I ask that of each one. Nothing yet."

"What about their families?" Landon had been rocking gently. Now, she stopped. "Whitney resents Phil's connection with your mom. Others may distrust this type of product. Or they could suspect a family member revealed a criminal secret."

"Mother's discretion was above reproach."

"The killer didn't think so." Bobby held out his notebook and a pen. "Please, Nigel. If this person is suddenly afraid of exposure, they may eliminate other threats. We need to give the investigators all the help we can."

Nigel studied him for a long moment before accepting the writing implements. He covered multiple pages without stopping.

Landon shared a wondering look with Bobby. For all she knew, he wrote with the same rapid-fire pace. But that was his imagination. Nigel held these details in his head on command.

Mind like a steel trap. If he knew half as much as his mother, that trap could contain a killer's identity.

He stood. "I must get ready for work. You young ones be careful asking around."

"You too." Landon mirrored his stance. "You drop out of sight for days. If you were hurt, we'd never know."

"Even a pro can be ambushed." Bobby stood too. He flipped through the notebook pages before stowing it in a coat pocket. "We should see Dee while we're here before we get this list to the police."

When they stepped out onto the porch and closed the door, he tapped Landon's arm. "He alphabetized that list. On the fly."

"No way. That's—"

"Amazing."

The porch gave a clear view of the physiotherapist's property. The client parking area held three cars. No opportunity there. Heading for the truck, Landon zipped her collar against the wind. "I guess we text and ask when she's free."

Bobby opened the passenger door and swept his arm in a grand gesture. "Your carriage, milady. Dee squeezed Gramp in end of day today. Ask her if one or both of us could tag along. We don't need a lot of her time—just a better picture of why she thinks this guy's back and if he could be involved in the murder."

Chapter 19

DUSK HAD BECOME almost full dark when Landon hopped from the truck at the physio clinic. Barely five o'clock. These short December days mocked her with the speed of their passing. Time was running out.

What they'd said to Nigel about a killer afraid of breached secrecy who might kill again—broadening the suspects to include the family and social circles of Vi's clients made an impossibly deep pool.

She stepped aside, giving Bobby room to exit the truck. He'd had the middle of the bench seat with only a hand on the dashboard to stabilize him on the rough road.

Roy rounded the yellow plow blade and circled back toward them. He wore a ball cap pulled low over his bristly white hair and a much-scarred leather jacket that must once have been a darker brown.

He gestured toward the clinic door outlined in white Christmas twinkle lights. "Tell her I'll be right in." Two more steps toward them, limping. "Damp's playing havoc with my leg. The storm's still a few days out, no matter what the weather folks say. Arthritis never lies. Landon, take my arm?"

Bobby chuckled. "I can take a hint. See you inside."

When Landon approached, the old man clasped her shoulders in gloved hands. Backlit by the building's exterior

217

lights, his features held shadows. A faint glimmer marked his sea-blue eyes, pale and focused.

"Can you forgive an old fool?" His grip tightened. "I made a false assumption and hurt you both."

Her throat burned. "You kept me from making a big mistake."

"No, girl. Talk to him. For all our sakes."

Over Roy's shoulder, Landon saw the door close behind Bobby. "Do you think he'll choose wrong? He's pretty sensible."

He huffed. "That choice doesn't matter. You do. So does he. Talk to him."

Landon drew a shaky breath. "No more words. It's for the best."

"It's not what you—"

"Roy, stop. This is killing me. Come on, Dee's waiting." She shook off his hold and spun to stare out at the darkened water. They were here for clues. For Nigel, maybe for Dee if her ex was unconnected with Vi's death. Personal heartache had to wait for later.

After Roy's footsteps scuffed toward the clinic, Landon caught up with him, and they entered together.

Bobby peered at his grandfather, brows tight. Roy concentrated on hanging his coat on the rack and lowering into one of the bright-turquoise plastic seats.

At the desk, Dee was processing the previous patient's payment. A fabric snowman on skis perched on one end. Once the other woman left, Dee directed Roy to a treatment room and came to sit beside Landon. "I don't want Starr to know Toby is lurking around. She romanticizes him."

"Are you sure it's him? Why would he come back?"

"He called the clinic a month ago, wanting something he left behind. I dumped all his stuff when he left, but I played along, asked for an address. I planned to give it to the police. He said he'd come when I didn't expect him. And not to cross him." Dee twisted her fingers together. "He never let loose his temper on us when he lived here, but now? I'm afraid."

Across the waiting room, Bobby leaned forward, elbows on knees. "Has he made contact since then?"

"I thought I recognized him at the wagon ride. Yesterday, he let me see him out the bedroom window. Waved and ran off before I could take a picture."

Landon shivered. "Can he get in?"

"I changed the locks and installed an alarm system, but that won't stop him if he's desperate. What if he gets inside and finds out whatever he wants is gone?"

"You don't know what it is?"

"No." Dee slapped her palms against her knees and pushed to her feet. "If they catch him and prove he's the killer, it'll break her heart all over again. For Starr's sake, it'd be better if he disappeared."

Landon focused on the physiotherapist. "Roy's waiting, but do you really think this guy's the killer?"

"Vi always had a key to our house. Which she clearly did not provide. If he lashed out and she fell—" Dee's eyes narrowed. "I took the key back from Nigel after that. Toby didn't find it when he searched later."

"According to Nigel, Vi said your ex couldn't come back. She knew why."

"Then Nigel was wrong." She hurried down the hall toward the treatment rooms, ponytail bouncing.

Landon moved over to sit beside Bobby, leaving an empty chair between them. Easier than meeting his eyes, and she could talk quieter in case Dee reappeared. "I didn't ask in case the police haven't mentioned it, but what about the calls from Vi's phone? Could Toby have done that?"

"Hope's card was lying around. That's an easy first shot at misdirection."

"What about Freesia? I don't think he was around when her dogs were seized."

"He might have been following local news in case his name came up. He'd know she had motive and guess Vi kept her contacts stored on her landline."

"I guess."

After a minute, he asked, "What'd Gramp want?"

"Don't worry, your secret's safe. He apologized again. I think he's worried about your decision, but I told him you'd choose right."

"Without knowing the details." Bobby's knee started to bounce. "Thank you. I'm nearly certain. What's getting me now is what you'll think."

"I'm going to think, 'Wow, my best friend prayerfully considered a big step, and I believe in him.' Number one cheering section, right here."

She clapped a hand to her mouth. The poisonous girl from his past, the one who looked like her—she'd been a cheerleader. Whatever she'd done, the scars were still raw. "Forget what I said. Supporter. No cheering."

"Even if it means I reverse direction on something I told you before?"

Landon's heart dropped like a rock. And cracked on impact. He'd said he loved her. That he'd stick around as a friend. She'd told herself he'd moved on, but the confirmation left her desolate.

She shut her eyes, too dry for tears. Forced herself to unlock her desperate grip on the edges of her seat. "You have to be true to yourself. And to God. Things change. That's life." The words burned her throat.

"See, you're already upset. I should—"

"You should do the right thing. Forget about me. I don't factor into this."

"It's not—"

The connecting door to the house eased open, swinging the reindeer wreath hooked to the top. Starr's curly black hair appeared around the edge.

When the girl's eyes popped into view, Landon waved. "Hi, Starr."

"Shh. I'm not supposed to interrupt." The door swung a

220

little wider. "Come visit."

As they started to rise, she hissed, "Her. Landon."

Bobby subsided, hand splayed across his elf shirt and his eyes dramatically large. "Rejected. Even though I dressed for fun."

"I don't want to laugh today." She ducked back into the house.

Landon followed and eased the door shut behind her. "Hey, what's the matter?"

Angling forward on her crutches, Starr heaved a teen-worthy sigh. Heaved was the right word. She leaned into the launch and seemed to watch a weight of emotion thud to the floor at Landon's feet. Where Landon had dressed drab today, a grumpy troll sweatshirt echoed the lines of Starr's countenance.

Landon stepped forward and stooped to hug her. "Another day, you have to let Bobby see that shirt."

With a half shrug, the girl pulled away. "He can tell them where you've gone. Come sit by the tree." In the living room, Starr made for the big leather recliner. "Sit beside me."

The supple material moulded around them, and Starr hit the control to elevate the footrest. Landon put an arm around the girl, tightening as Starr snuggled into her.

Quiet Christmas tunes set a gentle ambience. Head back, top-hatted snowman-themed tree twinkling, Starr's warmth nestled against her side, Landon could pretend all was well.

Except for the girl's sadness. "Starr, if you want to talk I'm here."

"Miz Vi was my friend. Like a grandmother. She kept my secret and didn't look down on me like most people."

"You miss her a lot." Landon squeezed tighter around the girl's ribs.

"I miss Toby too. More, now that Mom's so stressed. He could always make her laugh. I wish he'd come back."

"Did Vi think he would?"

"She helped me remember the good times and said he

loved me." Starr squirmed, jostling the chair, and thrust a hand in front of Landon's chin. "See this? It was his."

A coin worn shiny silver from use or touch. Holding the image of an unfamiliar ship.

The girl's fingers curled around it again, and she drew her fist to her heart. "His lucky coin. He used to do magic tricks. Pretend to find it in my ear or my hair."

"Did he leave it for you when he went?"

"Miz Vi found it." Starr's sigh came out long and low, lonely like a deflating soul. "Mom hates him. But I'm scared for him without his lucky coin."

"Could I see it again?" Had he come back for this? Collector coins could be worth thousands. Or more.

Tentatively, Starr offered her open palm.

"I've never seen one like this. May I take a picture?" Easier than trying to describe it to Dylan.

"What are you two studying?"

At her mother's question, Starr whipped her fist away and jammed it into her pocket. "Shh."

The hiss barely reached Landon's ears. She hugged the girl and smiled at Dee. "I hope you don't mind. Starr was feeling lonely, and this chair is a dream."

"Not at all." Dee's eyebrows pinched into a straight line. "What do you have, Starr?"

She stopped in front of them like a teacher calling out the class troublemaker. "I'm waiting."

Landon swiped along the side of the chair for the control to bring it upright. Her fingers brushed a button and sent them farther back. Slipped off the smooth plastic. Dropped them more. Her cheeks burned.

Starr's arm nailed the control, gliding them upright. Her body arced forward.

Fists planted on hips, Dee blocked Starr's escape. "Show me."

The girl tucked into Landon's side. "Promise you won't take it."

One brow curved up. "At least it's not insect season." Dee's gaze flickered to Landon. "Last summer it was beetles."

Back to her daughter. "Now, Starr."

Slow as an ancient, rust-seized machine, the girl extended her arm. Instead of creaks and groans, tremors vibrated from her frame pressed against Landon's ribs.

Compelled by the force of Dee's stare, Starr's fingers relinquished their protective hold one by one.

Almost at once, they curled inward again, but Dee caught her wrist and plucked the coin free.

"You promised!" Starr's wail shook with tears.

"I did no such thing." Dee shook too, visibly. Face beyond pale, she closed her eyes as if summoning control. "This proves he's back. I didn't want you to know."

Starr shot upright in the chair. "He came home? Really?"

At the wistful ache in the girl's voice, Landon spread her palm flat on the girl's spine. Supporting. Steadying. Comforting.

"This is not his home." Colour flared in Dee's cheeks. "He may have killed Vi. He'll be furious he dropped this. Unless he meant it to frighten us."

"Miz Vi found it after he left. She let me keep it at her place so you wouldn't dump it down the well with his other stuff."

"He used us—both of us. Tricked us and stole everything. From you most, Starr-ling." Dee focused on Landon. "What I couldn't sell or give away, I threw down the well with all his booze before we filled it in. Good riddance."

"You said we got the money repaid."

"Our insurance covered your trust account. His name was on the others, and there was nothing I could do. The good people of this town gave out of their own pockets."

"That coin belongs in my pocket. Please give it back. Or I'll hate you forever."

Starr maintained an upright posture. No more tears, no burrowing into Landon's embrace. One strong will engaging another.

The gentle Christmas background music suddenly sounded tinny like a carnival.

Dee blinked. With a laugh that tinkled like shattering icicles, she dropped the coin into her daughter's outstretched palm. "Consider it an inheritance. You can sell it when you get older. For now, keep it out of my sight. I don't want those memories."

She stalked away, giving Starr and Landon room to stand.

Leaning on one crutch, Starr hid the coin in her pocket. Her expression matched the grumpy troll on her shirt.

Landon pointed to the shirt. "Come show Bobby. If they're not already in the truck waiting for me."

"Will he be mad I didn't want him to come in?"

"He has to respect girl time. The troll will make him laugh—especially if you make the same face."

After a quick march through the house, they stepped into the client space.

True to Landon's prediction, Bobby admired the sweatshirt and showed Starr his snowboarding elf. When Roy produced a candy from his pocket, Starr's smile appeared at nearly full strength.

Landon hugged her again, and they all thanked Dee for fitting them into her day.

Roy executed a clumsy two-step. "Now, I can cut a rug over the holiday. Say, if anyone gives me good news."

Bobby passed Landon her coat. "Your pocket buzzed a couple of times."

"Thanks."

Buckled into the truck, she checked her cell. A text from Dylan, three missed calls from the same unknown number. One phone message. The mystery caller finally decided to talk?

Or she'd hear dead air and a click. Frowning, she cued her messages while Roy set the truck in motion.

A female voice spilled from the phone. "Landon, please pick up." Hushed, shaky. Near panic. "I'm at the Lunenburg

Esso. I can't stay here—I have to see you."

Recorded fifteen minutes ago.

Fifteen minutes could be a lifetime. Not bothering with Dylan's text, Landon returned the call.

"Hello?" The whisper carried an echo.

"This is Landon. Are you safe?"

Bobby twisted sideways. His elbow jostled her. "What's up?"

She strained to hear the woman's reply. "Yes. I'm hiding in the bathroom."

"Do you need to call 9-1-1?"

"No. Just to get this over with."

"I'll be there in—hold on." She lowered the phone. "Roy, how long to town? Will you take me?"

"Fifteen minutes." The plow blade bounced as he jostled onto the paved road and picked up speed.

She relayed the time, then put the phone on speaker. The men should hear this. "Are you safe? We can keep the connection open."

The woman drew a sniffly breath. "Call me when you're here. Meet me in the bathroom."

"Uh-uh." A sharp poke on top of her thigh accented Bobby's soft negative. Head shaking, he held eye contact, his brow tight.

Mirroring Landon's caution. Caring, like any friend would.

She rubbed the spot on her leg, the denim rough under her fingertips. "I'm not comfortable with that. If you don't want to be seen talking to me, let's meet in the parking lot."

"Alone?"

"Friends are driving me. We can talk where they can't hear, but it has to be in plain sight."

"They can keep us safe?" A thin hope threaded the shaky question.

Landon's vision misted. She allowed herself to lean into Bobby's shoulder. "They're the best. But if you're hiding out, we need the police."

"No cops. Please. It's not like that." The call ended.

Roy let out a slow whistle. "Girl, what've you gotten yourself into now?"

"I've had a few hang-up calls, but this is the first time she's spoken. It must be about the investigation."

He huffed. "Good sense, refusing to meet her in private. We fellas could land in a heap of trouble escortin' you into the ladies'."

The deliberately thickened Lunenburg drawl settled Landon's nerves—a little. She grinned. "Are you speaking from experience or trying to keep out of jail for the holidays?"

One gnarled hand lifted from the wheel. "Try to pay a compliment, and this is the thanks I get?"

"Seriously, thank you for driving. And for having my back when we get there."

"We want you around for the holidays too." Bobby's words came out low and strained.

The quiet pain in his tone brought memories of their reunion on the rainy September night when he'd thought she'd been killed. How secure she'd felt in his arms, nestled against his still-racing heart. His selfless comfort anchored her then, and it would now, even after his feelings had changed.

Both hands gripped her shoulder belt. She'd give anything to go back there now. Knowing she loved him while he felt the same.

In the close quarters, he must have sensed her bracing herself. His knee nudged hers. "Hey. It'll be okay."

Over everything inside her that screamed denial, she forced a reply. "I know."

All would be well. God wasted no hurt. In the meantime, she'd focus on justice for Vi. And hope this frightened woman could provide a clue.

Clue. The truck rocketed past Dylan's favourite coffee

shop. Almost to town but with a few minutes to share what she'd learned.

"Guys, if Dee's ex is prowling around, I might know why." She described Starr's coin.

"If he's out of funds and it's valuable, that could answer the why-show-up-now question." Bobby shrugged. "Nigel said the man won't return. Dee claims he has. No disrespect to Dee, but of the two of them, I can't see Nigel being wrong."

"He might have come back to kill Vi to eliminate the threat of whatever she knew."

They approached the town limits. Roy slowed the truck. "Phone your friend and tell her the cavalry's here."

Two minutes later, they rolled into the gas station lot.

A parka-clad figure with a backpack left the convenience store. Under a bulky winter coat, hood up, it could be anyone. The figure's jerky glances left and right and the swift pace to the far corner of the pavement spiked Landon's pulse.

"That's her. Let me out here? And stay close."

Roy grunted. "Call her away from that corner. Out toward the road. In case she has an accomplice waiting."

She released her seat belt and opened the door. "Now I know where Bobby gets his imagination. Will do."

Chin tucked against the cold, all senses on full alert, she walked toward the street edge of the lot.

Chapter 20

THE WOMAN'S FEAR meant there could be watchers. Someone who'd know what the conversation meant. Who'd be threatened with exposure and who might act decisively.

Or it was a trap.

As Landon angled toward the farthest roadside corner, she waved the stranger to join her.

The woman beckoned toward her own location but surrendered and trudged forward.

Landon stopped under a street light, chin up now and arms loose at her sides. Recognizable if this woman knew her, and nonthreatening regardless.

Close up, the careworn forty-plus individual she'd expected bore a much younger face. Blue eyes staring, features taut and pinched, but barely over twenty.

"Do you have information about Vi's death?" Landon tried to pitch it as a gentle invitation.

The girl flinched, teeth catching her lower lip. Tears sheened her eyes. "Death?" The question was a pained puff of night air.

Tension pulled at Landon's forehead. Not the murder after all. What, then?

She smoothed her features. "I didn't mean to frighten you. I'm helping a friend. His mother was killed, and we're trying to find clues."

Way to sound like a cartoon mystery show, but this girl looked ready to faint.

Framed by the faux-fur-edged hood, her wide, fear-filled eyes... might be familiar.

"Why have you been calling me?"

The girl's breath rasped. "I had to see you."

"Why?"

"I had to know if you're truly okay. If you're okay, I can be too." Her arms crossed her body, bare hands white against the dark coat. She clutched her elbows.

Landon reached out, red-mittened palms up. "Do you need help? Can you tell me what happened?"

"Nothing—yet. But I'm so sick of being afraid."

The girl lowered her heavy hood, revealing mussed brown hair cut in a short, nondescript style. She tucked both hands into her pockets, shrinking like a child with an angry teacher. Or a prisoner before a judge.

Landon gasped. It was like staring into a fun-house mirror. Distorting her features to painful thinness, superimposing a tousled brown wig.

Holding the girl's gaze, she moistened her lips. Unlocked her voice. "Lacey?"

A tiny nod and trickling tears.

Landon squealed. "Lacey!"

She launched at her sister, arms locking around the bulky coat, squeezing the dense filling until she felt the slender person inside.

They stood there, embracing and crying in the night, until the cold crept through Landon's jeans. She eased away but kept hold of her sister's hands. Studied her face to commit it to memory. Sniffled.

Lacey slid a hand free and drew a tissue from her pocket. Wiping her cheeks, she kept the eye contact. "When you were taken and Dad went to find you and the guy killed him—Mom went into hyperprotection mode. The fear came in, and it never left. It's killing me."

That soul-sucking void lurked on the edges of Landon's consciousness. Yet now she stood in the light of freedom and faith. No matter what happened, nothing could separate her from God's love.

"There's hope. It takes work, and it's too much to unpack now. Short answer, I'm whole, I've been made whole, and I'm becoming whole. Triggers still happen." She stomped her boots for warmth, each impact firing a dull pain through her chilled feet. "How did you get here? Where are you staying?"

Lacey pointed toward the gas station. "Bus. They drop off here. My room's nearby."

"Mom said you wouldn't leave the house, and here you are. Lacey, this is huge. Look at you! You're braver than you know. There's space at the inn. Cancel wherever you booked and come with me."

"No. I need to be alone and crash. This has been—"

"Will you feel safe there?"

"As safe as anywhere else with doors that lock."

Tires whispered on the pavement. Plow blade rattling, Roy's truck eased closer, stopping a car length away. Lights angled not to blind them.

Lacey went rigid.

"That's my friends. They probably want to get home for supper. Why don't I smuggle you into the inn and tell everyone to leave you alone until you come out?"

"Let me do it my way."

Inhaling slowly, Landon resisted the urge to push. "Can we drive you? Fighting fear doesn't mean you have to walk alone after dark in a strange place."

"Okay."

Landon beckoned the men out for introductions. They seemed to pick up Lacey's emotional overload. Even Roy limited his greeting to "Glad to meet you." No jokes, no attempt at even a handshake.

The truck wouldn't fit four, so they left Bobby in the

parking lot for the short drive to Lacey's accommodations.

Landon sat in the middle, a buffer against an unusually subdued Roy. She managed to extract a promise that Lacey would contact her in the morning and consider coming to Anna's inn. "If you're scared in the night, call me. I mean it. We can talk till dawn if that's what it takes."

With a grim smile, Lacey thanked them both and marched toward the entrance to one of Anna's competitors. The place had a good reputation, which made it easier to let her go.

Roy waited until the building door shut behind her before easing onto the road. "That took guts."

"I'll fill you both in once we pick up Bobby."

Circling the block, Roy whistled a monotone rhythm. "You okay?"

Same question as Lacey's. Same answer. Landon couldn't untangle the swirling reactions. "I thought I'd lost my family. God gave me a chance to rebuild with Mom and Lacey. Does it make me ungrateful that it hurts more now about Leyna? Or just crazy?"

"Or human."

Her throat tightened. "She's out on her own somewhere with who knows what kind of guy. From what Mom said, it could be bad. It's all because of what happened to me. That's what caused Mom's and Lacey's trouble too."

Roy's gnarled hand left the wheel for a brief grip of her knee. "God knows. What kind of guy. Everything else. And He's watching like He watched you. Give Him time. Meanwhile, maybe don't take responsibility for other people's choices."

His set profile betrayed his concern. The truth might be simple to state, but that didn't make it easy to apply.

"How'd you get to be so wise?"

"The trick's in not dying young."

"A worthy goal." Landon flexed her toes. The truck's heater had finally penetrated her shoes.

By the time they collected Bobby and half a tank of gas,

she'd warmed up to mostly comfortable. She explained what she could about Lacey. "Mom told me they've finally both started therapy. I had no idea how deeply my trauma affected the whole family."

Roy grunted. "Anna's been after your mom about it from day one. Glad they're getting help."

The truck swept around a sharp bend on the way out of town. In the middle seat, Bobby braced against the dash. "Seeing your sister again is good news. The bad news is the mystery caller wasn't about Vi after all."

"I forgot Dylan texted me." Landon brought out her phone and skimmed the terse lines. "Phil gave them ten minutes with Whitney. Guarded, stiff, and unproductive. Plus, an earful of ridicule about wasting time harassing a woman in her condition."

Bobby shifted on the truck's bench seat. "They have to check even the faintest clues but Whitney? That's really reaching."

"She may be no bigger than a minute, but never underestimate a pregnant woman." Roy chuckled. "Your grandmother was downright fierce if anyone crossed her when she was carrying your dad."

When the truck slowed to navigate the inn's driveway, the Christmas candle glow in each window wilted Landon into the stiff vinyl seat. Like water down a drain, she could slide right down onto the floor mat. "I'm beyond done. Thank you both so much for delaying your meal to help Lacey."

As she stepped from the truck, Bobby slid sideways into the spot she'd vacated. "Slow cooker stew gets better with time."

"This detecting is hungry work." Under the cab's dome light, Roy rubbed his stomach.

Before he'd finished turning the truck for home, Landon scooted across the paving stones to the deck and into the inn.

If Anna and Gwen didn't intercept her, she'd scarf a quick bite before breaking the news about her sister's surprise arrival. Then pyjamas, hot chocolate, and the most mindless movie she could talk the others into. Right now, Roy's fireplace channel sounded perfect.

Instead, they met her at the door. Leaving her plate spinning in the microwave, she faced them around the kitchen table. She was easing into telling her mother Lacey was in town when her cell rang.

Lacey? It would have made so much more sense for the girl to have come home with her.

Different number. Same sense of anxiety from the female voice on the other end. "Landon? It's Whitney Kirkwood. Ciara gave me your number."

It took the last of Landon's willpower to lever herself from her seat and excuse herself from the kitchen. She felt twin stares until she escaped into the hallway.

With Kenzie upstairs, the guests' common room offered a quiet corner. "Sorry, Whitney, you sounded like this might need privacy. Is there trouble?"

"The police came today. Asking me about Vi. As if I'd hurt anyone!" The words rushed out, sharpening as they took flight. "They sent their biggest officer to intimidate me."

Landon collapsed in the club chair, sliding forward until her head leaned against the back rest. Her eyes drifted shut. "Constable Zerkowsky? He's a pussycat. Honestly? If they ever have to question me, I hope he's the one."

"He was kind and polite but—Landon, I'm scared they'll keep digging. There's something Phil doesn't know, and... he's out. Will you come? Please?"

"Now?" Had that plaintive whine come from her? Landon stretched her arm skyward, fingers spread, then dropped her palm on her forehead.

"Phil's meeting goes until ten. Ciara trusts you. So does Dee's daughter, Starr."

Starr also believed her mother's ex was one step lower than the angels. Landon caught the retort before it passed her lips. Teeth clenched, she pushed herself upright in the chair.

The leather whispered against her jeans.

"Whitney, I can tell you're upset. Could you call Ciara or a friend to stay with you until Phil gets home? We could meet tomorrow when he's at work. It's been a rough few days."

A faint sniffle came through the speaker. "I'm sorry to be such a burden. If the police come again—" Another sniffle, louder. "I have to talk this through with a safe listener before Phil finds out."

"We're talking now."

"No, in person. So you'll see I'm not lying, and I can be sure nobody else hears."

Landon's brain started to engage. Stumbling, clunky, but definite motion. Insisting this could be important. She pinched the bridge of her nose, then let her hand fall to the armrest.

Eight o'clock now and all she wanted was to collapse. Someone else could help this porcelain-doll woman. Yet... "Is this about Vi?"

Silence. Finally, a whisper. "Yes. Please come."

"Forgive me." The question caught in Landon's throat. She coughed it loose. "Whitney, you didn't hurt her?"

"No! But they won't believe me. I lied."

"Okay." Heaving herself upright, Landon tried to inject energy into her tone. "I'll find a drive. Give me half an hour."

"You're a lifesaver. I didn't know what else to do."

Landon tucked the phone into her pocket and followed the hallway to the kitchen.

When she entered, the women broke off their conversation. Anna's expression held concern. "What's wrong now?"

"Whitney. Phil's wife," she added for her mother's benefit. "She's upset, and it's connected to Vi's death."

Gwen stood and snaked her arms around her ribs. "Did you tell her to call the police?"

"They're what's scaring her. Mom, she's fragile at the best of times, and she's, like, seven months pregnant. In her forties."

"That doesn't mean you have to rush out in the night to hold her hand." Gwen strode to the microwave and removed Landon's reheated supper. She set the plate on the table and waved Landon nearer. "That's what she wants, isn't it?"

Drawn by the scent of chicken, Landon sighed. "Will one of you take me? I'd hate to drag Bobby or Roy out again after—"

She dropped into her seat. Inhaled deeply as if the aroma could fill her stomach. Caught Anna's gaze, then focused on Gwen. "I was starting to tell you what made us late. Anna, those hang-up calls I was getting, the ones I asked you to watch for on the inn line? In case it was information about Vi?"

"Yes?"

"She finally spoke. She wanted to meet after we left Dee's."

Filling her lungs with air, she gripped the taut denim that wrapped her thighs. "It wasn't about the case at all. It's Lacey. She came in by bus today and wanted to stay on her own tonight to process. She said she'd phone in the morning."

Gwen gasped.

"We'll put her in the room beside yours." Anna's plans flowed. Ideas, options, a thread of hurt that their visitor would stay anywhere else for even one night.

Half listening, Landon watched the emotions play on her mother's face. Each nuance of muscle movement and colour bespoke an aspect of her struggle. Gwen's arms locked even tighter around her frame, her back-and-forth motion somewhere between rocking and a vibration.

Finally, Gwen sat taller, neck straight, eyes bright. A tiny smile thinned her lips. "I want to hear every detail. You can tell me on the way to debrief this next witness. I'll need an address for my navigation app."

Anna rose, tears glinting from her lashes. "You two, go.

I'll have fresh muffins and tea waiting for you."

Landon ate supper too fast to do justice to the savoury chicken.

In the car, she and her mother talked non-stop until the sight of the Kirklands' home reduced Gwen to a hushed, "Wow."

She parked hugging the edge of the double drive, gazing at the two-storey yellow Victorian as if it had materialized from a fairy tale. "She won't want a stranger in the conversation, but do you think she'd mind if I came inside and waited?"

Landon replaced the mittens she'd removed in the car's heat. "You can't stay out here. It'll get cold fast."

Sliding her keys into her purse, Gwen grasped the door handle. "Let's go."

"First, I'll text her we're here. I don't want to startle her with the bell."

As they crossed the wraparound veranda, the front door swung open, and Whitney beckoned them into the elegant foyer.

The woman's careful makeup couldn't hide an underlying pallor, and her mascara emphasized the extra rounding of her eyes. Their tawny depths and her half-parted pink-blush lips held uncertainty.

"Whitney, this is my mom, Gwen. I don't drive."

With a tinkling laugh, the woman fluttered her fingers and laced them together like a butterfly landing on her rounded belly. "I don't either, these days. I can barely reach the pedals." She tossed a vague wave toward the display room on their left. "There are seats in there and things to look at while Landon and I speak privately."

Privately but within earshot of a yell. Landon had been sure of a killer's innocence before. Dylan was right. She couldn't defend herself against a pregnant woman and risk harming the babies.

They left Gwen admiring a cabinet of blown-glass

sculptures and passed through into the room where they'd spoken during the Christmas party. Tonight, a thick red candle burned on a pillar beside the grand piano. Without the extra chairs and crowd, the space felt wide yet intimate.

Footsteps silent on the Persian carpet, Whitney crossed to the divan and lowered herself to sit, spine supported by the back rest on one end. Easing her feet up onto the brocade upholstery brought a whispered sigh. "I'm so grateful for the babies, but it's hard on the body. Now, this horrible stress..."

Landon edged an armchair nearer and sat facing her. "We're trying to find the person who killed Vi. For justice and to ensure everyone else is safe. What is it you weren't comfortable to share with Corporal Zerkowsky this afternoon?"

Whitney focused on smoothing the pastel blue maternity sweater over her belly, then patted it gently as if tucking the twins under a blanket. One hand curved protectively on top. "This pregnancy is high risk. My doctor wants me to avoid being upset, and then my home's invaded."

The words shot Landon forward in her seat. "When? Were you here?"

A thin crease appeared between Whitney's eyebrows. She pressed her fingertips to her mouth. "Not an attack invasion. I meant the trouble came in—right into the heart of our home."

She gestured to the expansive windows. "You can't see them now, but in summertime the roses are so beautiful. This is my safe space. Or it was. I can't even play the piano now—it's choking the music."

Resettling herself in the chair, Landon delved for patience. No need to ask which parent gave Ciara the drama-queen gene. At least the brief adrenaline jolt had pierced the day's exhaustion.

"When you say trouble came into the house... is this connected with Vi's death?"

"They're going to blame me—and I didn't do it. They'll

take my babies and send me to jail, and I'll lose Phil—I'll lose it all."

Fat tears cascaded down her cheeks, splotching dark circles on her sweater.

Landon scooted her chair nearer and took Whitney's hand. The woman's fingers trembled in hers. "Hey... the investigators have been interviewing a ton of people. Coming here doesn't mean they're accusing you."

Between police with integrity and a lawyer husband, Whitney should be fine.

For this, Landon had dragged herself and her mother out in the cold. Yet the poor woman needed support, and Landon was here. She stroked the back of Whitney's hand, praying for patience and some words of comfort.

A hiccupping sob jerked Whitney's frame. "I was there. That day. I swear I didn't hurt her."

"How did you get there? Phil was at his office, and you're not driving."

Eyes brimming, mascara daggers beneath her lower lashes, Whitney gave a tiny headshake. "I did drive. To see her. She chased me off, and I was angry and unhappy and—"

She rooted a tissue from her pocket, rescued her hand from Landon's, and blew her nose. It barely made a squeak. She dabbed a second tissue at her face and crumpled both into her fist. "An officer stopped me. To check if I was impaired. It'll be in their records, and they'll find it. They'll know I lied about being there, and why would I lie about that if I hadn't killed her?"

Because she didn't want to be a suspect. The same as Freesia and Hope.

Landon picked up a tissue box from a nearby end table and balanced it in Whitney's lap. "People lie for all kinds of reasons. Can you tell me yours?"

"Phil would be furious. If I got in an accident, steering-wheel impact could harm the babies. We agreed I'd take a taxi if I went out alone."

"Okay, I'm asking as a friend, no blame—What caused you to take that risk?"

"That woman knew details from my husband's past that I didn't know. It wasn't right. How could I help him after Kenzie's malicious trick if I didn't have the full picture?"

Of all the days to pick to have it out with Vi. "How did Vi learn the story?"

"She used to clean for us. When the cards started coming—at Christmas, of all times—Phil says he didn't want to worry me. She stuck her nose in and asked. Pulled out his pain and hooked him on her herbal *remedies*"—her fingers carved air quotes—"to manage his tension. Tension he wouldn't have experienced without that girl's appalling behaviour."

"Didn't he tell you about the accident?"

Whitney twisted her arm to plump the pillow at her back. "Eventually—that part. Not about the baby—his daughter." Her eyes welled again. "He saved that for the town secret keeper."

"I never met Vi, but some people have a way of drawing out information we don't intend to reveal." What belonged in a therapist's tool kit could be highly unwelcome in a housekeeper.

"She was a snoop." Whitney's hand covered her heart. "I felt so betrayed—exposed—to see my husband exposed like that when she knew it all and I had nothing. Nothing—his own wife."

Her mouth firmed, curved down. Her chin set. "So I went to confront her. To find what I had a right to know. I couldn't ask Phil. He was devastated. Secrets separate. I couldn't lose him now—not when we're finally pregnant."

"How did Vi react?"

"She said I'd hear it from him or not at all. I wish Kenzie had never come."

Landon exhaled slowly. "Kenzie's had it rough too. Can you imagine finding out your father is not only not dead but is the guy you've sent hate notes to for years?"

"She's an impertinent brat. Now, I have to accept her because he does." Her arms curved around her belly. "We'll have our own children soon. He doesn't need her."

"Like—" Landon snapped her teeth together, lips pressing tight. Like Whitney didn't need Ciara, her own child from a different father? Her chest rose and fell in a desperate breath for calm. Whitney did need Ciara. Mother and daughter were working it out, and the babies made a surprising bond.

She grasped for words. "Like you said, it's old pain. They'll need to figure out their relationship. I'm sure it won't change his feelings for you and the twins."

Worst transition ever. Ignoring Whitney's narrow-eyed scrutiny, Landon bounced her knuckles on the chair's padded armrest. "Vi was alive when you left her. Did you see inside the house? Any sign she had another visitor? Or did she say she expected anyone?"

"I went in, and she, she—patronized me. Wouldn't listen to reason and told me to get out. I'm glad there wasn't anyone else there to witness the humiliation. And no, she didn't show me her day planner."

Eyes closed, Landon rubbed two fingertips up and down the middle of her forehead. "I'm sorry to focus on such a painful experience, Whitney. I'm trying to think of what the police might ask. You might have observed a clue and not known it. Anything that points to the killer points away from you."

"We don't have to tell them, right? We can wait for them to find the traffic report. If they don't, they'll never know I lied."

Landon shook her head. "I have to report this. Like I said, you may be able to provide a clue. Talking about it the first time is the hardest. Next time, you'll be calmer, and your subconscious may offer a key detail in response to a skilled questioner. Officer Zerkowsky truly is the best when we're scared."

"Has he ever interrogated you?"

"I had to tell him about Ciara being attacked. It triggered bad things from my past, and he talked me through. That's all they'll want to do with you—talk. Here where you feel most secure."

"Does Phil have to know?"

"I'm not sure. Why don't you phone the station tomorrow once he's gone to work? I'll give them a heads-up tonight."

The woman studied her manicure. "I shouldn't have called you."

"Whitney, the police know how to be discreet. They need everything we can give them to solve this murder, and that starts with the truth."

"They'll be angry."

"Probably. We still need to do the right thing."

Whitney swung her legs sideways and eased her feet to the floor. Standing produced a soft grunt. "Ciara didn't tell me you were so bossy."

"Thank you for trusting me." Landon replaced her chair and went to join her mother.

Freesia, Hope, Whitney. Who else had visited Vi that final day and kept silent to protect themselves?

Chapter 21

Wednesday

SUNRISE FOUND LANDON in the inn's kitchen. She doused the lights and carried her second cup of coffee through to the breakfast room windows to watch the new day creep across the water. Mid-size waves rolled heavy and sullen beneath thick grey clouds that foreshadowed the coming snow.

Amid too many bizarre dreams of clues and secrets, she'd spoken twice with Lacey.

Her sister may not have slept at all. Yet apart from those spikes of fear and Landon's reassurance, Lacey's talk raced on a current of excitement. Hope. Dreams and plans and possibilities. All that she'd been holding herself back from.

Hurdles loomed ahead, but Lacey's therapist had laid a good foundation. Landon's efforts to add a faith perspective had passed without comment. That was okay. They'd have time.

This morning, bleary-eyed and headachy, Landon balanced a quiet joy and a burden for her other sister. "God, You've given me so much, restored so much. Touch Leyna too. More for her than for us, but make our family as whole as we can be without Dad."

Her breath steamed the window, and she watched it clear.

Trouble was like that. It brought fog, but the fog didn't last. At least in terms of eternity. In the here and now, everything looked murky. One missing sister, one broken heart, and an elusive murderer without the decency to leave a single clue.

Dee's ex sounded good in theory, but Nigel had enough of his mother in him for uncanny insight. If he blamed a local, local it would be.

So, zero clues.

Just a blizzard they said was bulking up before it pounced. Nigel would have Christmas without closure. Dylan wouldn't find out what was going on with his father. With the roads buried under snow, the investigation would stall. While Landon kept getting one day closer to Bobby's departure.

A quiet rattle from the kitchen announced Anna's presence.

Landon shuffled to greet her friend. "Lacey says she'll come. I told her we'd pick her up around ten."

Anna's smile lit her countenance, sparkling in her eyes. "God answers prayer. Sometimes faster than others and often not the way we ask, but He answers."

They finished breakfast prep and settled Kenzie with a golden ham-and-cheese omelette with no sign of Dylan. Landon's text last night had said her news was non-urgent. No reply was no surprise, but she hadn't wanted to risk falling back asleep this morning and missing him. If Whitney called the station and they sent an angry Constable Ingerson, the confrontation could push the fragile pregnant woman over the edge.

Finally, an engine sounded outside. Instead of Dylan's tread on the deck, the front door chimed.

"Hello?" A timid voice.

Landon dodged around Anna into the hallway.

Freesia stood inside the entrance, a bushy fabric sunflower pinned in her hair today. She waved. "I hope it's not too early."

"No, we're serving breakfast. Would you like tea and a muffin?"

"No thanks." Her rounded eyes disagreed. "I'm on my way in to the shelter. I have information."

"About Vi?"

"Maybe. You know when they took my dogs it included the one I had from Dee? The one she was so heartless about?"

"Yes."

"They all went to the shelter where I have my community service. So I snooped in the records last night. That sweet beagle was adopted two days after he arrived." Freesia stared at the floor. "He wasn't in very good shape. I couldn't provide for them like they needed."

"It's good he found a home."

"Yes, but people don't take animals until they're healthy. The shelter doesn't like to let them go either. There's a note that he paid extra to clear the vet costs and signed a promise he'd get little Weasel all the care she needed."

"I don't understand. That's good, right?"

"He wrote his name as John Smith and his street address was for a cheap motel."

Landon pressed a finger into the bridge of her nose, then rubbed up and down her forehead. "Are you afraid he took the dog for something bad?"

"Dee's ex loved that dog. If he saw the news about my poor pups, what if he came back to get her? Or maybe never went far away?"

"Everyone was looking for him."

Freesia's mouth flattened. "Disguise is easy. Especially for a cheat."

Dee did say she'd seen him. He could change his appearance, but an ex-partner who knew him well would recognize his stance or the way he walked.

"I'll pass this on, Freesia. Good work. There's an outstanding warrant out for him. He could even be involved in Vi's death—if it's really him."

244

"I heard he's been lurking around. That's why I peeked at the records. It was risky, but I want to help. You mustn't let my supervisor know what I did. Tell the police to check up on the dog but let them find out about John Smith through the office."

Once Freesia left, Landon looped through the breakfast room to check on Kenzie. "Can I get you anything else?"

"I'm good, thanks. I am so going to miss Anna's cooking. I hope Phil puts me up here if I come again. Sharing a roof with Whitney would be tough. Plus, there'd be crying babies."

"You'll always be welcome. I'm glad you and Phil have connected. Not too many people get a father for Christmas."

Kenzie's mouth twisted. "Now, I have to tackle Mom."

"I pray God will give you wisdom in how to bring it up and help you two work it out."

"You think He cares about stuff like that?"

"I do. That doesn't mean it'll be easy." Landon removed the girl's empty plate and left Kenzie to linger over her coffee. "I'll pack up a couple of muffins for the road."

Last night, she'd told Kenzie about visiting Whitney and her sense the pregnant woman had told the truth about leaving Vi alive. Reassured that Phil wouldn't be dealing with his wife's arrest, the girl had decided to fly home. She'd arranged to meet him for one last lunch before heading to the airport.

As Landon dropped two plump carrot muffins into a paper to-go bag, her phone vibrated on the table.

A text from Dylan: *On my way. You awake today?*

If not awake, at least vertical. She sent him a thumbs-up.

Gwen had gone upstairs to get ready to pick up Lacey, still shaking her head at the girl's solo venture.

Landon snagged Anna's tea towel to finish cleanup. "I'd rather do this than process check out. Go do your thing."

By the time Dylan arrived, Kenzie had gone upstairs, and the kitchen was spotless. He tapped on the door and let himself in.

Anna called out a hello from her sitting room but didn't follow him to the kitchen.

Eyebrows asking the question, Landon waved a tall reindeer mug at him.

"Yes, please." He draped his coat over the back of a chair and sat at the table. "Sorry I didn't get to you last night. You said non-urgent, and we had a situation."

She filled the mug and set it in easy reach, then took the seat diagonal to him. Grey shadows underlined his slow-blinking eyes, and vertical lines bracketed his mouth. She touched his sleeve. "People have no idea how hard you all are pushing to solve this."

"We've hit nearly everyone on Nigel's list. Nothing." He slurped the dark brew. "What's up?"

"Mom took me to see Whitney last night."

His brow tightened. "Phil doesn't want her upset."

"She was already upset. She's going to phone the station this morning, but I told her I'd give you a heads-up. Can you send Zerkowsky again?"

When she finished the account, he scrubbed his palms over his cheeks, eyes closed. Then he cupped his mug and stared into the depths. "I don't peg her as a killer, but I hope she can give us something useful. Give me a minute to catch Zerkowsky."

"He has to wait for her call though. She doesn't want Phil knowing. Do I need to go too?"

"Would you? See if there's any difference in her story. Plus, she trusts you."

Lacey was coming this morning. She didn't need all three of them to pick her up, and she'd be here when Landon came home.

"Sure."

Dylan made a quick contact with Zerkowsky, then told her to expect a call. "Sorry to drag you out again."

"It's fine." Before she could tell him about her sister, he

needed to know about the shelter dog. She warned him to be careful not to implicate Freesia. "Her supervisor's the one to sign off on her court order compliance. She's already picked out a puppy. Any disciplinary action now could ruin the whole thing."

One side of his mouth tugged downward. "We'll check it out, but here's our situation from last night. We caught the lurker near Dee's place."

"Is this solved? And you're stringing me along?"

"Don't I wish. Get this. He was hired—he thought by the homeowner, Dee—as a private security guard. Five hundred dollars a night, details texted from a number that doesn't match hers. Instructions were to arrive on foot and find the cash stuffed in a can at the property's treeline. And to stay out of sight unless there was trouble. Dee had no idea."

"Could Nigel have hired him? Maybe he has a cell just for texting."

Dylan snorted. "Nigel would have picked an experienced hunter who wouldn't be spotted. And he'd have arranged it in person."

And he probably didn't have that kind of money. "Didn't the man you caught wonder why Dee didn't make contact directly?"

"The initial texts claim she doesn't want her daughter frightened by the need for someone on patrol after the murder across the street. This guy takes odd jobs on the side, and he says this is nowhere near the oddest."

Landon flattened her palm on the table, fingertips tapping. "So Nigel's right and Dee's ex isn't around."

"We'll check into the dog anyway. The ex could be on the fringes pulling strings. Someone is."

"Dee's sure it's him. Whoever it is, this fits the pattern of setting up other people as suspects. And who better than someone the whole town already blames for a previous crime? If you hadn't caught this guy before his assignments stopped, we might have believed her ex did return briefly."

Dylan carried his mug to the sink. "I need to hit the road. Unless you have any other tidbits for me."

"Kenzie's leaving today. And my middle sister's in town."

He shrugged into his coat. "Here I am, breaking up the reunion to send you with Zerkowsky."

"So bring us cinnamon buns later. I'll introduce you. Dylan, this is huge, but you don't have time to hear it right now. Go catch a killer."

He flashed a wry smile and headed for the door, then looked over his shoulder. "We could use a little divine insight on this one. If you and Anna could ask."

"Already on it."

~~~

With no role to play beyond moral support, Landon observed Zerkowsky's approach to a skittish witness. His calming demeanour and body language, the slow and gentle speech. The questions that drew out nuances and memories.

Sadly, none of Whitney's words provided a single clue. As she'd told Landon the night before, she'd arrived and left without seeing anything useful.

On the way back to the inn, Zerkowsky aimed for the positive. "At least we've narrowed down the time of death."

Unless Whitney had in fact killed Vi, which he agreed was unlikely. "She wouldn't be able to hold it together if she'd committed murder. Too highly strung."

He dropped Landon off, declining her invitation for coffee, and drove away "to rattle the bushes and see what I can shake loose."

Landon trudged along the slate path. This weighed on her as an amateur trying to help. How heavy must it be for the career investigators? Especially at Christmas when they wanted not only to bring closure but also to be with their loved ones?

Dylan and Zerkowsky both radiated strain and an underlying discouragement. She'd jumped in and done everything she could with nothing to show for it. There was no sign her prayers were helping either.

Anna met her at the door. "Lacey's upstairs asleep—I hope. Poor lamb was exhausted. Courage takes it out of you."

"She didn't sleep last night. I'll stay downstairs."

Landon hung up her coat and joined Anna and Gwen in the sitting room. Nestling into a corner of the couch, legs tucked beside her, she leaned an elbow into the armrest. "Nothing this morning except watching a pro at work. I feel so bad for Nigel."

She'd brought her burden into the room—when they needed to celebrate her sister's step toward healing. Shifting to sit straighter, she smiled at them both. A true smile, if not high energy. "Christmas Eve tomorrow. Did Lacey say what she'd like to do today?"

Gwen shrugged. "Rest and reconnect. If the snow holds off until late tomorrow like Roy says, we'll stay for the feast before leaving. I wish we had longer, but work needs me."

"You can always come again." Anna lowered the footrest on her recliner and stood. "Let's have a bite of lunch. Landon, if you're home for a while, your mom and I can hit the grocery store. I need more ingredients for tomorrow, and we told Lacey there'd be someone home when she woke up."

"Works for me." Landon yawned. "I might nap right here."

Instead, once they'd gone, she brewed a cup of apple spice tea and opened the *Christmas Carol* audiobook on her phone. She'd left off with the Ghost of Christmas Present.

Her phone's ringtone startled her from a half-doze. She'd have to rewind. "Hello?"

"Landon, it's Dee. Is Starr with you?"

Her feet hit the floor, and her spine stiffened. "She's missing?"

"Don't freak out—she left a note. She didn't say where she went. Then there's Nigel—"

"What about him?"

Dee's breath whooshed. "Nobody told you? He's in the

hospital, and they say it's bad. He was attacked and left for dead."

"No!" Landon sat hard, fingers pressed to trembling lips. She had to be quiet, not wake Lacey.

Not more pain for Nigel. Not more violence. "Starr—Dee, you're sure this person didn't hurt her too?"

"Positive. But she found him. Nigel. Why she went over, I don't know, but if he lives, it's because she found him in time."

Landon knuckled her forehead and tried to focus. "What happened?"

"I made a quick run to the store, but it's a zoo. When I came home, there were three cop cars at Nigel's, lights flashing. I ran over, and they told me Nigel was taken by ambulance to Bridgewater—unconscious."

Please, not another death. It must be an outsider after all. Locals would know Vi hadn't shared anything incriminating with her son.

Dee continued, "Constable Ingerson said Starr appeared fine after a long talk about it all and insisted on going home. Claimed I'd arrive any minute."

"They let her stay alone after a trauma like that?"

"You know how stubborn she gets. She promised to lock herself in and call me. Instead, she left me a note that she's safe with friends and doesn't want to talk to me."

Unease slithered in Landon's gut. "Did she write it herself?"

"Her regular sloppy handwriting. A bit jagged, but she added a frowny face. She wouldn't do that under duress." Dee expelled a sigh. "We had a major blowout. We both needed space, so I did the errands alone. How could I have known there'd be a crisis like this while I was gone?"

"Have you called her friends?"

"They'd lie for her. It's happened before. I thought if she'd gone to you, you might be able to make her listen to reason."

"She's not here. So what will you do? Wait for her to calm

down and get a ride home?"

"I have to find her. On top of the upset over Nigel, I took her coin. The one from Toby. If he came for it, I wanted her out of the equation."

"But the man they caught last night wasn't him."

"I didn't know that then."

"So she can have it back? It did seem to comfort her."

"With a strong-willed daughter like mine, consistency is key. If I reverse on one decision, she'll push for it on the next."

The phone buzzed a message alert. Landon ignored it. "Let me know when she's home safe? Or if you hear an update on Nigel? I'll see what I can find out on my end."

She finished the call and texted Dylan. *Heard about Nigel. Praying. Does Elva know? Text when you can.*

She opened the other message that had come in during Dee's call.

A text from Bobby. *Phone when you get this? Or come over.*

He picked up on the second ring. "Are you home?"

"Yes, but I have to stay. Mom and Anna went out, and Lacey's sleeping. I need to be here when she wakes up."

"We'll come to you. Starr's with us, but you can't tell Dee."

"She just called and she's frantic."

"Gramp says protect the most vulnerable. That's Starr. Did... Dee tell you about Nigel?"

"Yes. I'm waiting to hear from Dylan. Elva needs to know too. I was going to call her next."

She gathered her hair with her free hand and let it fall. "No wonder Starr's upset, but wouldn't her mother—"

"She refuses to go home. It's not all Nigel. There's more, but she won't open up to us. She might talk to you."

"Tell her I'll make hot chocolate." Landon ended the call.

Starr was angry enough at her mother to run away. Avoiding her friends so she couldn't be traced. How had the girl ended up at Roy's?

Dee may have been wrong to take her coin, but they'd have to convince Starr to go home. To an isolated house where the neighbours kept being attacked.

A sudden thought froze Landon in place halfway to the kitchen. Did Starr see a clue at Nigel's? Something she kept from the police out of spite toward Ingerson?

Chapter 22

WHEN ROY'S TRUCK rattled into the parking lot, Landon spooned hot chocolate powder into the steaming milk. By the time she'd whisked it smooth and dropped creamy truffles in to melt, the door opened from the deck.

Low conversation filled the entrance, along with the shuffle of winter coats and boots. Landon stuck her head around the corner and held a finger to her lips. "Starr, my sister's sleeping upstairs."

The girl's black curls bobbed. She kicked off her boots and used a crutch to nudge them onto the drip tray. Her eyes seemed huge in an unnaturally solemn face. No impish spark, no secret glee. Downturned mouth, downcast eyes... Finding her neighbour attacked was no experience for a child.

Landon bent to hug her, then took her coat to the closet while the men followed with their own. "Come into the kitchen for treats, and we can talk."

They gathered around the square pine tabletop with brimming mugs and a plate of Anna's frosted snowman cookies. Starr's mood seemed to weight them all.

Landon squeezed the girl's shoulder. "We're all concerned for Nigel. It's a good thing you went."

"I found him lying on the cold ground in his root cellar." Her mouth quivered, and she scowled her features into submission. "The kitchen door was bolted. So was the one outside. Even if he woke up, he'd be trapped. He could have frozen to death."

"Honey, it's okay to cry." Landon kept her arm around the trembling girl.

"I'm not going to cry. Not yet." One huge sniff, then another. A taste of hot chocolate that brought a quick flash of light to her eyes. "This is good."

Bobby and Roy added approving sounds.

Bobby bit the point off a snowflake. "You two don't know what you're missing."

Roy saluted with his mug while patting his stomach. "We had ice cream after I picked this young lady up. She knows what she wants, and let me tell you, she's not a cheap date. Sprinkles, nuts, all the mix-ins."

"No wonder you were gone so long." Bobby shot Landon a look she couldn't interpret. "I was on a call when Gramp shook the truck keys at me and took off. Starr and I've been playing video games waiting for you to come home."

"Did she beat you?"

"No. But she could if she tried."

Landon angled sideways in her chair and propped her heel on the chair rung. "Starr, why did you contact Roy?"

The girl raised her mug in both hands and drank in silence.

"Told me she was scared. When I got there and saw the police presence, I was scared too."

A thick line of frothy chocolate coated Starr's upper lip. Landon hid a smile. "Your mom's worried about you. I know you're mad at her, but she's upset all this happened while you were alone."

"I wrote a note that I'm safe. You can't tell her I'm here."

A rebellious child suddenly afraid of her parent... "Did you do something for payback for your mom taking Toby's coin? Do you think you're in trouble?"

The girl scowled again, fiercer than before. The remaining chocolate in her mug should have boiled. She tugged a battered coil notebook from her hoodie's kangaroo pocket. Clutched it before plopping it on the table next to Landon.

Landon let out a soft puff of air. Always give the written stuff to the dyslexic. She could process it, but her brain felt like rubber after the past few days.

Inside, rows of cramped but tidy writing—names, sentences, dates.

She passed it to Bobby, but her gaze held Starr's. "Is this what I think it is?"

The dark curls bobbed again. "Miz Vi's orders. And maybe journal."

"And you found it...?"

A single tear cracked Starr's iron control. "Mom had them. This is the newest." The frown reappeared full force. "I know her hiding places. When she went out today, I took back my coin. And I found the books. She shouldn't have them."

Roy's sea-blue eyes glistened. His wide jaw bulged, thinning his lips. Bobby's nostrils flared, his head making a tiny side-to-side negative. They must see similar horror in her expression.

Landon took a deep breath and waited for one of the men to say what she was thinking.

Roy cleared his throat. "There could be a valid explanation for this."

"I have to give it to the police, don't I? And tell them where I found it."

The resolution in the girl's voice tore Landon's heart. She reached for Starr. "You won't be alone, and Roy's right. It doesn't mean your mom hurt Vi, but we have to be sure."

"Will you call for me? Don't say where I found it." She sniffed. "Not yet."

The station dispatcher promised to send an officer to interview Starr and collect the notebook.

Roy wiggled his chair away from the table. "While we're waiting, this old body needs a softer seat. Like one of Anna's recliners." He tugged at Starr's curls. "Did I ever tell you it was a squirrel attack that busted my leg and sent me to your mom for physio? Without that squirrel, I'd have never met you."

"Squirrels don't attack people."

"Mama squirrels do when they think a human's after their babies. Jumped on my head and dug in her claws. Startled me so bad, I fell off the ladder."

With the barest squeak of a giggle, she stood and fitted her arms into the cuffs of her crutches.

In Anna's sitting room, the lights twinkled on the Christmas tree. Starr ignored it. Roy pointed her to one of the teal recliners, but she pulled Landon toward the couch. When they sat, she pressed in close.

Landon draped an arm around her waist, increasing the contact. Through the hoodie, it was like hugging a statue.

Bobby dropped into the empty recliner but didn't push back. "The notebook is evidence, but where's the motive? Aside from everyone having secrets, what could Dee have against Vi?"

Roy's fingers rasped against his brush cut. "She could have found it and be covering for a friend. Or for blackmail. Bad either way, but nowhere near as bad as the alternative."

"You and Vi spent a lot of time together." Landon cuddled Starr nearer. "Did she and your mom ever argue?"

"Only about me and Toby. I missed him so much. Miz Vi said I should keep going to the well like Weasel did before she died. Toby and I used to hang out there after dark to watch the stars and make up stories—he told the best stories."

She sniffed. "It helped me feel better. But Mom didn't like it. The day Miz Vi died, the three of us were talking out front, and she told Mom to stop glaring at the well and let it go. She was always saying things like that. Sharp bits of advice. Like a cranky granny who loved us. Mom used to get so mad. She'd take off for a run or long walk to let the steam out. Then they'd be friends again."

A line appeared between Bobby's brows. "Did she take off

that day? Didn't you say she'd been out when you saw the car leave Vi's?"

Landon held in a gasp, feeling the girl tremble at her side. Dee had been out, and Dee knew the back trail to the Foley home. She stared at Bobby, silently pleading for him to be wrong.

"She did." Starr's hands clenched into fists. "It was nothing new, no big fight. Miz Vi knew Mom dumped all Toby's stuff down before she filled it in."

Bobby had gone statue-still. No jaw-stroking supervillain pose, no hair-mashing like when he wrestled with his thoughts. Instead, a waxy pale and that deepening line in his forehead—matched now with a strained set to his lips.

"Had Vi mentioned the well to her before?" His gaze locked on Landon, his blue-grey eyes intense, desperate to communicate. Words he couldn't say in front of Starr?

Landon stared back helplessly.

"She said we'd better not." Starr crossed her arms, clamped her fists tight to her ribs. "You know something. You're shutting me out like I'm a child."

"Except you are. Smart and brave, but a child." Bobby's fingers thrust into his hair, tugging it into a thatched mess. "Involved in something that's over all our heads."

The front door chimed.

"Hello? Landon, are you here?"

Dee.

Landon gasped. Starr's arms circled her like a tight belt. She peeled them free. "Starr, let me go meet her. The guys will hide you."

Roy had already reached the window. He hauled the vertical blinds wide and thrust it open. "Bobby, take her and run. Elva's place. Cops might already be there about Nigel. I'll call 9-1-1."

"Gramp—"

His anguish stopped Landon at the door.

"I know, boy. Go. My leg can't take the drop."

The jump from Anna's ground-floor window to the frozen ground would jolt a younger person but not harm them. Picturing Roy folding himself through the window gave Landon a brief snicker amid the panic.

Dee called out again, louder.

Bobby hurtled through the window. As Roy lowered Starr out, Landon stepped into the hallway.

She shut the door behind her.

"Did you find Starr?" Get the first word in. Play innocent.

Dee approached, and Landon hurried to meet her in the hall. Blocking the way to the sitting room but glad Dee had left the stairwell base—with its access to Lacey.

The woman's body language held no threat. No visible weapons, just a light purse dangling from her shoulder. Arms free, hands peeling out of black leather gloves she stuffed into her coat pockets. Tension around her eyes and an uncertainty to her mouth, but any mother would have those if her child had run off.

"I came to see if she'd called. When I saw Roy's truck outside, I hoped—she'd been snooping in my files. She could have found his number. He might have brought her."

"Roy's waiting for Anna." No lie. He wouldn't leave now. "Starr's not here."

The afghan they'd grabbed from the couch wouldn't be much protection for her against the cold. And Bobby ran in his socks. Elva and Hope would take them in—if they were home. The thought undercut Landon's confidence. If not, Bobby had his phone and the common sense to use it. A hero always found a way.

She studied Dee. The picture of a concerned, if exasperated, mom. Surely, they were wrong. They had to be. Yet Landon's body remained on high alert. "Did you have to go after her before, or did she come home on her own?"

"Her friends' parents bring her once they find out she's run away. It's no comfort to me in the waiting." Dee's nostrils flared. "Starr presents well to outsiders, but she has a volatile imagination. When she's angry, you have no idea the stories she'll tell. Right now, with Nigel's injury on top of Vi's death, she could say anything—about anyone. I need to see about stronger medication."

The wildest imagination or mental illness couldn't conjure a notebook out of thin air. Unless the girl had hidden it all along, for a reason that made sense in her head, and brought it out now to punish her mother for taking the coin?

No. Starr's physical reactions confirmed she believed what she'd said. Maybe a type of paranoia could have set this up, but there'd be other signs. Everything else the girl said made sense—other than her refusal to believe Toby had taken their money and run.

"She's highly strung for sure. Is that why she can't let go of your ex?"

Pinch-lipped, Dee rolled her eyes. "She followed him around like a dog."

Like his dog that returned to the well. Where Vi found the coin. The one Toby wouldn't leave behind. The well Vi told Starr was a connecting point. And told Dee to stop glaring at.

A current zapped from the back of Landon's neck to her core. Tremors rocked her stomach.

If Dee killed Vi... then Dee had killed her ex. Buried him in the well. And discovered Vi knew. This must be what Bobby realized in the sitting room. What he hadn't wanted Starr to know.

Molars ground together, Landon tried to anchor in the here and now. To keep her features calm. To see this woman as a frustrated mother—not a killer standing within reach.

Where were the police? Roy would have warned against sirens.

They couldn't use the rear entrance without being seen. The front door, solid with glass panels to one side, would cover their approach. Then what? How to get in without spooking the suspect? Were they waiting for her to leave?

Landon scuffed one foot against the pale floorboards. Looked past Dee. Eye contact right now was impossible. "I'd offer you tea, but maybe you should go home. You'll want to be there when she arrives."

"Landon?" Behind Dee, Lacey appeared at the foot of the stairs, sleep-rumpled and cautious. A thin grey cardigan hung loose over her fleece pyjamas. "Is everything okay?"

Fear arced from Landon's stomach to her lungs. Her indrawn breath hissed.

Dee must have heard. Must see the blood drain to leave her cheeks chalk white.

Blanking her expression, Landon locked the emotions away. Stood taller. Mustered a smile.

"Lacey, you startled me." She pushed on before the others could speak. "This is Dee. She's on her way out. Dee, meet my sister."

Why couldn't Lacey have stayed upstairs? The door chime or their voices must have wakened her.

Dee angled sideways, her back to the wall. "My daughter's missing. You haven't heard a child? She could have tricked Landon and be hiding."

Lacey sucked in a gasp. She retreated onto the stairs, visibly trembling, and clutched the railing. If she registered Landon's quick headshake, she ignored it. "Then it wasn't a dream. I saw—I saw a man running into the woods. Carrying a child in a blanket." Tears tracked down her cheeks.

Red splotches formed high in Dee's cheeks. "An old man? White hair?"

Eyes wide, Lacey shook her head.

"Then Bobby's in on it too. You're playing her game. Whatever she said is a lie. She needs help. She needs her mother." Lips pressed tight, Dee blinked away tears. "I should never have trusted you near my child. Starr is my life. My career—I went into physio training to help her after the accident. She's all I have."

She twisted her purse strap, her narrowed eyes glinting.

"Where is she?"

"They were going to Elva's. You can find her there." If the police weren't waiting on the other side of the front door, another 9-1-1 call would let them head her off. Protect Starr and everyone else.

Landon moved nearer, urging Dee toward the entrance.

The woman sidestepped. Hooked an arm around Landon's throat, arcing her backward. Dee's other hand pricked a sharp blade to her spine.

The pain brought a gasp and a fury that erased all Dylan's self-defence coaching. Dimly, she realized struggling would get her stabbed.

"Not a sound. From either of you." Dee's voice hissed in her ear. "We'll go together. Exchange you both for Starr. She has to come with me."

Lacey's stricken face, her frightened whimper—Roy wouldn't hear. If he did, he couldn't help.

The knife point twisted against Landon's back. Beside her spine, below her ribs. Aimed at something vital.

Dee had the strength and desperation to push it home. She'd still have a hostage. Unless Lacey escaped.

Landon strained to swallow against the pressure squeezing her larynx. Choking on saliva, her body arced.

The knife bit deeper.

Dee loosened her hold, allowing shallow breaths. "Don't even think about calling for Roy. A bleeding hostage will work even better. I want my daughter."

Warmth trickled from the burning cut. Landon grit her teeth. "You only need one of us. Leave my sister here and let's go."

"Nice try. I'm taking you both. Now, move."

Landon made eye contact with her sister. Walked steadily toward the door. "Lacey, it'll be okay. I'm living proof, remember?"

Lacey was crying now, silent tears that shook her shoulders. Her fists stretched the pockets of her thin cardigan.

As Landon reached for the door handle, an ear-splitting electronic wail shattered the space.

The sound bounced off the walls. Dee's hold wavered.

Landon shut her eyes. Remembered Dylan's calm instruction in her ear, his breath on her cheek. Twisted to the side and down like they'd practised.

She broke free, spun, and tackled Dee to the floor. The knife skidded across the hardwood.

The front door burst open. Uniformed officers poured in.

Roy's feet pounded up the hall. The old man skidded to a stop.

Writhing and screaming, Dee nearly bucked Landon off in a desperate lunge for the knife.

Landon kicked it out of reach and moved aside for the officers. Panting, she scrambled to her feet.

Constable Ingerson pinned the struggling woman's shoulders to the floor while Dylan cuffed her nearer wrist. Together, the officers rolled her onto her side to bind her hands behind her.

At the metallic clicks, Dee wilted. Hollow-cheeked, she speared Landon with a tear-glazed stare. "Miss Know-It-All Girl Detective. You didn't solve this. Starr did. It's your fault I'm losing her."

Dylan glanced up from where he knelt at Dee's side, dark eyes warm but strain lines cramping his smile. "Well done. You okay?"

"Looks like blood on the back of her sweater." Roy squeezed her arm through the sleeve. "Girl, that was too close."

Leaving Dylan to haul the sobbing Dee to her feet, Ingerson approached Landon. "Step around the corner and let me see."

Landon scanned the crowded space and found her sister, partially hidden behind Zerkowsky. Who knew the girl's fear meant she'd carry a panic alarm? She must have stuck it in her pocket before coming downstairs. Or did she keep it on her all the time?

"Lacey, you're amazing. Perfect timing on that alarm."

Lacey's skin tone resembled an old sheet. She flashed a shaky thumbs-up.

Following Ingerson into the breakfast room let Landon see the police vehicles lining the drive. "If Anna and Mom come home to this, they'll panic."

"Dispatch says Roy already notified them. There's an ambulance on the way, but let me see your wound."

Landon lifted the hem of her sweater. The motion brought a twinge of pain.

"The EMTs will want to check, but it's not deep." Ingerson folded up a paper napkin from the nearest table and pressed it into Landon's palm. "This will do for now. Unless you have a first aid kit at hand."

The wound stung. "In the kitchen. This way."

Ingerson's touch taping the gauze in place didn't ease the frost between them. She'd be blaming Landon for interfering. Again.

Landon twisted her hair into a rope and released it with a sigh. "This wasn't my idea. We called about Vi's book before Dee came."

"If the child had simply taken the evidence to our team at the Foleys' or called from home, none of this would have happened."

"Agreed. Unless her mother caught her with the book." Landon drew her sweater into place around her hips and turned to Ingerson. "But you wouldn't know about the body in the well."

The officer went rigid, her features sharp. "Tell me now."

"Bobby figured it out too. He couldn't say anything in front of Starr. We think Dee's ex didn't leave town. If she's capable of killing Vi, she's more than capable of killing the man who cleaned out her daughter's trust account."

As Landon ran through the list of clues, the disbelief faded from Ingerson's stance. "We'll add this to our conversation when we book her."

Dylan had cleared Dee from the hallway. Ingerson followed him out.

Landon introduced Lacey to Zerkowsky before hugging her close.

Dry-eyed, Lacey trembled non-stop. Yet she stood tall and didn't collapse in the embrace. "I survived. Something terrifying happened, and I survived."

"More than that. You saved the day. It'll have an effect—for both of us. But we can rebuild."

Zerkowsky clapped them both on the shoulders, his large hands firm. "Give yourselves plenty of downtime and a healthy dose of Anna's comfort food. We'll follow up with you. See what official resources you may need."

He moved toward the door. "Ambulance is here. Once everyone else clears out, Constable Price will bring Starr and Bobby for their coats and boots. Your co-sleuth is one agitated man. Starr wouldn't let go of him to come back. We've already radioed that the situation's secure."

Roy coughed. "I texted him and Anna both. Didn't dare show myself earlier in case Dee felt threatened, but I kept my ear to the door and a line open to 9-1-1 dispatch. They fed everything through to the squad at the front."

Landon bundled him into a hug. She kissed his leathery cheek. "Thank you."

When she let go, he rubbed the spot, his eyes damp. "We could've lost you. Again."

After a soft-spoken EMT cleaned and dressed Landon's cut in the downstairs powder room, they emerged to find Dylan standing at the base of the stairs with Lacey and Roy.

He stepped in front of Landon, searching her eyes. "You okay for a debrief?"

Tipping her chin, she pulled a deep breath. The sooner they walked through everything, the clearer the memory. The sooner she and Lacey—and the others—could begin to put the experience behind them.

She set her shoulders and tried to control the tremors in her chest. "Lacey, Roy, let's do this while it's fresh. Dylan? Cookies and tea? Comfort food—Zerkowsky's orders."

He allowed a crooked grin. "Coffee for the cop, for Pete's sake. It's been a bear of a day. You civilians have no idea what it does to us when you get in the middle of events."

Roy grunted. "It was no picnic on this side either, sonny."

Dylan led the old man toward the common room. "Let's get started. You're tough enough to handle me without my caffeine."

Lacey held Landon's hand on the way to the kitchen. She might have her colour back, but her wide eyes held trouble.

Landon squeezed her fingers before releasing. "It's over now. We can get through the rest."

Waiting for the water to boil, she sent Bobby a quick text to prove she was alive and well. *Hey, hero. Travers would be proud. We're giving statements. See you soon?*

Knowing Bobby, rather than thinking of the girl he rescued, he'd be beating himself up for running from danger.

As she poured boiling water on the tea, the back door slammed. A hollow-eyed Gwen raced to clutch her daughters, stroking their hair, speaking in broken whispers. "Roy promised you were safe. The police didn't want us here until they'd taken her away."

Behind her, Anna explained they'd been in a long check-out line in one of Bridgewater's bigger grocery stores.

The scent of coffee tickled Landon's nose, but caffeine was the last thing she needed on top of adrenaline. She slipped from Gwen's embrace. "Dylan's taking Roy's statement now, and I promised them drinks. We'll tell you everything once he says we can."

Anna's smile wobbled. "In the meantime, perishable groceries need refrigeration. We may have bought enough for the whole neighbourhood. I'll start bringing them in."

With a shuddering sigh, Gwen released Lacey. It must be

killing her not to ask questions. Instead, she stared into Lacey's eyes, then across the room at Landon. Then she followed Anna outside.

After carrying two steaming mugs to the men, Landon sat with Lacey in the breakfast room. Dylan called her sister first. Then it was her turn to tell her story in the common room. The sharp evergreen scent and festive decorations clashed with memories of the day's events and worry for Nigel and Starr.

She answered all his questions, then asked one of her own. "Did Ingerson tell you about the body in the well? It's the only thing that makes sense. Why Dee would suddenly kill Vi."

"So you think Vi knew all along."

"And kept the secret for Starr's sake." The woman had reported Freesia to protect innocent lives. She could well have seen silence as the best protection for the child. "If Vi hadn't told Dee to stop glaring at the well, she'd still be alive."

Dylan rubbed his eyes. "Tough break for the kid. And at Christmas."

"Any word on Nigel?"

"Hold that thought. The others will want to know too. Are we done here?"

"I am."

He excused himself from the room and returned with Lacey and Roy. "Anna said to catch her and your mother up later as long as Nigel's going to be okay. They're elbow-deep in food prep out there. I hope you're hungry." He gave Lacey the background, then said, "Nigel hasn't yet regained consciousness. We're hoping he can identify his attacker. My guess is Dee, but why now?"

Landon pressed her palms against the sides of her head, cradling her crowded brain. "I told her he knew from Vi that Toby couldn't return. We thought it was because of Vi's influence. We didn't know he was dead."

"When?" Dylan scratched a note in his book.

"Yesterday." She caught her lower lip between her teeth. "I sent her after him. Until then, she believed Vi's secrets died with her."

Standing beside the Christmas tree, Roy slapped his thigh. "None of that. You may have given her the information, but you did not send her."

"Yes, Gramp."

The old man let out a hoot. "She called me Gramp. In the presence of witnesses. It's official."

Lacey squinted at him. "What's official?"

"Been trying to adopt this young lady for months now, and she's finally given in."

"If you'd ever asked, I'd have said yes sooner." Fists on hips, Landon shot him a mock glare. "I adopted you. I got tired of waiting."

His eyelid dropped in a slow wink. "Welcome to the family."

Dylan shut his notebook and tapped his pen on the cover. "Starr's grandparents are flying in ASAP. Until then we need a safe place for her. We'd like to avoid placing her with Social Services over Christmas. Poor kid's been through too much already."

"You know what Anna will say. Kenzie's room's vacant. If the stairs are too much, we'll work it out."

"I'll talk to her before heading out to get started on my reports. And I'll give Price the all-clear to bring Bobby and Starr for their belongings." Dylan held out his hand to Lacey. "It's a pleasure to meet you. I hope we'll see you again when you can enjoy the best of Lunenburg."

After a quick handshake, he strode into the hallway.

Landon grinned. "He said the same thing to me when we met—over another crime. Really, Lace, it's usually safe and quiet."

Lacey huddled deeper into her cardigan, pulling the sleeves down over her hands. "This has been awful but kind of okay. I need to talk to my counsellor."

Barely three minutes later, another police cruiser arrived. Roy snorted. "If they weren't sitting in the car waiting for the call, they were at Elva's front door."

The car behind it stopped Landon's breath. Choking on a cough, she dodged the Christmas tree for a clearer view.

A compact cobalt-blue Kia. Her eyes misted. "Roy, it's Elva. It has to be. With Hope."

He stepped behind her. "By gum, it is. Now, who's this Roy fella? Did you forget your old Gramp so quickly?"

She smiled. "Never. Lacey, Elva's the neighbour they ran to. She had a bad experience here in her teens, and she refused to set foot on the property since. This is huge. Huge like you coming to Lunenburg."

Roy tapped her arm. "Best you don't mention it. She won't."

"I know. But she's here. For a terrible day, good's been happening."

"Talk to my grandson, girlie."

"I will. To thank him for rescuing Starr."

Roy's exhale told her what he didn't bother to say. He shuffled toward the door to greet the women.

As expected, Elva entered the inn as if she'd been a frequent guest. She drew Landon into a stiff hug and hissed, "Hope insisted on coming. It was this or give her a clue about her paternal line."

Landon kept a light touch on the woman's arms, meeting her unsmiling eyes. "This is healing. Well done."

When they eased back into the knot of people in the entrance, Landon introduced Lacey.

Bobby and Starr rushed along the hall from the rear, Starr's crutches thumping on the hardwood. She wore the sitting room afghan draped around her shoulders.

Sorrow etched the girl's face, yet she soldiered through the adults to Landon. She pressed her curly head against Landon's side. "I'm glad you're okay."

268

Landon slipped her arm around the thin shoulders. "I'm so sorry, Starr. I wish things worked out different. Your friends are here for you."

Were they? For how long? Her grandparents would take her to a new home in another province. She'd have to start over. Yet staying here would mean living where everyone knew her mother's crimes.

Spotting Bobby on the edge of the group, Landon flashed a quick salute.

A slow smile spread his lips.

Anna called out from the breakfast room. "Impromptu celebration. Everyone, come find a seat."

Bobby maintained eye contact. Eyebrows up, he inclined his head toward the common room.

Landon faded back and allowed the others to move across the hall. "Your feet okay after the frozen ground?"

"After facing down a killer, that's on your mind? What about you?"

"What about Starr? And Dee."

Gaze tracing her features as if he needed visual proof she was okay, he jammed his fingers through his hair. Then stuck his hands in his pockets and looked away. "I won't keep you from the others. Can we talk soon? That call I was on when Gramp took off to get Starr—I decided to go."

Landon spun toward the tree, reaching to finger a polar bear ornament in a Santa hat. Trying to work moisture into her mouth to speak.

"When do you leave?" She kept her focus on the ornament.

"After New Year's."

Emotions locked behind a bland facade, she studied the little bear—somehow disconnected from the tree and lying in her palm. "I can't do this. Not today."

"Neither can I." His breath whooshed out in a faint whistle. "Thank God you're all right. Nigel will be too. But I'll be a mess until I know you understand."

"It doesn't matter how I feel about it. I support your decision."

"It matters to me." He moved toward the door. "Travers would say it's an integrity issue. Plus, I'd like to be able to share my excitement with a friend. Gramp knows, but I didn't tell Mom and Dad in case it falls through."

Landon hooked the ornament back on the tree. Friends. Even long distance. She'd follow his example and fight for that friendship—listen to his plans very soon—even if her heart bled out.

Chapter 23

Thursday

L AUGHTER AND CONVERSATION, flickering candles, and the mingled savoury scents of a turkey dinner shaped an atmosphere of home. Family. Even though few of them shared blood ties.

Landon surveyed the people gathered in the inn's breakfast room. Roy and Bobby. Anna. Gwen and Lacey. Elva and Hope. Starr waiting for her grandparents' arrival. Anna's neighbouring friends the Dyers—Blaine and Tricia and their teen grandson, Quinn, his surly expression triple-strength. Freesia had chosen to stay with her furry friends at the shelter, but she'd assured Anna she'd spend Christmas with her parents—not alone in her isolated trailer in the middle of a blizzard.

Rather than the standard four small groupings, they'd shoved the tables together to seat everyone around one large square. It made talking across the table difficult, and they'd already had more than one laughing shout to pass the salt.

It felt good to be one big, mostly happy family at Christmas.

Anna had risen before dawn to wrestle a huge turkey into the oven. The inn's occupants, Starr included, had spent the morning preparing for this feast. Christmas Eve dinner at noon, so the travellers could get home before the impending storm. Dylan was already gone, relieved he'd be able to see his father for the holiday after all.

When he'd phoned to say goodbye, he shared the basics of Dee's confession. As they thought, she'd killed Vi and tried to kill Nigel to cover up Toby's death. She'd hired the lurker after all, to convince the police of her ex's return so Toby would be blamed. The day she'd discovered the missing funds, she confronted Toby at home. He was woozy with migraine meds but packing to leave. When he laughed about emptying her child's trust fund, she snapped. Then he was dead, and she had no way to recover the money—only a burden she couldn't risk sharing.

More details would come out over time. For now, Landon relished the chance to focus on the present—and her friends and family here at the inn.

With soft Christmas carols in the background and plates heaped with all the trimmings, Anna had crafted a safe haven after yesterday's drama. Starr's presence in their midst deterred everyone from discussing Dee's crimes.

Along with celebrating the season—and the Saviour who came into a lost, struggling world to bring light and hope—the unspoken goal was to keep Starr from dwelling on her shattered life.

They'd kept her at the inn last night. The girl insisted on sharing Landon's room and declared the aged-honey four-poster bed worthy of a princess. When Starr finally fell asleep, Landon lay holding her for hours. Praying and rocking her whenever the whimpers started.

The one spot of joy this morning came from Constable Zerkowsky, who'd tracked down the man who adopted Weasel. When they surprised Starr with a visit, her reaction moved everyone to tears—even the grizzled beagle owner.

Pale and subdued, the girl sat now between Roy and Bobby and picked at her food. Respecting her sorrow didn't keep Roy from the odd anecdote. Occasionally she rewarded him with a sad smile.

She kept angling to see out the window. "No snow yet."

Roy squeezed her shoulder. "Your grandparents will be here in time."

Beside Landon, Gwen scooped mashed potato from the serving bowl. "I'm counting on you, Roy. According to the weather guy, Lacey and I should have left hours ago."

"Ha. Storm's coming up from Boston, and the worst won't hit till tonight. You'll be snug in bed at home before it starts."

Hope tented her white linen napkin like a mountain peak. "Everyone wants a white Christmas unless they're travelling."

"White, yes, but this is shaping up to be a major dump." Roy chuckled. "I'll don my Santa hat before heading out in the morning. Quinn and Bobby, it's all hands on deck. Up at five if you want to open any presents before we start on the driveways."

Quinn lifted a bony shoulder. "If it's bad like they say, the road won't be done. You'll have to plow yourself a lane to reach me."

"Then I'll expect to see your steps and walkway already clear. And you waiting with a flask of hot coffee." He winked at the teen. "No slacking at Christmas. You never know who might show up."

"Taskmaster." Bobby elbowed his grandfather. "I was hoping the snow'd hold off until I was gone."

Hope glanced along the table at him. "Heading south for some sun?"

Landon cut a piece of turkey she couldn't taste. So few days before Bobby left. Grief turned the hours to ash.

"South-ish. To the US for meetings. Book stuff."

Landon froze. Reminded herself to chew and swallow. Found the words she wanted.

Before she could speak, Anna asked, "How long are you gone?"

"Two weeks, tops. If the weather's good, I'll fly to Ontario afterwards, see my parents, then drive my winter car home. Stop ride-sharing with Gramp."

"You're still on for plow duty." Roy's blue gaze shifted to Landon. He raised a lazy white eyebrow.

Landon focused on her plate. Meetings. Book stuff. He was coming back.

Her food had flavour again. Cranberry sauce. Gravy. Everything. The hope dancing in her stomach didn't leave much room for it.

Around her, the conversations flowed on. Inside, she considered. Imagined.

How to speak privately? His trip. He wanted to explain his decision.

Finally, after second helpings for some and dessert for most, Anna portioned out the leftovers into cardboard take-away boxes and set the dishwasher running. Most guests drifted for the door with suspicious mutterings about the scattered snowflakes already falling.

Elva claimed a box for Nigel, who'd regained consciousness but remained under observation in the hospital. "Hope asked me to spend the holiday in the city with her family, but Nigel has nobody now."

After he'd guarded Elva's hospital room this summer, she probably saw this as a chance to repay his care. Plus, springing herself on Hope's husband and teen kids for Christmas might feel awkward.

Gwen's suitcase stood at the front door with Lacey's backpack. She had to be on duty at the care facility tomorrow morning—snow or no snow. Roy had lent her a pair of snowshoes in case she needed to walk the few blocks from her house.

She pulled Landon into a quick hug and retreated, eyes damp. "See you soon?"

Landon reached for Lacey. "You two drive safe. Text me when you get home?"

The five-and-a-half-hour trip meant they'd cover the last

stretch after dark. Hopefully, any wildlife would be finding shelter ahead of the storm, not wandering onto the highway.

"I wish you could have stayed for Christmas." Landon hugged them each again. "We barely started rebuilding."

Gwen blinked away a tear. Her lips firmed into a smile. "But we did start. I'm trusting you and Anna to pray for our wandering one."

With everyone else gone, Landon, Anna, and Roy scrubbed the pots and roaster pans. Bobby distracted Starr with a video game until her grandparents arrived.

The travel-rumpled couple had caught a dawn flight, claimed one of the last car rentals at the airport, and raced the storm to get here. Less than twenty-four hours after being informed of the charges against their daughter, they bore tight grief lines at their mouths and a dull glaze in their eyes. As one, they swooped to gather Starr in a lingering embrace, like twin brooding hens bent on sheltering her forever.

The way her fingers clutched their coats eased Landon's concern. Starr loved these people and trusted them. She'd be in good hands.

Straightening, Starr's grandfather made eye contact with each adult. He stared longest at Bobby, who'd carried the girl to safety. Dee wouldn't have harmed her daughter—not when protective love drove her. But she could have taken her and fled, increasing Starr's trauma and everyone's panic. Anything might have happened.

The grandfather shook each one's hand. "Thank you is inadequate, but it's all I have. We'll never forget your kindness to our Starr-light."

His wife held Starr close to her side. The girl leaned into the embrace, her eyes closed.

This wasn't goodbye. They'd be staying at Dee's until the investigators finished processing with Starr—and until everyone dug out from the looming blizzard.

The weight of their sorrow was a tangible force. A child

cut off from her mother. Parents from their daughter.

Landon swallowed hard. She knew about loss. Betrayal. But not like this.

Crying, Starr hugged each one before following her grandparents out into the falling snow.

They all stood in the doorway, waving, until the car drove out of sight. A damp chill curled around their ankles.

As Anna shut the door, her shoulders lifted and fell with an audible sigh. "I hope they'll be all right."

With a clumsy pat on her back, Roy shepherded her toward the rear of the inn. "God's got this. You need to sit after slaving to feed an army."

Landon's pulse quickened. Heavy-hearted or not, this was her chance. She stepped closer to Bobby. "Want to walk off the turkey? Tell me about your opportunity?"

A corner of his mouth lifted. "Sure."

Bundled against the cold, they strolled toward the mixed forest behind the inn. Fat snowflakes drifted down, already thicker than before. The slow, silent descent carried a hush. Like the whole world was waiting for the storm. Or for this conversation.

The evergreens trapped some of the snow, but not the leaf-bare hardwoods. Walking among the trees with Bobby, Landon held out her palm to catch a fluffy flake. The white melted against the red fleece.

She reached for another. "What Roy said that night—I thought you were taking a job somewhere."

"And break up our sleuthing act? You're not getting rid of me that easily."

He picked up a fallen branch and tapped it against the grey trunks they passed. Swished it through any low-limbed evergreens. "It's Travers. A screenwriter contacted my agent, and this guy sounds like he actually gets the characters. Like he could translate the books to screen without ruining or reinterpreting everything."

"And...?"

"And what?"

"You were concerned I'd—I don't know—disapprove?"

His stick clattered against a smooth, thick trunk and broke. "I'd just told you Travers would never go to Hollywood. He may not anyway, for a number of reasons, but am I selling out to consider it?"

"What does it cost you to talk? A plane ticket? Bobby, you care about Travers like he was real. You won't sell him out."

His exhale formed a big cloud of steam. "That's how I feel, but I don't want you to think I can't keep my word."

They'd wandered to the property line. Beyond, the trees grew closer, underbrush crowding the space between. Angling left, they continued to walk, boots occasionally scuffing a pine cone or snapping a stick. The frozen ground silenced their footsteps.

Lacy snowflakes filtered through the tall trees. Landon glanced skyward, and one landed on her cheek. A cool watery kiss for luck.

She drew in a lungful of winter-flavoured air. "About keeping your word. And things that change."

Several paces later, he asked, "You going to finish that?"

"You said if my feelings changed to let you know." Her heartbeat pounded in her throat. "I—" She couldn't say it. "You made a promise. I release you. Like in *A Christmas Carol*."

"You want me to go. Because of the tattoo incident. I torpedoed our friendship." He kicked a tree trunk. "I am such an idiot."

Or she was. Release from a promise, yes, but for Scrooge, that meant a broken engagement. She'd botched her attempt at a hint.

"Bobby..." Could he hear her angst?

She stopped. Clapped her mitts over her cheeks. Gulped more air. "Did you promise to stay?"

"No. I promised..."

His face contorted, brow puckered and eyes pinched, a

storm of mental effort.

Then his features smoothed, the tension ebbing and a soft glow lighting his eyes. He swept an invisible hat from his head and flowed into a low bow worthy of Dickens himself. "Lady, may I speak my heart?"

A sweet thrill chased through Landon's chest. "Speak, sir."

Bobby took her mittened hands in his. Raising them to waist height, he stepped nearer. Opened his mouth, then shut it again with a chuckle and a shake of his head. "The writer is at loss for words."

He drew a deep breath. "Here goes. When I look at you, I see a beautiful woman of God, strong and loyal and willing to fight for what's right. I love you. If that doesn't scare you, I'd like to explore where this could go."

She could seriously get lost in those blue-grey eyes.

Snowflakes landed on her lashes, and she blinked them away. Not breaking the contact. "Between being human trafficked and then the recovery process, I missed the normal experiences or rites of high school passage like learning to drive and falling in love—until now."

He pressed their joined hands to his heart. "You deserve so much better than me."

"You are a hero and a gentleman."

"I was so afraid I'd blown it."

"Bobby, that touch... you have no idea. That's when I knew. But I thought you'd moved on." She giggled. "Maybe you kept your promise too well."

He reached for the nearest tree trunk and mimed breaking off a twig. "Invisible mistletoe." With a cheeky grin, he held his pinched fingers above his head. "An invitation—if you'd like. No pressure."

The naked adoration in his gaze tilted the forest floor beneath her. Landon rested her palms on his shoulders to steady herself.

Eyes drifting closed, she leaned forward to kiss him.

His lips warmed against hers, tender. Pure. Welcoming.

As his arms drew her nearer, she melted into his embrace.

Standing beneath the trees, snow falling like a blessing, Landon nestled her head against his shoulder. "I never expected this. To be so happy."

"Me either." His breath stirred her hair. "If Gramp hadn't made you think I was leaving, we could have done this a week ago. Interfering old coot."

"He felt bad about that. He's been nagging me ever since to talk to you."

"Then let's go make his day. And Anna's. They both need to stop meddling, but this is one time I'm glad they'll get what they want."

Landon drew a slow contented breath. "Did everyone but me see this coming?"

"I did... for a few hope-filled weeks. Until you told me you'd be single for life."

Hand in hand, they neared the inn. Landon's steps slowed. The warm, expansive glow in her spirit met cold reality. She stopped, peering ahead through the trees. Her teeth trapped her bottom lip.

He stopped at her side. "You okay?"

"I'm kind of scared."

"You're scared? I'm downright terrified. Like crest-of-the-roller-coaster, tracks-out fear."

"I come with a lot of baggage."

He squeezed her fingers. "We'll unpack it together. With counselling if we need to. It's—now that romance is part of the plot, what if a proper Prince Charming comes along? They don't write fairy tales about guys like me."

"You wish you were Travers, don't you?"

Bobby glanced down at their joined hands. "Not now."

He peeled off one of his gloves and raised his fingertips to caress her cheek. Wide-eyed like a child with the best Christmas present ever, unbelieving but radiant, he stroked her hair and drew her forehead against his own. "Now, there's this."

"Your mother will think I'm a liar."

"I'll tell her my natural charm won you over. Which I guess it somehow did." A bemused grin washed across his face.

Then his eyebrows pulled together in a mock-serious frown. "Please tell me it's not the car."

"It does make you more interesting." Or so his former girlfriend had claimed. Landon nestled into the circle of his arms. "No, it's not the car. Or Travers. Or your crazy shirts. It's you. Your heart. And your goofy sense of humour." She feathered a kiss onto his lips.

As they emerged from the trees, he swung their hands in a high arc. "I could get used to this."

The orange cat waited on the inn stairs, watching their approach. When they reached the deck, he butted his head against Landon's leg, then Bobby's. Then Landon again.

She stooped to run a hand along his bony spine. "Hey, Mister. I guess you approve."

"Good thing. I'd hate to run afoul of the pirate cat."

"He's not a pirate cat. Even if he walks like one. He's a wounded warrior."

"Like you. Only a lot less pleasing to look at." Bobby reached for the door handle. "Truck hasn't left. Gramp doesn't miss a thing."

They hung up their coats and followed the Christmas carols into the sitting room.

Anna and Roy each occupied a recliner. They both looked up, Anna studiously neutral and Roy with a jaw-stretching smirk.

Bright-blue eyes pinpointed their joined hands. He saluted Landon. "It's about time. I thank you. His publisher thanks you. Not a lot of writing going on these past few days, just a pile of misery."

Bobby groaned. "Gramp."

Roy wagged a crooked finger at Landon. "You weren't much better. Thought I'd have to instigate a fight so you could kiss and make up." He squinted at his grandson. "You did kiss her, right?"

Red flared across Bobby's cheeks. "Gramp!"

Landon grinned. "I kissed him."

Bobby squeezed her hand. "Yeah, but who found the mistletoe?"

~ The End ~

Author's Note

Human trafficking is all too real a problem, both for sex and for labour. It's possible for survivors to heal as well as Landon is healing, but I didn't find very many positive reports. The truth is ugly and frightening, and sex trafficking victims can be girls and boys as young as 12. Or younger. One way to fight back is to support your local programs for at-risk youth.

A few sites for background information:
- Canadian Centre to End Human Trafficking canadiancentretoendhumantrafficking.ca
- Public Safety Canada canada.ca/en/public-safety-canada/campaigns/human-trafficking.html
- Canadian author K. L. Ditmars lists more resources on her website: klditmarswriter.com/resources

If you are or someone you know is a victim of human trafficking, please reach out for help!
- In Canada: Canadian Human Trafficking Hotline canadianhumantraffickinghotline.ca
- In the US: National Human Trafficking Hotline humantraffickinghotline.org/get-help
- In any country: in your internet browser, type "human trafficking help" and add your country.

To end on **a brighter note**: The as-yet untitled **novel 5** in this series will be another winter story. I hope you'll come back to the Green Dory Inn when that book releases. For **advance notice** of future releases, be sure to subscribe to my mailing list at janetsketchley.ca/subscribe or follow me on Bookbub at bit.ly/JanetSketchleyBookBub.

Thanks for reading *Deadly Burden*, and I hope you've enjoyed my imaginary friends. It's a huge help to authors and other readers when you take time to leave a brief (spoiler-free) **review** online or in talking with your friends. It doesn't have to be scholarly, just mention what you liked or didn't like, and why. That will help the next reader know if they might like it. Life's too short to sample every book ourselves.

Thanks for reading!

Janet

PS: The next pages include discussion questions for *Deadly Burden*.

Acknowledgements

This book has my name on the cover, but it only reached this stage with the help of many:

Huge thanks to Deirdre Lockhart at Brilliant Cut Editing and Emilie Haney at E.A.H. Creative.

Thank you to patient and keen-eyed early readers Ruth Ann Adams, Heidi Newell, Matthew Sketchley, and Russell Sketchley for significant developmental input and proof-reading. And to Andrea King for help with the title.

I rely on my friends and fellow writers in the Metro Christian Writers group and The Word Guild for insights, encouragement, and prayer.

Russell, Adam, Amanda, Nathan, Harper, Andrew, Adrianne, and Matthew. Mom W and Mom and Dad S. And the extended branches on both sides of the tree. My family makes life precious.

Lastly but most importantly, I thank our good God for the privilege to create with words. If anything in this book has touched your spirit or encouraged you, that's an answer to prayer. Anything amiss is my shortcoming, and anything excellent has His touch.

Discussion Questions

1. What makes a perfect Christmas feast for you? What are some of your favourite traditions of the season?

2. Is there a particular character in this story you feel a connection with? Or one who troubles you? Who and why?

3. Nigel, Freesia, and Vi seem a bit "odd" at first glance. How does building relationships with people who are different from us help us see past the externals and into their hearts? What gifts do they bring into our lives?

4. Anna's support for Landon crosses into interfering. How can we show our love for others while respecting their choices?

5. Was there something in the story that particularly touched you? What was it, and why?

6. When Kenzie says Phil doesn't deserve forgiveness, Landon suggests bitterness hurts us more than it hurts the offender. Is it easy or hard for you to forgive? If you make that choice, do you sometimes have to make it more than once?

7. This story has plenty of unexpected reunions. How do you think they'll work out? Has there been a significant reunion in your life? Are you still waiting for one, like Landon is with her runaway sister Leyna? How can you pray and prepare in hopes of that day?

8. When Dee's impulsive retaliation killed her ex, she "had to" cover it up so she wouldn't lose Starr. What might she have done instead? How would it feel to realize you'd gone too far and could never undo it?

9. Lacey was a prisoner to the fear of what might happen to her. When she witnesses Landon being threatened and is nearly taken hostage, she discovers the strength to act. Surviving the traumatic experience seems liberating for her. What do you think she'll do going forward?

10. Landon is encouraged to find her identity and value in knowing and believing what God says about her. The more sure we are of God's loving and unchanging nature, the easier it is to receive these truths. What are some of your favourite things about God? How does knowing Him give you security?

BOOKS BY JANET SKETCHLEY

The Green Dory Inn Mystery Series:

Unknown Enemy
Hidden Secrets
Bitter Truth
Deadly Burden

The Redemption's Edge Series:

Heaven's Prey (book 1 expanded anniversary edition)

High octane Christian suspense meets women's fiction in this battle of wits between the prayer warrior and the fallen hero.

Ruth Warner is broken. Her adult niece's violent death at the hands of a serial rapist-murderer leaves her bitter. Tempted to reject her faith, Ruth instead finds healing through praying for the victims' families. But pray for the predator himself? Never. Until she does—and then a botched kidnapping pegs her as his next victim.

Ruth has invested too many prayers and tears to give up now. Not when his coming to faith is the only way to save her life.

Secrets and Lies (book 2 expanded anniversary edition)

A widow in hiding. A vengeful drug lord. And a teenage boy ready to come of age.

Carol Daniels is afraid to be found. Starting over in a new city to escape an anonymous threat, the single mother is desperate to protect her sixteen-year-old son. But a chilling phone call from a local crime boss reveals a menace she can't outrun.

Terrified and out of options, she agrees to find her convict brother's hidden fortune. Facing this crisis alone is overwhelming, but the one man she wants to trust has a past she can't accept. With the clock ticking, will Carol break under pressure or survive to forge a stronger life with her son?

Without Proof (book 3)

"Asking questions could cost your life."

Two years after the plane crash that killed her fiancé, Amy Silver has fallen for his best friend, artist Michael Stratton. When a local reporter claims the small aircraft may have been sabotaged, it reopens Amy's grief.

Anonymous warnings and threats are Amy's only proof that the tragedy was deliberate, and she has nowhere to turn. The authorities don't believe her, God is not an option, and Michael's protection is starting to feel like a cage. How will Amy find the truth?

Daily Devotions:

A Year of Tenacity
365 Daily Devotions to Warm Your Spirit and Encourage Your Heart

Tenacity at Christmas
31 Daily Devotions for December

Readers' Journals (print only):

Reads to Remember: A book-lover's journal to track your next 100 reads

~~~

For advance notice of new releases, connect at janetsketchley.ca/subscribe or follow me on BookBub at bit.ly/JanetSketchleyBookBub.

JANET SKETCHLEY

 **Janet Sketchley** is an Atlantic Canadian writer who likes her fiction with a splash of mystery or adventure and a dash of Christianity. Why leave faith out of our stories if it's part of our lives?

She's the author of the Green Dory Inn mystery series, the Redemption's Edge Christian suspense series, and the daily devotional books, *A Year of Tenacity* and *Tenacity at Christmas.* She has also produced a fill-in reader's journal, *Reads to Remember: A book lover's journal to track your next 100 reads* (available in print only). Find her online at janetsketchley.ca.

You're invited to subscribe to Janet's newsletter at janetsketchley.ca/subscribe or follow her on BookBub at bit.ly/JanetSketchleyBookBub.

www.ingramcontent.com/pod-product-compliance
Lightning Source LLC
Chambersburg PA
CBHW020231260626
47156CB00002B/632